BODYGUARD COWBOY

DANIELLE M. HAAS

Harlequin
ROMANTIC SUSPENSE

MIX
Paper | Supporting responsible forestry
FSC® C021394
www.fsc.org

Harlequin® ROMANTIC SUSPENSE™

Recycling programs for this product may not exist in your area.

ISBN-13: 978-1-335-18503-7

Bodyguard Cowboy

For questions and comments about the quality of this book, please contact us at CustomerService@Harlequin.com.

Harlequin Enterprises ULC
22 Adelaide St. West, 41st Floor
Toronto, Ontario M5H 4E3, Canada
www.Harlequin.com

HarperCollins Publishers
Macken House, 39/40 Mayor Street Upper,
Dublin 1, D01 C9W8, Ireland
www.HarperCollins.com

Printed in Lithuania

1 2 3 4 5 6 7 8 9 10 LIT 28 27 26 25

Dax stood in front of her, his hands shoved in the front pockets of his jeans.

He'd left his cowboy hat at his place, and his dark hair stuck out in a sexy way that made her want to run her fingers through it.

He rocked back on his heels. "Thanks again for having dinner with me. I know it wasn't the ideal first date, but Pops enjoyed your company as much as I did."

"I think he liked Frankie more than he liked me, but that's okay. I get that a lot."

Dax's lips curved up at the corners. "I doubt that. The dog's nice and all, but..."

"Good answer."

"Well, I guess I should get going." His tongue swiped his bottom lip, eyes locked on hers.

Oh, dear Lord, anticipation made her batty. She didn't want to wait any longer to find out what he tasted like. Standing on her tiptoes, she rested her palms on his chest and pressed her lips to his. Excitement zipped up her spine, making her giddy.

She pulled back but kept her face close. "Was that okay?"

"Okay? More like great."

Dear Reader,

I love it when a plan comes together. When I've made my lists and set my schedule and the stars seem to align, making all the pieces of the puzzle magically fit together. Sometimes, if I'm really lucky, that happens with a book. I dream up a world and visualize how I want things to go, and once I sit down to type, it all just works.

Other times, I'm not as lucky. I *think* I have everything planned out, only to realize the characters have another idea entirely.

For *Bodyguard Cowboy*, I had a spark of an idea that just poured out. Every detail snapped into place, and I created two characters who came alive. Dax and Vanessa practically begged to be written. When I wasn't at my computer, I had to type out words on my phone. When I wanted to sleep, they demanded I get up and finish writing their story. They were alive in my mind, and I'm so excited that their story has now found its way into your hands.

I hope as you read *Bodyguard Cowboy*, Dax and Vanessa come alive for you like they did for me, as the adventures continue in my favorite town of Cloud Valley, Wyoming. Happy reading!

With all my love,

Danielle M. Haas

Danielle M. Haas resides in Ohio with her husband and two children. She earned a BA in political science many moons ago from Bowling Green State University but thought staying home with her two children and writing romance novels would be more fun than pursuing a career in politics. She spends her days chasing her kids around, loving up her dog and trying to find a spare minute to write about her favorite thing: love.

Books by Danielle M. Haas

Harlequin Romantic Suspense

Sunrise Security

Wyoming Bodyguard
Personal Bodyguard
Bodyguard Cowboy

Matched with Murder
Booked to Kill
Driven to Kill

Visit the Author Profile page at Harlequin.com.

To my true-blue bestie, Samantha. Thank you
for making both my words and my world better.
Swan sisters for life!

Chapter 1

Sheets of rain and another clap of thunder couldn't dim Vanessa Kemp's shine as she finally pulled down the long lane that led to the home she'd always wanted.

Her grandfather's home.

And now, due to a host of unforeseen tragedies, it belonged to her.

She'd waited twenty-five years to finally step foot on the property where her mother had grown up in Cloud Valley, Wyoming. A dream her mother had all but forbidden; the place of her childhood forever cloaked in an air of mystery.

But that cloak had been yanked away when her mother passed away last year, leaving her with a broken heart and a lifetime of unanswered questions.

The gray French bulldog she'd inherited from her mom barked from the passenger seat, as if sensing they'd finally made it to their destination. François, or Frankie as she liked to call him, had been a champ over the two-day voyage from their Chicago apartment, but they were both in dire need of stretching their legs.

"All right, buddy. Let's get you outside. Try to be quick with your business. I don't want you tracking in a bunch of mud to my new house." She glanced behind her at the boxes loading down her small SUV and sighed. "I can't mess with this now. Let's check the place out before getting to work."

Frankie tilted his head from side to side, as if trying to figure out what she'd said, then gave one decisive bark.

She chuckled and opened the door. Her mom had loved Frankie as much as her own daughter—doting on him way more than she ever had Vanessa—causing bouts of irritation with the furry rug rat. But when Frankie refused to leave her mother's side while she fought the cancer that took her life, he'd stolen Vanessa's heart. She'd promised to love him as fiercely as her mother had; an easier feat than she'd anticipated.

Cool rain slanted inside the car, urging her to move quicker. She waited for Frankie to jump out before grabbing her purse and closing the door. A shining light beamed from the old farmhouse. Red shutters stood out against the white siding and a wide porch wrapped around the house like a welcoming hug.

A sense of peace she hadn't felt in far too long filled her. She closed her eyes, breathing in the clean, fresh air, and reveled in a contentment that told her she'd made the right decision.

She'd finally come home.

Frankie's frantic bark broke into her moment.

She opened her eyes, water soaking through her clothes and plastering the dark hair that had slipped from her ponytail to her cheeks. Lifting her face toward the sky, she let the rain wash over her for a few more seconds before she burst into laughter and ran for the cover of the porch.

Excitement built deep in her soul. She found the key and pushed open the front door. Silence might have been the only thing to greet her, but that silence was filled with a million stories and whispers and memories.

Memories she would never make with the grandfather she'd never had a chance to meet.

"Nope. No time for feeling sorry for ourselves, Frankie," she said as the little dog pranced into the narrow hallway. "Grandpa wrote me so many letters, I probably knew him better than most kids ever knew their grandparents. And now that we're here, I can really find out who he was. I can find out who Mom really was. And who knows what else we'll discover along the way."

A familiar ache pulsed through her excitement. There was so much she didn't know. So much that had been kept from her. Her mother had had her reasons, she was sure, but she was tired of not truly knowing where she came from. The gift of her grandfather's property had come at the perfect time, and now there was no reason not to dive in and uncover whatever she could about the family she'd never met.

A low growl rumbled from Frankie's throat. He stood rigid, the fur along his back stretching toward the low ceiling.

She crouched and ran a palm over his head, taking time to scratch behind his ears. "Everything's okay. Just an old house with lots of creaks and groans."

Staying low to comfort the dog, she glanced into the front room to her left. White cloths had been draped over the furniture and burnt brick surrounded the fireplace on the far wall. Cream-colored curtains hung in front of the picture window, blocking the muted light from reaching the far corners of the room.

Framed photographs on the hallway walls lifted her to her full height. Black-and-white shots of a bride and groom laughing in front of a church, surrounded by family and friends, lifted her lips. Her grandparents? Great-grandparents?

Needing to know, she lifted the ornate metal frame from the wall and turned it over to open the back. Faded writing spelled out the names of her grandparents and the year they'd been married.

She traced the tip of her index finger across the letters. This writing was larger than what she saw in her grandfather's letters, the curves more ornate. Unexpected tears stung her eyes. She'd never seen her grandmother's writing before, never held a piece of the woman who was woven into the very fabric of her being.

A boom of thunder shook the house, and her heart jumped to her throat. She yelped then slapped her hand on her chest. "Okay, so the storm's making us a little jumpy."

Frankie growled again. He crouched low, as if ready to pounce.

Returning the frame to the wall, she sighed. "You can't get upset over every litt—"

Thundering footsteps barreled down the stairs and a figure cloaked in black rushed toward her. Her scream combined with Frankie's snarls and growls. Time slowed and sped up at the same time, and fear stole her ability to move.

She braced herself seconds before the figure slammed against her and knocked her to the ground before fleeing out the door, swallowed by the deafening storm.

Dax McKay strolled through the sheet of rain to his truck, parked in front of the house he shared with his father. The old ranch might not be a working cattle farm anymore, but that didn't mean there wasn't work to be done.

And with his brother consumed with his security business and his father's health declining daily, it fell to Dax to keep the ship running.

Not like he could complain; in the last year he'd been the one who'd pushed to board horses on the property to bring in extra income. It also helped him carve out time with the ones he trained, giving him full access along with the flexibility to continue working as a security specialist at Sunrise Security.

By the time he yanked open the driver's-side door, water soaked the bottom of his jeans and seeped through the material of his black cowboy hat. The bite in the early spring air was the only thing that kept him from standing in the refreshing showers just a little bit longer.

"What the hell you doin' out there, boy?" His dad stood on the porch, leaning on the cane Dax and his brother Madden had forced on him. "Didn't your mama teach you any sense?"

Walter McKay was a stubborn old man filled with as much pride as he was piss and vinegar. Parkinson's disease had crept in, silently stealing his ability to physically navigate his world. He'd been forced to give up so much already, and Dax was determined to make sure he could enjoy every last bit of the life he had left.

And if that meant standing outside and yelling at him, so be it.

He shut the door until only a sliver remained open and grinned up at his old man. "Mama gave me sense. It's my father who raised me to be a pistol."

Walter's snort of laughter cut through the constant ping of raindrops against the hood of his truck. "Where you off to?"

"Meeting Madden at the office. He wants to go over some new cases with me. See if I'm interested."

Working with his big brother had been as high on his list as shoveling manure from the barns, but when Madden had reached out overwhelmed and understaffed months before, Dax had offered to help. He preferred to be outside, the mountains his backdrop and horses his coworkers, but had been surprised with how rewarding using his brain to fix a problem had been.

And hell, he was actually good at it.

"You better get goin'. Don't want to piss off the boss."

Dax rolled his eyes, enjoying the sound of his father's ornery chuckle as he climbed into his old pickup and headed to town. The skies may be gray and dark, but it didn't dim the beauty of the land as he drove past rolling hills and gurgling brooks. Buds sprouted on the trees, promising beauty and renewal for another year.

The slopes flattened and houses dotted the landscape, the space between them decreasing the closer he got to downtown Cloud Valley. Neighborhoods and small businesses welcomed him into the city limits. He turned onto Main Street, the storm keeping tourists away from the normally bustling sidewalks. Colorful awnings stretched away from storefronts, water sliding down the fabric and splattering on the ground.

Sunrise Security's main office didn't boast any fancy fabric, but large golden letters scrawled across the front window. The lack of traffic gave him a first-class parking spot in front of the office. He slid in, parked, and jogged inside.

Peggy Reynolds, the office secretary and surrogate mother to all, glanced up from under her bifocals. Her gray hair skimmed the top of her shoulders and pink lipstick stained her lips as well as her white coffee mug. "Aren't you a sight for sore eyes."

He grinned and touched the brim of his hat in mock gratitude. "No matter what I do, I'll never be as pretty as you, Peg, so why even try?"

She waved a hand through the air, showing off pastel-green nails with tiny flowers somehow painted on them. "I'm not going to fall for your charm, so don't even start. Your brother was called out somewhere or another and took Ben with him. He said if you could hang tight for a few minutes, he'll be back soon."

Dax gritted his teeth. He and Madden had worked through a lot of their issues, but his brother could annoy him more than anyone else on this planet. He'd hauled ass to finish what needed doing this morning to make it to the office on time and Madden couldn't even shoot him a text to let him know he'd be out.

"I know that look," Peggy said. "Don't go getting all upset about something outside of Madden's control. Mr. Bailey came busting in here like a fox in a henhouse, making demands and causing a scene. Madden and Ben jumped into action, knowing you wouldn't have to wait long. So, have a seat, grab a cup of that fresh coffee I just made, and let's have a chat."

Biting back a sarcastic comment, he stalked over to the credenza shoved against the wall that Peg had set up as a coffee and tea station. He filled an oversized mug then settled on the couch in the sitting area. He hooked his ankle over his knee and leaned back against the soft, leather cushion. "Might as well enjoy some good conversation. Tell me what Mr. Bailey was all bent out of shape about."

The front door swung open and a dark-haired beauty with long legs and dangerous curves hidden behind a canvas raincoat stepped inside. Big, olive-colored eyes dominated her face, her expression tight with fear.

Dax set his mug on the coffee table and rose to his feet. "Hello there. Can I help you?"

She darted her gaze between him and Peggy. "I hope so."

Something wiggled beneath her jacket and a small gray head popped out.

Dax chuckled. "If you need a vet, there's one down the street."

Swallowing hard, she shook her head. "I don't need a vet. I need my home secured. I just moved in, and someone was inside the house when I arrived. I need to make sure that won't happen again."

He took a step closer, amusement about the funny-looking dog melting away, along with his irritation with Madden. He didn't know who this woman was, but something stirred inside him that he hadn't felt in a very long time.

Something that should have him running in the opposite direction instead of closing the distance between them and extending his hand. "I'm Dax McKay. I'll do whatever you need to keep you safe."

Chapter 2

Warmth seeped into Vanessa's palm, chasing away the chill clinging to her bones. Something about the way this man stared at her, earnestness in his deep, blue eyes, made words impossible to form in her brain.

Frankie whined, wiggling to be free of her confinement.

Humor ticked up the corner of Dax's mouth. "He doesn't look happy."

Sliding her hand away from his, she hoisted Frankie in her arms and placed a quick kiss on the dog's head. "It's been a long few days followed by one hell of a welcome home. We're both a little shaken."

The older woman from behind the desk stood and hurried over. "You poor things. Both of you. Why don't you take a seat and tell Dax and me everything? I can grab a bowl of water for your dog. Go ahead and set him down. What's his name?"

"This is Frankie," she said, setting the little ball of muscle and fur on the ground.

The woman crouched and scooped Frankie against her. "Hi, Frankie. I'm Peggy. And your name, dear?"

"Oh right. Sorry. I'm Vanessa Kemp. I just moved to town, today actually."

Frowning, Dax tilted his head to the side the same way Frankie did. "Kemp? Any relation to Earl Kemp?"

Her grandfather's name created a lump of emotion that lodged in her throat. "He was my grandpa."

Peggy's mouth formed a small O, and she abandoned the dog to fold her into a hug. "I'm sorry for your loss, honey. Earl was a good man. Loved by everyone in this town. We'll all miss him so much."

Vanessa blinked to keep the unexpected tears from falling. The trauma from earlier, combined with her exhaustion and excitement, leaving her on shaky emotional ground. "Thank you."

Dax swept his cowboy hat from his head and clasped it over his heart with his big hand. "My condolences."

The gesture was so small and simple, but the clear respect he paid to the man she loved twisted her gut. "I appreciate that."

"Are you moving into his place?" he asked.

"That's the plan," she said, a short, high-pitched laugh lifting her voice to an unnatural place. "But I wasn't expecting to show up and find someone inside."

As if suddenly reminded of why she was there, Peggy hooked an arm around her shoulders and led her to the couch where Dax had been seated. She'd hoped he'd reclaim his seat beside her, but he remained on his feet with his arms crossed over his broad chest, hat now dangling from his hand.

"Go on and tell us what happened," Peggy said.

She drew in a shuddering breath, her earlier fear coming back to hit her over her head like an anvil. "Frankie and I just got to town. It's my first time here, and I was so excited to see the place my mom grew up—the home my grandparents shared."

Dax's dark eyebrow hooked toward his hairline, but he didn't interrupt.

"We got inside, and Frankie started growling," she continued. "I figured he was spooked by the sounds of the old house. But then someone flew down the stairs, knocked me off my feet, and ran out of the door."

"Did you call the police?"

"Yes. Sheriff's deputies came and took my statement then checked the house. Everything seemed fine, but I'm not sure how safe I feel. I'm already a little uneasy being in a new place, but now..." She shrugged, hating the anxiety snaking up her spine. Moving to Cloud Valley had been a huge leap of faith, and now she was second-guessing uprooting her life and starting over from scratch.

Maybe she should sell the house and land, pack Frankie into the car, and head back to Chicago. Back to the concrete jungle with its sky-high buildings and friends she'd left behind.

Sensing her worry, Frankie hopped onto her lap and nudged her hand with his wet nose.

"I understand how upsetting that must have been," Dax said, cutting into her thoughts. "But this is a safe town with good people. I'd hate to think some clown messing around in a house that's sat empty for weeks would chase you away. Not if you really want to be here."

She tucked her bottom lip between her front teeth. The past years of pain and grief returned in a flash. So much loss. So much heartbreak.

She needed a fresh start like she needed her next breath. Tucking her tail between her legs and giving up before she'd really tried wasn't an option.

At least not yet.

"I really want to be here," she said. "But not if I'm afraid someone will burst into my house or be waiting for me when I come inside. It's difficult enough to find comfort in a new place. I'm not sure how to do that now, when this space has already been violated."

"Anyone would feel the same way," Peggy said. "Sunrise Security can offer several services to secure your home and maintain your safety as well as your peace of mind. The owner, Madden, had to step out of the office. But we can go over some options with you until he gets here."

"Why waste time?" Dax said, covering his close-cropped dark hair with a hat of the same color. "I can head to your place, see what we're working with, and suggest some things we can do to help."

The thought of being alone with the devilishly handsome cowboy made heat creep up the back of her neck.

Calm down, girl.

A good-looking man was the last thing she needed to focus on. He was just offering to do his job, which was exactly the reason she'd come here.

"Is that a good idea?" Peggy asked. "Madden would want to meet the newest resident of Cloud Valley before she decides if she'd want to use our services or not."

The pointed look Peggy aimed at Dax had Vanessa bouncing her gaze between the two of them. She was clearly missing something, but she couldn't bring herself to care about someone else's problems right now.

A low, menacing rumble poured from Dax's throat that should have her running instead of almost swallowing her tongue. Maybe they should wait for the owner. Hopefully he was a short bald man with a beer gut and a wedding band.

"Why waste time?" Dax spit out. "She needs to know

what her options are. I can give her a better idea of what we can do when actually at her house, not sitting here giving her generic information. As long as that's what she wants."

Peggy struggled against a grin. "Whatever you think's best. I'll let Madden know what's going on when he gets back."

"Well?" Dax turned expectant eyes her way and butterflies flapped like crazy in her stomach. The hard lines of his face broadcasted his irritation, but he softened his features as he waited for her response.

She couldn't turn back now, couldn't let fear of the unknown—or of the hot security specialist—rule her life. Fate had brought her here, and she wouldn't walk away from the life she craved. "You want to ride with me or meet me there?"

Dax stepped out of his truck and slammed the door shut. The earlier downpour had slowed to a lazy drizzle. He waited for Vanessa to lead the way to the porch before walking up the stone pathway. Weeds wedged between the loosened rocks, cracks showing the lack of maintenance that had poisoned a lot of properties in the area.

The ugly little dog with his scrunched face and oversized ears stared at him, his breaths wheezing from his nose.

"He okay?" Dax asked.

Vanessa glanced over her shoulder at the dog before unlocking the front door and stepping inside. "He's fine. He always breathes like he's about to drop dead from a heart attack." She took a few more steps and pivoted to face him, twisting her hands in front of her.

He wished he could wipe away her anxiety, but nothing would erase the memory of what had greeted her when she'd first stepped into this house. But he could put measures in place so it wouldn't happen again.

"So, do you want to look around?" she asked. "I could give you a tour, if you need it, but honestly, I haven't even gotten the lay of the land yet. My boxes are still in the car."

"Seriously?" He shifted to get a better glimpse of the living room to his side.

She swished her lips to the side and lifted one shoulder. "I didn't have time. I parked the car, came inside to check the place out, then was blindsided. After you leave, I'll bring in a few things. At least enough to get me through the rest of the day."

He shouldn't worry about what she'd do with her time, but he couldn't help but be intrigued by her. She'd admitted this was her first time in Cloud Valley. Why had Mr. Kemp left her his home instead of the son who'd lived in town his whole life? And what had made her leave everything behind to live in a place she'd never stepped foot?

A strong desire to know more about her kept him talking. "Did you bring more than what's in your SUV? Furniture? A giant television?"

"Nope. I brought what I couldn't leave behind and figured anything else I'd need would be here waiting for me."

He glanced up the stairwell, anger tightening his hands into fists at his sides. "I can install a top-of-the-line security system. Will keep out anyone you don't want in here. Maybe a camera at the front door to see who's coming around."

The lines of her face relaxed for the first time since he'd set eyes on her, a small smile lifting her full lips. "That'd make me feel a lot safer."

"Good. Do you mind if I poke around a bit? Make sure all the windows are secure and locks are in working order?" Okay, so checking locks and windows wasn't usually on the checklist, but she had no one looking out for her.

Unless her uncle planned to stop by and offer his assistance, but he didn't foresee that happening. Chip Kemp wasn't exactly known around town for his warm and fuzzy nature. If he'd never showed a nurturing side to his own daughter, Dax doubted he'd make an appearance for Vanessa.

She wrapped her arms around her middle. "I'd appreciate that. Since I don't know where anything is anyway, I'll follow you."

He started up the stairs and Frankie leapt into action, nearly tripping him as he mistook his movement for a race to the top. He gripped the oak railing and waited for the little rat to win the race before continuing, the old steps squeaking with each movement.

"Sorry about that. He's got a lot of pent-up energy in him."

"I've got plenty of experience with energetic animals, it's the size that I don't know how to handle. He's more like a fat cat than a dog."

Vanessa laughed. "Don't let him hear you say that. He's very sensitive."

"Dogs aren't supposed to be sensitive," he said, scowling down at the panting dog with the tongue hanging out the side of his mouth.

Frankie's tongue snapped back into his mouth, and he lifted his stubby snout in the air.

"See, you offended him."

"I'll buy him a bone later. For now, let's check out these windows."

He poked into one of the four closed doors to find a small room with blue walls that matched the blanket on the twin bed. He crossed over the threadbare rug to the lone window. Satisfied it was secure, he repeated the process for what he assumed to be the primary bedroom and a bathroom before dipping inside the remaining space.

"Oh my God." Vanessa's voice was quiet, and awe-filled.

The tears hovering over her dark lashes caught him off guard. "Are you okay?"

"I think this was my mom's room. It doesn't look like Grandpa changed anything after she left." She stepped past him and stood in the center of the room, rubbing her fingers against her collarbone.

He studied the light pink walls and white-eyelet cover over the bed. A tall jewelry box collected dust on the long, white dresser and browned tape held up faded posters all around them. He didn't know anything about her mom or their relationship, but her reaction kept his mouth closed as she took it all in.

Nothing but the sound of Frankie's heavy breathing filled the room. Dax watched her as she lightly touched the bed then opened the closet door.

"She left clothes hanging in here. Shoes on the floor. There are boxes stacked to the ceiling. Parts of her I never got a chance to know are waiting for me to uncover, and I'm not sure if I'm ready."

Her tortured tone had him forgetting logic or reason, or hell, even acting appropriate with a woman he'd just met, and he made his way over to the closet. He rested a hand on her shoulder and squeezed. "All this has been here for years. It's not going anywhere. Take whatever time you need. One day, you'll be ready. And when you are, it will all be waiting for you."

"Thank you for that. I don't even know you and somehow you managed to say exactly what I needed to hear."

"Good, and now that I've said what you needed to hear, let's check out the rest of the property and see if there's anything else you need me to do."

She scrunched her brow, deepening the V between her eyes. "Where else would I need a security system besides the house?"

"You've got the barns. Not sure if anyone would venture in there, but we should visit the goats and make sure nobody's messed with them."

Her jaw dropped. "I have goats?"

He couldn't help but laugh at her surprise. Vanessa Kemp was proving to be interesting as hell, and a feeling in his gut told him he hadn't even scratched the surface.

Chapter 3

Vanessa stared at the four-legged creatures with their beady eyes and long moustaches while Frankie vibrated at her feet. "Huh. I have goats."

"I'm surprised no one told you," Dax said. "Who's been feeding them?"

She rounded the closed-off pens and kept her eyes on the small herd. The smell of wet hay and mud hung heavy in the air. The large red barn shielded them from the continuing rain, but she pulled her jacket tighter around the middle to keep away the chill.

The goats stared back, expecting God only knew what from her.

"I guess my uncle or aunt. They've been taking care of the property since Grandpa died."

Dax leaned over the barrier and patted the top of a tan-and-white goat with glassy blue eyes. "Chip didn't mention anything about caring for these guys to you?"

"Not a word."

Frowning, he stared down at her. "What about the rest of the property? This hasn't been a working ranch in a while, but there's a lot of land that needs tending. Most of the animals are gone, but he kept a couple sheep, and I think he still has Bessie."

"Bessie?"

He turned in a circle then walked down the wide aisle. His boots slapped against the concrete as he moved further away and then pointed toward the far corner. "There she is."

Vanessa followed him, a mixture of dread and excitement weighing down each step. She loved animals, even Frankie with his heavy snoring and judgy looks had grown on her, but she didn't have the first clue how to take care of farm animals.

A knee-high cow with big brown eyes and shaggy tan bangs stared up at her, and her heart melted. "Oh my goodness. She's adorable!"

Dax's chuckle glided over her skin. "I figured you'd think that."

"Can I pet her?" Asking permission to touch her own animal might be ridiculous, but she didn't want the furry little creature to turn feral and bite off a finger.

"Sure can."

Slowly, she ran her fingers through the crop of hair at the top of the cow's head. "How do you know so much about my grandfather's land?"

Hooking his thumbs in the front pockets of his jeans, he shrugged. "Small town. I've lived here my entire life. Not much happens around here that folks aren't aware of. Especially when someone buys a miniature Highland cow. Not exactly common in these parts. Bessie was a big hit with the kids, and the ladies."

He shot her a wink that curled her toes.

Not wanting him to catch the light blush in her cheeks, she rested her forearms on the top of the wooden door that caged Bessie in her hay-filled home. "I have no idea how to take care of her, or the goats, or hell, even all this land that's suddenly mine."

An invisible weight crashed down on her, stealing every ounce of joy at starting this new adventure. Who was she kidding? She had no knowledge of how to live on a ranch, and absolutely no support system.

At least, not one who could do a darn thing to help her.

Bessie shook her head and a long, low moo echoed off the aluminum roof. Frankie bounced around, yapping in response.

"Good news is you already have one hell of a farm dog." Dax scooped Frankie into his strong arms and the dog instantly quieted. "The rest you can learn. It's not too hard."

She wrinkled her nose, mostly because of her doubt but also in response to the foul smell suddenly coming from Bessie's backside. "Sure. I'll just hop onto YouTube and watch a few videos. Easy peasy."

He ran his hand along Frankie's back, inducing a round of enthusiastic kisses Dax was forced to dodge before setting the dog back on his feet. "What about your uncle? You said he's the one who's been out here taking care of things. I'm sure he helped your grandpa the last few years as his health faded. Won't he give you a hand?"

"Maybe, but I've only spoken with him a couple of times over the phone and through email. He wasn't exactly forthcoming with information. He didn't seem all that excited to meet me." Another stab of disappointment. A reminder that family bonds were something she'd probably never have, no matter how much she yearned for them.

Not wanting Dax to think she was looking for pity, she forced a smile. "Back to the YouTube plan it is."

Scowling, he shook his head. "I'm sure you can figure

out plenty of stuff by watching videos but not tending a ranch and all that comes with it. I'll show you."

His offer made her heart lurch. "You will?"

"Sure, why not?"

"Because we just met. Because you don't know anything about me. Because you have your own life and responsibilities to look after."

He batted away her concerns with a flick of the wrist. "We're neighbors. You're new to town and didn't exactly get the best welcome. Least I can do is lend a helping hand to get you started. Besides, there's not a ton to do around here. I might not know much about you, but that doesn't mean we can't be friends."

Unexpected tears stung her eyes. She blinked to chase them away. "Thank you."

He dipped his chin then glanced into Bessie's pen before retracing his steps back to the goats, Frankie at his heels. "Looks like they've been fed. Since the rain's slowing down, they'd probably like to go out in the pastures a bit. Get some fresh air and burn off some energy."

"Okay, how do I get them to the pasture?"

"Chances are they know the way. You've just got to give them a chance to show you. Or let Frankie be a sheepdog and show them where to go."

Frankie's ears twitched at the sound of his name.

"I think he'll need more training than I do," she said, studying her furry little companion. "I guess let those little ones out."

Dax unlatched the gate and a chorus of maas and bleats made her smile as close to fifteen goats leapt and sprinted forward.

She couldn't stop the rolling laughter as the animals

formed a chaotic line toward the door that Dax swung open, freeing the lively crew into the attached yard.

"Go ahead and let Bessie out, too," he said.

She hurried to the little cow who'd stolen her heart and freed her.

Bessie ambled forward, stopping when Frankie sprinted to her side, barking the whole way. The cow lowered her snout and gently brushed it against the dog, sniffing.

Frankie's barks quieted and he licked Bessie's nose before following her into the yard with the goats.

"Looks like he made a new and unlikely friend."

She couldn't help but look up at his handsome face and smile. Frankie wasn't the only one who'd made an unexpected friend. She just hoped all the bad was behind her and the rest of her time in Cloud Valley would only get better from here.

Dax grinned at the joy pouring off Vanessa in waves, her eyes fixed on her new herd. Her yappy little dog wagging his butt and weaving through the annoyed goats and sheep. The rain had stopped and the sun peeked out behind the cover of clouds blanketing the gray sky.

"I can't believe I own all this," she said, awe filling her voice. "What the hell did I get myself into?"

At least her panic had gone away, or enough of it that a little bit of excitement filled her voice.

Hell, the majority of the land his family had owned for generations had been sold out from under his feet when he was still a teenager. He'd spent years soaked in bitterness for the turn his life had taken—the turn someone else made for him—and would give anything to have a chance to make his mark at the McKay Ranch.

That dream would never become a reality, but time had dimmed the pain enough for him to forge a new path.

"Are they okay out here alone?" she asked. "Seems like the pasture goes all the way to the mountains."

"How do you know it doesn't?"

She turned to him with wide eyes and her mouth open.

Chuckling, he strolled back down the aisle of the barn. "They're fine. Let's get those boxes inside before the rain starts again. The way the sky looks, it'll be back before we know it."

She jogged to catch up with him, reaching him before stepping outside. "You really don't have to do that."

"I don't mind. Once we're done, we'll bring the animals back in then we'll head to the office. I can grab the equipment we need to get your house secure, and talk about cost. My brother, Madden, is the one who'll discuss that with you."

"You work for your brother? That's so cool."

He barked out a humorless laugh. "Not really, but that's a story for another time."

"Can't wait."

He hated how much he hoped she was being sincere, but he didn't dwell on it as he carried box after box from the silver SUV into the house. Vanessa kept pace with him every step of the way with the lighter boxes he purposely left behind. Stacks of her personal belongings cluttered the dusty living room. Sweat dotted his hairline and his muscles ached.

When he grabbed the last box, Vanessa slammed the door closed and followed him into the house.

"I can't thank you enough." She stood near the doorway with her fists planted on her hips. "Can I grab you something to drink? I assume there are at least glasses and water in the kitchen."

He glanced at his watch. As much as he'd like to linger, the three missed calls from Madden told him he needed to return to work before his brother showed up and kicked his butt.

Not to mention he still needed to get the security system installed for Vanessa.

"Appreciate the offer, but I've got a bottle of water in my truck. I better get back. If you tag along, we can make everything official then get the security system installed before dinner. Any chance you know which one of these boxes has towels?"

Frowning, she studied the mounds of boxes. "Why?"

"Frankie's going to be head to toe in mud. You'll want to wipe him off before he gets in your vehicle."

"Oh crap. I didn't think that through. Most of these are labeled by room, so towels should be with the bathroom boxes—wherever those are."

He swallowed the laugh at the horror etched on her face and instead moved around her belongings to help locate what she needed. Finding one that fit the bill, he picked it up and carried it to her. "The black marker says 'bathroom' and it's pretty light. Might be what we need."

She tore open the packing tape and lifted the flaps before turning wide eyes on him. "Seriously, are you some kind of cowboy angel or something sent to help a flailing damsel."

He couldn't stop the laugh this time. "Just a good neighbor. Now, let's get the animals in the barn and grab that mutt."

Marching outside, he hurried to the barn and made sure the animals had water in the pens before letting them inside. Frantic barking reached his ears before he made it to the door, and he quickened his pace.

"That sounds like Frankie," Vanessa said. "But far away. How much area do they have out there?"

"Not sure, but maybe they ventured further than Frankie liked or maybe he's just playing."

Stepping into the pasture, he noted Bessie surrounded by a handful of goats in the right corner as well as a couple sheep chewing grass, mud marring their white coats. But no Frankie.

"Frankie! Come!" Vanessa shouted, but to no avail.

Dax stalked through the muck and puddles. The yard stretched in front of him, but not so far he couldn't see the barbed-wire fence around the perimeter.

But still no dog.

Shit.

He jogged toward the continued yapping until the fence stopped him.

Vanessa kept pace beside him, her ragged breaths tearing from her mouth. "I don't understand. Where are the rest of the goats and Frankie?"

Mangled wire caught his attention and he crouched low to study it.

Double shit.

"Oh my God, the fence!" Vanessa dropped beside him, her knees hitting the muddy ground. "Did they tear it?"

Anger boiled his blood, and he pointed toward the busted fence. "See this metal? It's not all jagged and strained. The line is smooth and intentional."

Her eyelids slid closed. "You think this was done on purpose?"

He nodded. "Yes. Somebody cut this fence. Now we just need to figure out who and why."

Chapter 4

"Frankie!" Fear clutched Vanessa's throat as she yelled for the dog she'd never even wanted. But now that he was hers, she'd fallen hard for the darn pup. He wasn't just the pet she'd taken in after her mom's death, he was her best friend. "Come on, boy!"

Dax stood and held out a hand to help her to her feet. "We don't want to damage the fence even more and no way we can climb over. The barbs will hurt like a bitch."

She accepted his help then ran after him as he headed to the barn. Thick mud latched onto her sneakers. The curious gazes of the animals still in the pasture followed her. "What about them?"

"They're pretty content. If we're quick enough, we shouldn't have to worry about them getting out."

Not knowing what else to do, she stayed a step behind him. They ran down the wide aisle of the barn until they made it out the other end.

Dax headed for his rusted pickup truck.

She skidded to a stop. "What are you doing?"

"Grabbing some supplies. Those goats are going to be scared and confused. Herding them all the way to the front of the barn will be a pain. Getting them through the fence will be easier, but I need to make that safer, then fix it as much as possible so they can't get back through."

Her mind spun as she watched him leap into the cab of his truck and rummage through a toolbox. He tucked a big pair of gloves into the back pocket of his jeans then secured some tools before jumping on the gravel lane.

"Let's go." He took off toward the cluster of trees on the other side of the fence.

She stayed close, sending silent prayers that she hadn't already failed the animals she'd found herself responsible for.

Frankie's frantic barks picked up, spurring her on. He was a city dog, used to leashed walks and tidy parks. Not muddy forest floors and a maze of wilderness that could swallow him whole. If he was hurt because she'd given him too much freedom, she'd never forgive herself. Hell, she'd repack all those boxes and head straight to Chicago.

The ground became uneven, and the canopy of leaves made the dreary day ever darker. Vanessa braced herself against the rough, sturdy tree trunks as she moved deeper into the forest. A thundering noise echoed around her. "What's that sound?"

"River," Dax called over his shoulder. "We need to get to the animals before they fall in."

She picked up her pace, not knowing what direction she headed. "Frankie!" she yelled. "Come here, boy!"

More barking sent shivers of panic through her entire body seconds before she spied Frankie standing on a log. His ears stood at attention on the top of his little head.

"There he is!" She pointed at her pup then opened her arms wide. "Come on, boy. Come see me."

Frankie stayed rooted to the spot, his barks only increasing as they approached. The cries of goats joined with the chorus of warnings from Frankie.

Dax leapt over the log, stopping to rest his large hand on top of Frankie's head. "I got it now, boy. Good job. Vanessa, walk slowly and quietly. Your little farm dog led us to the herd, and we need to get behind them before they get hurt. If you spook one of them, they'll all go a little nuts."

She walked forward, mindful not to snap any twigs or rustle fallen leaves. She spied a handful of goats. They chewed on branches and pawed at the ground. A wide river rushed by not too far behind them.

"I'll head to the right," Dax said. "You take the left. We'll push them forward until we get to the fence, then I'll figure out how to get them in the pasture."

Too nervous to speak, she nodded. She stepped over roots and pushed through weeds as she got into position. She glanced between Dax and the goats. When she stood behind them, she locked eyes with Dax. "Now what?"

"Fan out your arms, keep them wide. Try to keep the goats together as we take this one step at a time."

"Sounds simple enough, but what about Frankie?"

Dax grinned and his dimples flashed. "I don't think you have to worry about him. He's a natural."

She followed his sightline to her fat city dog. He stood at the head of the herd, ready to take the lead. "Well then, what are we waiting for?"

By the time they made it to the edge of the woods, the rain had started again. Big drops fell from the sky, soaking her hair and clothes. Mud and dirt splattered up her jeans, and the white of her sneakers was nowhere in sight. Her socks were cold and wet. But she couldn't help the flurry of giddiness that built with each step.

Frankie trotted to the fence. He turned to face them, as if telling them they'd arrived.

She stopped, grinning at what a wild turn her life had taken. She owned a home, a feisty little dog and a herd of animals. Not to mention a patch of land. And come hell or high water, she'd figure what the heck she was supposed to do with it all.

With a surge of accomplishment, she stepped onto the slick blades of grass and her feet slid from under her. Her arms went out to brace her fall. Her palms landed in a patch of mud seconds before her bottom smacked the ground. Dirt sprayed into the air, landing on her face and covering her shirt.

A deep rumble of laughter turned her in the direction of Dax, who stayed behind the goats, pressing them toward the fence. "You all right back there?"

She lifted her hands and drips of muck fell to the ground in clumps. Her own laugher joined Dax's. "Nothing hurt but my pride, I think." Climbing to her feet, she wiped her palms on the thighs of her jeans, but the motion just rubbed the dirt around more.

"Don't think that's gonna work." Dax grinned then fit the gloves from his pocket onto his hands and maneuvered the broken fence to allow the goats to slip into the pasture.

Her stomach did a crazy somersault as she watched him work. Muscles strained against the wet material of his shirt, and his cowboy hat made her think she'd stepped into some weird fantasy that was ripped from the pages of a romance novel. If Frankie wasn't standing beside him, his laboring breaths wheezing through his snout, she'd think she was dreaming.

Well, that and the way her bogged-down shoes squished against the grass with each step and the chill clinging to her bones. If she was in dreamland with a hunky cowboy, she'd prefer not to be covered head to toe in mud.

Glancing over his shoulder, Dax shot her another dazzling smile. "I can handle the fence if you want to head inside and clean up. Once you're done, we'll go to the office and speak with Madden. We'll get you right as rain before nightfall."

She debated staying and watching him work. The drizzling rain would hide the drool probably running down her chin. But there was no reason not to go inside. Dax probably had more to do today than handle her problems. She shouldn't make him waste more time with her than necessary.

"Okay. If you don't mind," she said.

"Go for it. I'll find you when I've got the animals in their pens." He swiped his hat from his head and wiped a forearm across his brow before replacing it.

Oh dear Lord. Chilled bones weren't her problem anymore. Dax McKay was, and he was one problem she wasn't sure she wanted fixed.

By the time Vanessa walked onto the porch shiny and clean, Dax had the fence patched and animals settled. Water soaked through his shirt and his jeans had taken on that annoying stiff texture that happens when wet. He wanted nothing more than to grab a hot shower and a change of clothes, but that had to wait.

"Wanna hop in my truck or drive?" he asked. "I might get ya all dirty again." He held out his arms to display the state of his clothes. He hadn't ended up ass-deep in mud like she had but traipsing through the wet forest had left its mark.

She fisted her hands on her hips, the motion making

her ponytail swing behind her. "I think Frankie and I can handle it. As long as you're not sick of us yet?"

"Not even close. Jump in. I'll let Madden know we're on our way."

Rounding to the passenger side, he held it open, waiting for her to run through the sprinkle of rain with her dog in her arms and climb inside before shutting it. He jogged back around and jumped behind the wheel. "Ready?"

"Yep."

Frankie curled into her lap and closed his eyes.

"He's worn out." Dax scratched the dog between his ears before reversing out of the driveway then heading for town. "He did good today. Surprised the hell out of me. Didn't think he'd have the instincts to get those goats to listen, but he came through."

She stared out the window, wide-eyed and with a ghost of a smile on her lips. "His were better than mine, but I'd be lying if I said it wasn't fun. Well, at least it was after I knew the animals were safe."

"See, you're a natural."

She snorted. "I'm not sure about that. I still don't know what I'll do with the property. I just kind of jumped in with both feet. I should have stopped and really given this some thought. Realized what I was getting myself into."

With his wrist draped over the top of the steering wheel, he cast her a quick glance before returning his attention to the road. "Nah. This land is in your blood. You're here to protect it, to cherish it, to hold it close and use it in a way that would make your grandpa proud. I have no doubt you'll do that."

"How can you be so sure?"

He shrugged. "Just am."

He wouldn't admit it, but he didn't know a damn thing;

he just wanted it to be true. She'd impressed the hell out of him by diving in and doing what needed to be done in the moment. Even when she'd plunged into the mud, she hadn't gotten angry or frustrated. She'd laughed and made sure everything was taken care of before washing herself off. As far as he was concerned, her tenacity was the number-one thing she'd need to make it on her new patch of land.

Comfortable silence settled between them. She stared out the window like a child about to tear into a candy store with an endless budget. He didn't want to disturb her, but a few minutes down the road, curiosity got the best of him. "You doing okay over there? If you press your nose any closer to the glass, you'll fog up my window."

She chuckled but didn't tear her gaze from the passing scenery. "I was too upset and on edge earlier to really take in my surroundings. Now I feel like I'm in a dream. I've read so many stories about this place. Grandpa described it so well, yet at the same time I never imagined Cloud Valley could be so beautiful."

"I've lived here my whole life, and I don't think I could ever get sick of the view of these mountains. This land's in my blood, and it's in yours, too. I'm sorry you never got a chance to experience it until now. I'm sure Earl would have loved showing you around."

More questions burned the tip of his tongue, but he held them back. He understood what it was like to have people poking around in his business. Judging things they had no understanding of then making him feel like crap in the process. If Vanessa wanted to explain why she'd only ever read about this town, she'd tell him when the time was right.

She sighed then faced forward while smoothing a palm over Frankie's head. "I wish he'd have had the chance, but there's no use living your life in regret."

"That's a damn hard lesson for most to learn," he said with a snort. The heat of her stare singed his cheeks, but he kept his eyes forward.

"Do you speak from experience?" she asked.

"Darlin', that's a long story for another time. Let's just say life lessons are never easy, especially for a stubborn son of a bitch like me. I've learned a few, and I'm sure there are plenty in store down the line. For now, I just take each day as it comes and try to make the most of it."

"And making the most of it includes helping a stranger wrangle goats in the rain?"

The laughter in her voice hiked up the corner of his mouth. "Sure is, but lucky for you the day isn't over."

"Oh really?" Amusement smothered the question. "And why is that?"

He motored down Main Street until he found a parking spot close to Sunrise Security's office. Pulling in, he shut off the engine then shifted to hook his elbow on the seat-back. "The way I see it, you've had a hell of a welcome to Cloud Valley. First the intruder, then the fence. I'm sure you have a lot on your shoulders right now, and I don't see many people 'round to share that burden."

"Not sure where that luck's coming into play." She frowned, pulling the deep V in the middle of her fore-head toward her nose.

He chuckled. "After I get your house all set up, I'm going to take you out to dinner, if you want, and show you how the fine folks of Cloud Valley like to welcome new-comers. With a cold beer and warm smile."

Her expression turned serious. "That's all I get for din-ner? I'm going to need something a little more substantial."

He burst into laughter. "I think we can handle that. Now,

let's figure out exactly what you need. The sooner we get started, the sooner we can finish."

She flashed him a smile that made his heart beat in triple time before she hopped out of his truck with her dog tucked under her arm. He watched her for a second before giving a tiny shake of his head and meeting her on the sidewalk. He had a funny feeling that as far as Vanessa Kemp was concerned, things were very far from over.

Chapter 5

By the time the security system was installed and the animals were settled for the day, Vanessa's growling stomach told her it was past the dinner hour. Twilight arrived just as the rain clouds parted, revealing a wide sky painted with streaks of purple and pink. Distant stars created a dazzling display unlike anything she'd ever seen.

If she wasn't so hungry, and the smell of the food from behind her wasn't so tempting, she could stand outside and stare at the sky forever.

"You comin' in, or should I bring you a plate of food to eat on the sidewalk?" Dax stood next to the brick building and held open the door.

She twisted her lips to the side as if giving the question serious thought. "Is that really an option?"

He grunted and shrugged. "If you want. But I'm cold and thirsty, and there's no place to sit out here. I'm heading in."

Grinning, she hurried to walk through the doorway and into Tilly's Bar and Grill. She wasn't sure which hit first, the scent of fried food or the feeling of stepping into a room ripped right out of an old Western she used to watch with her mom.

Square tables filled with patrons clogged the center of

the space with booths lining one wall. Backless stools were all taken along the gleaming wood bar, and neon lights flashed advertisements. She cringed at the mounted buck's head above the stone fireplace, even if the yellow rain hat between its antlers made it a little less intimidating.

Dax swept an arm through the air as if offering a glimpse of some foreign land's cave of treasures. "Welcome to Tilly's. The beer's cold, the food's good and the company's always entertaining."

A woman with auburn hair that fell down her back stood behind the bar and filled a pint glass with amber liquid. "Hat comes off in here, cowboy."

Dax swept his hat from his head and rolled his eyes. "You're making me look bad in front of my new friend," he yelled, then hovered a hand near the small of Vanessa's back to usher her to an empty table.

He didn't touch her, but his palm so close brought with it an awareness of his proximity, as well as an intense desire for him to erase the gap of space. Instead, he pulled out a chair and waited for her to sit before settling in across from her.

The bartender delivered the beer then rounded the bar to their table. She was small in stature, but she fisted her hands on her hips and stared down Dax as if she were ten feet tall. "You're a mess."

He grinned up at her. "What can I say? I'm a hardworking man. And this is my hardworking friend, Vanessa. Vanessa, this is Eve Tilly. She owns this place."

Eve turned her smile on Vanessa and offered a hand. "Nice to meet you. You helping Dax with some horses?"

"Horses?" she squeaked, accepting the outstretched hand. "Gosh, I hope I don't own any of those. The goats and Bessie are hard enough to wrap my mind around."

"Bessie?" Eve's face fell. "Oh, you must be taking over the Kemp place."

Yet another stranger who knew where she lived and who'd been there before her. How odd to have strangers know more about her property than she did. "Yes. I'm Vanessa Kemp."

"Relation to Earl, I gather?"

She nodded. "He was my grandfather."

"I'm real sorry about your loss," Eve said. "Your grandfather was a good man. I'm glad you're here to keep his legacy alive. When did you get into town?"

"Earlier today. It's been an eye-opening experience to say the least."

Eve hooked up one perfectly sculpted eyebrow. "And you already ran into this one?"

"She didn't have the most welcoming homecoming," Dax cut in. "Someone was in the house when she got there. She came into Sunrise Security for help. She didn't get a chance to meet Reid yet."

"Reid?" Vanessa asked, bouncing her gaze between the two.

"My fiancé," Eve said. "He's Madden's business partner. He had the day off. But enough about him. I'm sorry to hear about your troubles. You're in good hands with these guys. They know what they're doing."

"I hope so, because I sure don't. Frankie and I have an awful lot to learn."

Eve frowned. "Frankie?"

"Her farm dog," Dax said, sarcasm dripping from the words.

Eve turned curious hazel eyes her way. "So, you're already familiar with farm work?"

"Not in the slightest. I was born and raised in Chicago,

and my farm dog is a pint-sized French bulldog who's fast asleep at home because this day kicked his butt harder than it did mine."

"How about some food to ease the pain of that butt-kicking?" Eve plucked a menu from the corner of a nearby table and set it in front of her. "Anything you want, on the house tonight. Welcome to Cloud Valley. You need anything, all you have to do is ask. I'm always more than happy to lend a hand, and I know quite a few people who feel the same."

Dax grabbed the menu and flipped it open. "On the house, huh?"

Eve reclaimed the menu and hit him upside the head with it. "Not for you. And don't act like you haven't memorized everything we have to offer. I'll grab you a beer, Dax. Can I start you off with something to drink, Vanessa?"

"I'll have what he's having, and a water as well, if it's no trouble."

"None at all. I'll be right back with your drinks then I'll grab your order."

She watched Eve weave between the tables. She grabbed dirty plates and tossed out a few words or a smile to everyone she passed. "I like her."

"Yeah, she's pretty likable. Even when the rest of the town treated my family like outcasts, she always had our back. She's one of the good ones."

Tilting her head to the side, she studied the change of his facial features. Gone was the easy smile and drool-inducing dimples. In their place were hard lines and a flash of anger—a glimpse of a different side of him than she'd seen so far.

But what did she expect? Dax had been a lifesaver, but

she didn't know much about him. He was just as much a stranger as everyone else in this town.

"Why did people mistreat your family? From the sounds of it so far, everyone here is so nice."

He worked his jaw back and forth as he scanned the dinner crowd. "Not everything's always what it seems. People judge. They make assumptions. They paint you one way when they had no business holding a damn brush in the first place. Things are good now, but that's not how it's always been. But that's a story for another time."

Eve arrived with their drinks and a promise to be right back for their food order.

He lifted his glass. "Tonight is for celebrating your arrival in Cloud Valley. For working hard and shifting gears when the unexpected happened. It was a challenging day but a good one, because it's the day we met. Here's to you."

Unexpected tears filled her eyes. Her muscles ached, her brain filled with a hundred uncertainties, but her heart was full. After twenty-five years, she'd finally made it home. And she wouldn't let anything, or anyone, scare her away.

Exhaustion weighed down each step Dax took as he made his way up the porch steps to his house. After he'd seen Vanessa safely home, he'd had his own chores to finish. Thirty minutes after his return to the ranch, the horses were just as ready for sleep as he was.

Dried mud caked the bottom of his jeans, making the material stiffer than usual and uncomfortable as hell. His shirt may have dried, but the dirt and sweat mixed together to invade the fabric. He needed a hot shower and warm bed.

Night had fallen, bringing with it an inky-black sky and cascading stars. The air had grown colder, a cool breeze announcing the coming rain. Springtime always brought its fair amount of precipitation, but he was damn well sick of it.

Not like anyone cared about his opinion on the matter.

The subtle creaking announced the presence of his father before he climbed the last step. As much as his entire body craved heading straight inside, his conscience had him settling in the old, white rocking chair beside his dad.

Walter spared him a quick glance before returning his focus straight ahead, eyes either on the shabby old barn or the faint outline of the mountains in the distance. His ever-present pipe sat on the wide arm of the rocker. "Busy day?"

Dax snorted, his body relaxing along with the gentle motion of the chair back and forth. Most nights, he and his dad found themselves out here. Sometimes not even having a word to say between the two of them. But that didn't matter. They didn't need conversation to enjoy each other's company.

A familiar ache crept into his chest, squeezing his lungs. This would be what he missed the most one day.

"Well?" Walter barked. "Get mud in those ears of yours, too, or you just not in the mood to say much?"

Clearing his throat, Dax pushed away the awful thoughts of what life would be like without his father and focused on the question at hand. "Nah, just wrapping things up in my head. You know how it is."

"Had many days like that in years past. Not so much now, but that's all right with me. Don't have the stamina for too many shenanigans."

Dax fought against a laugh at the old man's word choice. "You and that wild crew of yours could get into your fair share of trouble if ya wanted. Weekly poker games seem to be all any of you old geezers care about."

Walter chuckled. “Of course it is. How else will I win all their hard-earned cash?”

“Fair point.”

“So, you gonna fill me in or what?”

Dax scrubbed a hand over his face, deciding where to start. Hell, he hadn’t exactly figured out why he’d spent so much of his time with a woman he didn’t know. How could he explain it to his dad?

“A woman came into the office this morning. She moved into the old Kemp house.”

“Related to Earl?”

“His granddaughter. You know anything about her?”

Walter kept the steady motion of his chair moving and nodded. “There’s been talk. Not much lately. Years ago. When his daughter left town.”

“Why’d she do that?” He couldn’t help asking the question even if he knew he shouldn’t. He liked Vanessa. Wanted to get to know her better, and if she had a story to tell, he should wait for her to tell it. But he couldn’t help but wonder if his dad could offer some insight.

“’Cause of the granddaughter you met. Her mama, Mindy, was young and wouldn’t name the father. Ignited a real uproar at the time. She took off and never came back. I’m surprised to hear the granddaughter’s here. I wonder what Chip thinks about her moving into the house. If I remember correctly, it sits on a nice little patch of land.”

“Yeah, land she doesn’t have the first clue what to do with.”

Walter picked up his pipe and put the end in his mouth. “And how would you know that?”

Dax bit back a comment about how he was wrecking his lungs. His dad had enough heath issues limiting not only his life span but his ability to live that life the way he wanted. Instead he quickly replayed the events of the day, sharing a laugh with the old man when he described her fall in the mud.

"She's got heart, I'll give her that," he said. "I'm not sure if she'll stick around, but I think she'll give it an honest shot. I told her I'd help any way I could. I patched the fence, and I'll stop by tomorrow to show her more details about caring for the animals."

"So, she's pretty, huh?" Walter took one more puff then blew a wisp of smoke in the air.

He rolled his eyes. "Didn't say anything about how she looks."

"Why else would you be so helpful?"

"Because I'm a good neighbor? Maybe you raised me right. Ever consider that?"

Walter chuckled and set his pipe back down. "Nope. Never crossed my mind. But I do hope whoever's giving her a hard time leaves her be. You think the same person who was in her house is the one who cut her fence?"

Dax tossed the idea around in his mind. He hadn't given it much thought, but it was a possibility. Hell, with everything that had happened today, he hadn't thought back to the fence at all after it'd been patched, and he'd moved onto the next issue. "Maybe. Not sure what the point of that would be."

"To warn her off. Make her think staying in town's not worth the trouble."

"If that's the case, there wouldn't be many people who'd benefit from her leaving. I'll keep that in mind, though. If she has more issues, it's a good theory worth looking into. Hopefully the security system I installed is enough to keep whoever's messing with her away."

"And you want to her to stick around." It was a statement and not a question.

A statement he couldn't argue.

"I feel bad for her. She's all alone. Well, her and that little dog of hers. It's not easy to start over. To pivot with your life and create a new path. I understand how that feels, and if I can make it a little easier for her, I will."

"Because she's pretty," Walter said again.

Chuckling, Dax shook her head. "Yeah, she's pretty. But she's interesting and smart and funny as hell."

"Sounds like her grandma."

Dax stopped rocking and glanced at his dad. "You knew Mrs. Kemp?"

"Son, I've known everyone who's lived in this town. Earl's wife passed years ago, back when both Chip and Mindy were young. Earl showed his support a lot when your mama passed. He understood what I was going through. Offered to lend a hand any way he could."

Frowning, Dax thought back to the days after his mom died. He'd been young but the memories from those days were strong. "I don't remember Earl coming around."

"Didn't say he did. Said he offered support, so I reckon you doing the same for his granddaughter makes sense. Brings everything full circle."

He let that settle in, and yeah, he'd be lying if he said he didn't feel as though the universe played some part in bringing Vanessa Kemp into his life.

The ping of raindrops against the tin roof combined with the crickets in the distance—a soundtrack to his childhood.

"Rain's coming back," Walter said. "We should head inside."

"In a minute."

His day had been long, and his bed beckoned him, but he'd savor this moment for a while longer because pretty soon he wouldn't have another chance.

Chapter 6

Vanessa's eyes slid open only to be attacked by bright streaks of light streaming through the living room window. She pulled the orange fleece blanket over her head and groaned. She'd opted to sleep on the old couch instead of heading upstairs. Something about the creaking house along with the wind whipping against the siding had set her nerves on edge.

Not to mention the constant claps of thunder and memories of the intruder who'd greeted her the day before.

A wet nose snuck under the blanket and rubbed against her cheek, routing around like a pig.

"I know, I know. You've got to go outside."

Frankie licked her chin, as if not convinced she'd actually get up and let him do his business.

Sighing, she sat and bundled the blanket around her shoulders. Her bare feet touched the cold wooden floors and a chill shot up her legs. She might not know exactly how she'd spend her day, but part of it had to include making a list of everything she needed to make this house her home.

Starting with cozy rugs, blinds, and the urgent need to choose a bedroom for herself.

Frankie leapt off the couch and faced her, his butt wiggling and tongue lolling out the side of his mouth.

Pulling the blanket tighter, she padded to the front door and aimed her index finger at Frankie. “Okay, you did good yesterday, but today’s a new day and I need you not to get into any mischief. I’m going to let you out without a leash. Please stay close.”

Frankie’s tongue disappeared back inside his mouth.

“I’ll take that as a sign of agreement.”

After disarming the alarm, she opened the door and a blast of cool wind blew inside. She couldn’t suppress a shiver and bundled deeper into the fleece as she stepped onto the porch. She didn’t trust Frankie enough not to at least keep an eye on him as he wandered around the yard.

A low moo sounded from the barn, reminding her Frankie wasn’t the only one she had to look after this morning. There was still a lot she didn’t know about tending this land—hell, she didn’t know about where her entire life was heading—but she had learned how to feed her new flock.

Once Frankie finished, she hurried him inside so she could get dressed and start on her morning chores.

A chorus of bleats and moos welcomed her into the barn. She breathed in the scent of hay and dirt and something a little smellier that wrinkled her nose. “Morning, everyone,” she called. “Please be patient and kind to me. I’m learning.”

The next twenty minutes were filled with eager goats chewing on the strings of her jacket and pant legs. Water sloshed on the ground and the hungry animals attacked the bundles of food she brought into their pens.

When everyone was fed, she leaned on the railing caging in Bessie. The little cow ambled toward her, resting her head on the fence.

Vanessa ruffled the soft fur on the cow's forehead. "I think you might be my favorite."

Frankie interrupted the moment with a fierce bark.

Laughing, Vanessa crouched to give her dog some love. "I meant among the farm animals. You, my friend, are family."

The crunch of tires turned her attention outside. Her heart did a silly pitter-patter. She only knew one person in town well enough that they'd stop by. Instinct smoothed her palm over her jacket, leaving a smear of dirt along the green canvas. The barn door was shoved open, allowing her a glimpse of a silver truck with an extended cab she'd never seen. Stabs of disappointment needled her gut with each step as she made her way outside to see who'd arrived.

The truck parked and a man stepped out from the driver's side. A brown cowboy hat perched on his head, he stood tall, his broad back to her. The passenger door slammed shut, followed by the murmur of low voices.

Curiosity moved her forward, Frankie at her side. "Hello? Can I help you?"

The man turned toward her, a scowl drawing down the corners of his mouth. Sprinkles of salt threaded through his dark beard. Something about him struck her as familiar although she'd never laid eyes on him before. "Vanessa Kemp?"

"That's me."

A squeal of excitement preceded two women who hurried around the front of the truck. The younger one had the man's black hair that fell in a straight sheet down her back, but the delicate lines of her face matched the older woman next to her.

"I'm Chip Kemp."

She barely registered the words before the women gobbled her up in a hug.

"And I'm your aunt Diane," the older woman said. "This is your cousin, Autumn."

Autumn, not much younger than Vanessa, squealed again and took hold of both her hands. "Oh my gosh, I'm so excited to meet you. I can't believe you're really here. It's crazy! We're going to be the best of friends. If you need anything at all, I'm just a phone call away. I'll give you my number, okay?"

Diane chuckled and smiled down at her. "You look just like your mama. Anyone ever tell you that?"

The compliment curved Vanessa's lips. "All the time."

Tears shone in her aunt's brown eyes. "It is so lovely to meet you."

"And you've got a little dog," Autumn said in a singsongy voice. She lowered herself to Frankie's level and scratched behind his ears. "What a little cutie."

Chip cleared his throat, scattering the two women like a pack of chickens. They hurried to his side, their smiles still present but a little uneasy.

"Doesn't look like much of a farm dog," Chip said.

Vanessa bristled at his harsh tone. Dax might have said the same thing yesterday, but he'd been mostly teasing. Her uncle sounded as though he'd like to punt Frankie straight into the river. "Maybe not, but he did a good job yesterday herding goats when they escaped the pasture."

Chip frowned. "How'd you let that happen?"

The bristling turned to raw, hard annoyance. "*I* didn't let anything happen. We let the animals outside and when we came back out, some were missing. The fence had been cut, and they managed to squeeze through. Frankie was a big hero."

"What do you mean the fence was cut?" Chip asked, skipping over the heroics of her dog. "I just checked it the other day and it was fine."

Inhaling a large breath, she worked on her patience. "Dax said it looked like someone cut it purposefully."

"Dax McKay?" Autumn squeaked.

Chip clicked his tongue. "You've been here one day and the property's damaged and you've managed to find riffraff to hang out with. Perfect."

Anger swept up quicker than a dust storm. Dax had showed her nothing but kindness yesterday. More than her uncle ever had, and from the sounds of it, ever would. "Dax came to this house to help me after I arrived to find an intruder inside the home. Which means, on *your* watch, the property was not only damaged, but the house wasn't properly secured. Something I fixed."

Diane took a step back and darted worried gazes between Vanessa and her husband. "Chip," she said, tugging at his shirt sleeve. "Give the girl a break. Sounds like she stepped into a bit of a mess, and we don't want that for her. She's family."

Yanking out of his wife's grasp, he pointed a finger in Vanessa's direction. "What I want is for her to go back where she belongs. This isn't her home. Never was and never will be. Now, let's go."

Her cousin ran forward and gave her another quick hug then squeezed a piece of paper in her hand. "Sorry about him. Here's mine and Mama's numbers. Call any time."

Vanessa watched as her newfound family climbed back in the truck and drove out of sight. Determination steeled her nerves. Her uncle was wrong. This was her home, and no one would chase her away.

Not even her uncle.

Dax wiped a bead of sweat from his brow with his forearm. He wasn't sure who was more exhausted, him or the young thoroughbred he'd just finished working.

Probably him.

The black horse pranced in the pasture, expelling any leftover energy from their session, while Dax slumped against the fence post and watched the other horses nibbling at the grass. He'd love it if the sky split open and dumped rain on him, but the forecast for the day promised some rarely seen sunshine.

It'd be a good day to work the Kemp property with Vanessa. Then she could get a feel for what she was up against and possibly form a plan on how she wanted to use it.

He shook his head and rolled his eyes. He had to get her off the brain or he'd creep her out. There was a difference between being a friendly neighbor and a clingy nuisance. She had enough on her plate without dealing with some guy badgering her.

Madden's truck pulled into the driveway. He parked then jumped out, strolling over the gravel lot to join Dax by the fence. Leaning against the railing, he mimicked Dax's body language and stood quietly for a minute while he watched the animals frolicking in the paddock.

"That's one handsome animal," Madden said, nodding toward the young horse. "How's he doing?"

"He's a stubborn one. And a little unsure of his purpose, as am I." Dax admired the sinewy muscles rippling along the horse's back and long brown legs. "He's not built for ranch work, and you've got to be one hell of a rider to handle him no matter how well he's trained."

Madden chuckled. "Reminds me of someone else I know."

"I'm not sure if I should take that as a compliment or an insult." Dax muttered the words under his breath. It wasn't that long ago that anything his brother said would have gotten under his skin. But in the last year, they'd worked through most of their issues.

Even if Madden could drive him nuttier than anyone else on this earth.

"Thanks for all the time you took with Vanessa Kemp yesterday," Madden said. "I wasn't planning on being out of the office for so long and you stepped in. Stepped up. I appreciate it."

Dax shrugged, hating the way his chest tightened at the praise. "Just doing my job."

"You did more than that, and we both know it." Silence stretched between them as they continued watching the horses, the mountains a beautiful backdrop in the distance. "You've been stepping up a lot lately."

Discomfort shuffled his cowboy boots against the ground, kicking up a cloud of dust. "I'm just out here living my life. Doing what I can when I can."

A heavy hand squeezed his shoulder. "It's more than that, and we both know it. Lily and I do as much as we're able but we're not around enough to help with the day-to-day for Pops. Most of the help he needs falls to you. It's not fair to put that on you."

"No one put anything on me," he shot back. "Pops doesn't need much. He's too stubborn to accept a hand most of the time."

"All McKays are pretty damn stubborn, and that's part of the problem."

Dax shrugged off his brother's hand. "So, now I'm a problem? What the hell are you trying to say?"

Madden scrubbed a palm over the dark whiskers on his jaw. "It's time to hire someone to come out to the house to take care of Dad. His Parkinson's is getting worse."

Anger fired in his blood. "I don't need anyone else here in this house, bustling around and getting in our way. Pops and I have been by ourselves for a long time. We do just fine, and we'll keep doing just fine. Why don't you keep lookin' after your business and stay the hell out of ours?"

Madden worked his jaw back and forth. "Listen, I'm not trying to get in the way or make things worse. Hiring an aide to come out here once in a while is for everyone's benefit."

"You might be my boss and my big brother, but that doesn't mean I have to listen to you when we're at my home. At my ranch. Where I'm here day in and day out making sure everything runs smoothly." He jabbed a finger in the direction of the old farmhouse. "Making sure our dad has everything he needs while he still has breath in his body."

"And you don't think I'm doing my part?" Madden shouted. "You think I'm just skipping around town, not scared to death about what's happening to Dad? I'm here, too, Dax. Maybe not as much as you, but I'm trying. This is a way that I can help."

Dax snorted his disgust. "By paying someone else to do what you should do yourself? Does that make you feel like a big man?"

Fire shot from Madden's eyes. "Screw you, man. I can't be here all the time because I'm running a business that's putting food on his table. That's paying his bills. I'm busting my ass every damn day."

Anger vibrated Dax's skin. He took a step closer to his brother until the tips of his cowboy boots met Madden's. "There you go again. Strutting around acting like you're everyone's saving grace when you helped create the problem by making decisions without letting me in—dictating my future without asking for my input. I don't need your business or your pity or your charity. And the work I do with these horses is in my blood—gives me back something that you helped take away. So, if you want to act all high and mighty, go for it. But don't expect me to fall at your feet. Don't expect me to step aside and watch you make decisions that affect everyone's lives. I did that once and lost everything."

Just staring at his brother turned his stomach. He wasn't a teenager with no voice anymore, not like the last time Madden had swooped in to save the day. He was a man, and he didn't have the heart to bring in a stranger to care for the man he loved more than anything on this earth.

Turning away, he stormed to the house. This conversation was over. His dad was fine for now, and nothing Madden said would convince him otherwise. He had everything under control, and he'd fight with his last breath to keep it that way.

Chapter 7

A myriad of emotions surged inside Vanessa as she stomped around the kitchen. She yanked open cabinets just to bang them shut as she looked for something—anything—to calm her racing heart. She was a fool. Coming here with the hopes of forming some kind of loving relationship with an uncle she'd never met.

He'd made it clear for twenty-five years he wasn't interested in knowing anything about her. Why would that change just because she lived in the same town? Heck, now it was worse. Now she wasn't just some long-lost niece, she was the enemy.

A familiar ache in her heart intensified and stupid tears blurred her vision. She slammed another cabinet, frustrated not to find something inside that would magically make her feel better. Like a pack of chocolate cookies or a jar of frosting.

Leaning against the counter, she sighed, choosing to look on the bright side. Her uncle was a dick, but her aunt and cousin were lovely. She'd focus on building a friendship with the women who'd welcomed her with enthusiasm and love and see what happened.

With one decision under her belt, she might as well push through and make another. She wouldn't find anything to satisfy her in the kitchen until she made a trip into town and found a grocery store. Until then, she'd ride the wave of emotions kicking up dust inside her instead of sweeping them under the rug and revisit her mom's old bedroom.

"Come on, Frankie. We've got to start somewhere." She climbed the stairs with Frankie a step behind her.

She trailed her fingertips along the dark walnut railing, her gaze fixed on the clutter of photos on the floral-wallpapered wall. So many unknown faces stared back at her. Faces of relatives and family she'd never known, never met. People who shared her name and blood and nothing else.

A strong urge to be around someone she really knew hurried her to the room she'd avoided since yesterday when she'd first stepped foot in it. In the moment, feeling the presence of her mother had overwhelmed her.

Now, she needed that presence. Even if the girl who'd left behind the boxes and trinkets wasn't the woman who'd raised her.

Opening the door, she walked inside and drew in a large breath. The pink walls and frilly bedspread brought a smile to her lips. The room her mom had lived in all of Vanessa's life had held neutrals and practical necessities. But she'd brought pieces of the girl from Cloud Valley with her, even if she'd never realized it.

She slipped the rainbow throw off the edge of the bed and wrapped the blanket around her shoulders as she stood in the middle of the room. A subtle hint of vanilla—her mom's favorite scent—clung to the soft fabric and brought tears to her eyes.

Frankie whined and stared up at her with his big, soulful eyes.

"You ready for this, boy?"

He cocked his head to the side.

"Where should we start?" Vanessa glanced around, not exactly sure what she was expecting out of this. Once she got a glimpse of the girl her mom used to be, would she feel closer to her or further away than ever?

"Well, Frankie, we might as well just jump in and see what happens. Standing around isn't going to do anything, and if nothing else, I need to get this house put together the way we want it."

Steeling her nerves, she opted to tackle the closet. She could pull out a few boxes and peek inside. If it was too much, she'd put them back and try again another day. The top box was light, and she set it on the floor in the middle of the room. She flipped open the lid and was greeted by old clothes. She pulled out T-shirts with the local high school's mascot—a bison wearing a cowboy hat—on the front and found an old cheerleading uniform.

She shook out the pleated skirt with alternating colors of gold and crimson and held it up to her waist. "You think I could pull this off, Frankie?"

Frankie's low, long whine seemed to tell her no, so she set it aside and kept digging into her mom's old possessions.

When she found a yearbook, she sat cross-legged on the shaggy rug and pulled the blanket tighter around her. She flipped through the pages, searching hungrily for a sighting of her mom. She found her on the page dedicated to the cheerleaders. Her smile wide and bright, her hair bigger than the mountain outside the window.

Vanessa laughed through her tears. She'd never seen what her mom looked like when she was younger. The images of her laughing with friends and cheering on the football team were like looking back in time. "She was beautiful."

Frankie grunted in agreement.

"You're wonderful, but I need to find someone who's a better conversationalist."

He rolled over and showed her his belly.

Laughing, she rubbed the velvety fur then flipped the page to find an old photograph tucked between the pages. Her mom stood between two boys. One had to be the younger version of her uncle, although his wide grin and cute dimples went against the memory of the stern-faced jerk who'd showed up earlier.

But it was the other boy who caught her attention. Her mom stared up at him, her admiration clear through the glossy paper, and his smile was full. His jaw chiseled and dark hair shaggy around his ears. Although it was the x's scratched over his eyes that she couldn't look away from.

A shiver raced down Vanessa's spine and a sudden urge to toss the box aside had her steadying her breath and returning everything back to where she'd found it.

Except the photo. The image stirred something in the pit of her stomach she wasn't quite ready to figure out but couldn't ignore. Standing, she stuck it in the corner of the mirror. She wouldn't pack it away. She'd keep it where she knew she'd find it when the time was right.

"Well, I think that's enough for one day, don't you?" she asked, staring down at Frankie. "Maybe we should go see our other farm friends? We can let them out in the pasture, as long as you promise to stay in the fenced-in area this time. I think I'll stay with you just to be safe."

Frankie barked then ran out the door, the clatter of his nails on the wooden floors echoing off the ceiling.

Shaking her head, she chuckled and followed him down

the stairs and out the front door. The sun had risen a bit higher in the sky, sending warm rays through the crisp wind shifting the nearby leaves. She zipped up her jacket to keep away the chill and hurried across the gravel driveway.

Frankie waited at the barn door. He jumped and pawed at the ground.

"You're so impatient today," she playfully scolded. "I'm coming."

He moved out of the way when she gripped the handle and shoved the door aside.

"Why's it so quiet?" Her intuition went haywire, and she ran to the pen at the front of the barn that housed the goats.

"Oh my God!" She stared in horror at the motionless animals lying on the ground, their eyes closed and no sign of life in their little bodies.

Dax stepped out of the cold shower, anger still sizzling on his skin. Starting the day off arguing with Madden wasn't ideal but also wasn't a big surprise. The two had butted heads for years. Just because the last few months had brought some peace didn't mean they magically saw eye to eye on everything.

Especially when it came to their dad.

As the big brother, Madden always assumed he knew what was best for everyone. He had an annoying habit of sweeping in and making decisions that affected everyone else, not caring that he wasn't the one in the trenches. Dax had been too young when Madden had made a life-altering decision before, but he wasn't some dumb kid now.

And he wouldn't let Madden waltz around the ranch with a puffed-out chest, demanding others adhere to his whim.

Drying off with a soft cotton towel, Dax hurried to dress

and get downstairs. By the time he poured a fresh cup of coffee, he'd calmed. Flying off the handle wouldn't prove his point. He had to stay in control of his emotions and show Madden that what was best for their dad was Dax continuing to keep watch and helping when necessary.

The thump of his dad's cane against the hardwood floor preceded him into the kitchen. "Morning. What's on the agenda for the day?" He settled into a chair at the round table in the middle of the room. A green tablecloth covered the table that was used at the weekly poker game.

Dax grabbed another mug and filled it, delivering it to his dad without being asked. If coffee was in the pot, Walter wanted it. "Not sure. I worked the horses already. I could take another run at that thoroughbred later. He's a stubborn one."

Walter took a sip then set his mug down. His hand shook just enough to slosh coffee over the side. "Sometimes it's best to give the stubborn ones some space."

Dax leaned against the counter and studied his dad's weathered face. Most days he struggled to hear the television at full blast, but there were times Dax wondered if he observed more than he let on. "Why do I have the suspicion you're not talking about horses?"

Walter shrugged. "Think what you want. No skin off my teeth."

Not wanting to discuss his argument with Madden, especially since it centered around Walter, Dax took his coffee to the table and sat. "What are your plans for the day?"

Walter snorted. "I've got a big day planned. Breakfast followed by some porch sitting. Ball game's on this evening. You watchin' with me tonight?"

"Are you going to yell at the TV?"

"Try and stop me."

"Wouldn't dream of it," Dax said, lifting his palms. "I'll be here."

The side of Walter's mouth inched up, not quite reaching a smile. "Don't cancel anything you might have going on for me. I don't need no company to enjoy a game."

Chuckling, Dax shook his head. His dad wasn't one to ever ask for company or request anything from his sons. Mentioning the game was his way of throwing out a line, and no matter how much he wanted Dax to take the bait, he'd never press.

But Dax would take that bait any chance he got.

"If I'm not here, there's no one to yell back at you. Count me in." The sound of his phone stole his attention. Vanessa's number flashed on the screen, increasing his heart rate. He raised a finger to his dad, indicating he needed a minute, before answering the call. "Hey, Vanessa. How you doing?"

"I'm sorry to bug you so early, but something's wrong with the goats."

Leaning against his chair, he grinned and aimed an exaggerated eye roll at his dad. Walter would get a kick out of some city girl's dramatics over a handful of farm animals. "What's going on?"

"I don't know," she said, her voice growing more frantic. "They were fine when I fed them this morning. But I came outside to let them into the pasture and they're just laying here. Eyes closed, and I don't know if they're breathing. What do I do?"

He jumped to his feet. "Have you tried giving them any water?"

"No. I can't get them to do anything. I'm freaking out."

"Stay put. I'm on my way." Disconnecting, he downed one more sip of hot coffee. "That was Vanessa Kemp. Says the goats are sick, possibly dead. She doesn't know what do, so I'm heading that way."

"Girl might not be used to farm life, but it ain't too hard to tell if an animal's dead or not," Walter said.

"It doesn't make any sense. They were fine yesterday."

"Might have eaten something they shouldn't. I think we've still got some activated charcoal in the barn. We'd give that to the animals from time to time if they got into something bad. Go take a look, and I'll find some Pepto-Bismol. If they got a hold of something, the charcoal will keep the poison from spreading and the pink stuff will coat the belly. You'll still need a vet though."

"Thanks, Pops." He ran down the hall, shoving boots on his feet as he made his way out the door. His dad might be old and ailing, but he had years of experience dealing with unexpected problems on a ranch.

He just hoped his assumption that the goats had gotten into something they shouldn't have was right. If not, he wasn't sure he could help the little guys.

Ignoring the curious gazes of the horses, he rushed into the storage room and scanned the dusty shelves. He spotted what he needed then sprinted back to the house.

Walter waited on the porch with a pink bottle in his hands. "I put in a call to Dr. Hatcher. She said she'll head out to the Kemp place right away."

Dax bounded up the steps and grabbed the medicine. "Good thinking. I'll call if I need more advice. Keep your phone nearby."

He hurried to his truck, but not before he noticed Walter's chest puff a bit at the request. His dad might be battling a nasty bastard that threatened to steal his dignity—and eventually his life—but he still had so much to offer.

And Dax vowed to do whatever possible to keep him around and happy for years to come, and God help anyone who stood in his way.

Chapter 8

As soon as Vanessa spotted Dax entering the barn, the bunched muscles around her neck loosened. She stayed on the hay-covered floor with a little white goat in her lap. Frankie stood at attention beside her. His ears perked up at the sight of Dax, but he stayed rooted to his guard post.

Dax jogged down the aisle with a canvas bag draped across his chest. "How many goats are down?"

"All but two of them," she said, unable to stop tears from filling her eyes. The poor animals had stirred since she'd first found them, but she wasn't convinced they could fight whatever ailed them much longer. "I don't understand what happened. They were fine. I was only away from them for an hour or so."

Dax swung open the gate and dropped to his knees beside one of the animals. He dug into his bag and pulled out little syringes. "This is a gel we need to get into their system as soon as possible. It's activated charcoal, which combats poisoning and has added electrolytes to keep them hydrated until we get a vet here."

Frankie walked over and sniffed the tube.

"They're not even moving. How do we get them to eat?" Vanessa asked.

"We force them." Dax pulled one of the goats onto his

lap. He cradled the animal like a baby and pried his mouth open, squirting a little of the substance in its mouth. "We'll get as much in them as possible. There are more syringes in my bag. Grab one," he said, tossing his bag toward her.

She rummaged through and found the charcoal then used the tip of the syringe to pry the little goat's lips apart just enough to squeeze some of the medication inside his mouth. His tongue moved, licking at the gel until it disappeared.

"He did it!" she said, hope beating back the dread. When she'd first spied the animals on the floor, she'd never imagined there was anything that could revive them.

"Get as much in him as possible then move on to the next," Dax said. He gently laid the white-and-brown-spotted goat on the ground and scooped up another sick animal.

Her heart continued to hammer against her breastbone. "I can't believe this happened. My uncle was right. I don't know what the hell I'm doing. I should just go back to Chicago. I mean, I might have killed my goats." Okay, so that might be a little bit of an exaggeration, but she couldn't help feeling responsible.

Once the little guy in her lap took in as much medicine as possible, she gave him a little kiss on his nose then placed him beside her. She picked up another sickly animal and repeated the process.

Frankie whined and sniffed at his friends.

Dax scowled. "You didn't do anything wrong, and if your uncle told you any different, he's a dick."

She snorted. "You might be right about that, but that doesn't change the facts."

"I want you to go over everything you noticed with the goats this morning."

Sighing, she poured over the details of her morning from the time she came out to the barn until she found the animals unmoving in their pens. "Did I feed them wrong? Do you think they ate something bad for them yesterday when they got out of the pasture? Maybe I missed signs last night that would have clued me in to things going on below the surface."

He shook his head, his scowl showcasing his thoughts. "If they'd gotten into something then, we would have known it fairly quickly. I'll take a walk back there later to scout the area, see if there are any poisonous plants. But if that was the case, some of the sheep would be sick, too. This looks deliberate. We need to look at their food. See if someone tampered with it."

Anger heated her cheeks. "Why would anyone do that?"

"Same reason they cut your fence," he said, shrugging. "To mess with you, scare you off or discourage you from staying. You mentioned your uncle. You told me yesterday that you'd had minimal communication with him. When did he tell you that you should leave?"

She ran her hand over the soft fur of the goat she held, focusing on getting her to swallow the medicine. "He stopped by earlier with my aunt and cousin."

"And?"

"And he told me to go home." Sadness pressed down on her shoulders and she struggled to put her feelings into words. "I didn't expect some grand welcoming from him, but I didn't think he'd be so nasty. He didn't show an ounce of kindness or happiness at meeting his niece for the first time. And do you know what the weirdest thing is?"

"What's that?"

"I went through some of my mom's boxes this morning, and she and Chip seemed to really get along. Lots of smiling and laughing in the pictures I found. I wish my mom was alive so I could ask what happened to cause such a rift—a rift so strong that he even hates her daughter."

"I'm sure he doesn't hate you," Dax said.

"I'm sure he does. The question is, would he deliberately hurt these animals to scare me into leaving?" The question took shape in her mind. Her uncle had access to the house and property. He could have been the one in the house, waiting for her to arrive to spook her. A deep pit of despair opened inside her and threatened to swallow her whole. "I'm a real treat. No mom, a grandfather I loved and never met, I have no clue who my father is, and my uncle might be actively tormenting me."

Dax lifted the corner of his mouth in a sad, half smile. "We're all from messed-up families one way or another. Sometimes it's just easier to see from the outside."

She studied his blue eyes. Something lingered behind the cobalt hues that told a story she longed to know, but now wasn't the time to pry. "Yeah, well, my issues have a freaking spotlight on them right now, and that's something I'm not used to."

"If it makes you feel any better, people in this town are used to knowing everyone's business—and that includes your uncle. Everyone knows he's a jerk, so try not to take it personal. The rest...well, you just have to figure out if it's worth it to stick around and see what you can build here."

His words touched a place in her heart. "How do you do that?"

He frowned. "Do what?"

"Say the exact right thing at the right time." The creature on her lap squirmed and maaed. She set her down and repeated the process with the next sick goat as Dax did the same.

"Well, you might be the first person who's ever told me that, but glad I can help."

The sound of tires crunching on gravel lifted her gaze to the driveway. Through the open doorway, she spied a large, white van. "Someone's here."

"Dr. Hatcher, the town vet. My dad called her."

Before she could thank him again, a middle-aged woman with her light locks pulled into a ponytail ran into the barn. "What's it look like, Dax?"

Vanessa kept working while Dax gave her the rundown.

"Have they all gotten activated charcoal in their systems?" Dr. Hatcher asked.

Dax dipped his chin to the goat in his lap. "This is the last one."

"Good work. Let's get them in crates in my van. I'll take them to the office and get IVs in them. Keep an eye on them."

Vanessa stood and held the animal tight. "Are they going to be all right?"

Dr. Hatcher aimed a pleasant smile her way. "I hope so. Sounds like you acted fast, which is key in these situations, and the McKays know a thing or two about keeping animals alive. You're lucky he was here."

Hurrying toward the van, Vanessa hung on to her thoughts. She agreed with the vet. Her last twenty-four hours had been filled with more lows than she'd anticipated, but one truth remained. Meeting Dax McKay had been one lucky break.

Dax wiped his palms on the thighs of his jeans and studied the neatly organized storage room. "All right. I think you're all set. We tossed out what you fed the goats this morning, and everything that's left in here is unopened.

You'll have to pick up some more goat food soon, because what you have left won't last long."

Vanessa sat on an overturned bucket and leaned against the wall. Dirt was smeared across her cheek, and her dark braid hung across one shoulder. "Does that mean you think they'll live?"

"Dr. Hatcher was pretty optimistic when she left," he said. "I'll call her later and check. Or I can give you her number to call yourself."

She let out a long breath. "I can call, and I'll pick up some food to put some positive energy in the air. I might just need to know where to go and what to buy," she said, scrunching her nose. "I'm a pain in the ass, aren't I?"

He couldn't help but grin. He had a thing or two to say about her ass, but he'd keep those thoughts to himself. "Nah. I like doing this stuff."

"What? Rescuing damsels in distress?"

His grin widened. "You're far from that, but no, I meant being outside. Working with my hands and helping to show someone the ropes. You've been given something special here, and it'd be a shame for you to walk away before you understand what all you have. If I can be the one to show you, great. Which reminds me." He held out a hand to her.

Eyes narrowed, she cocked her head slightly to the side. "I'm scared."

He chuckled. "Don't be. This won't be work. I actually think you'll like it."

She slid her hand into his and let him help her to her feet. "Oh yeah?"

Making sure to ignore the jolt of electrical currents shooting up his arm, he cleared his throat then broke the connection. "I want to take a walk to where the animals were yesterday and double-check nothing was back there that would harm them."

"How do you know what to look for?"

"City girl," he muttered, shaking his head.

She swatted at his arm and laughed. "I can't help where I was raised."

"Fair point."

Silence settled between them as they wound around the same path they'd traveled the day before. All of yesterday's rain made the ground soft. His boots made imprints in the long blades of grass. The sun sent warm rays onto his face and the song of the birds echoed in the sky. Buds blossomed on the trees, promising colorful life to come.

Vanessa stayed in step beside him. "It really is beautiful out here."

He glanced down at her, and the warmth of the morning sunrays didn't hold a candle to the heat simmering in his veins. A part of him screamed to turn around and head home. Between horse training, working for Madden and caring for his father, he didn't have time for anything else.

Especially a gorgeous stranger who might not even stay in town.

But he meant what he'd told her. He understood more than most what a family's land meant, and if her grandfather wanted her to have it, he'd do what he could to make sure she honored that wish.

"So, what did you do for a living back in Chicago?" he asked as the shadows of the trees welcomed them.

"I taught yoga," she said.

Images of her in formfitting clothes contorted into mind-blowing positions made him groan. "You planning on doing that here?" he asked, hoping she didn't pick up on the strangled quality of his voice.

She shrugged. "Not sure yet. Between the inheritance I got from my grandfather and life insurance policy from my mother, I don't have to figure out an income right away. I really want to take my time and see what makes the most sense. I know it sounds silly, but I'd hoped once I got here things would click into place. I'd just know what I should do. That clearly isn't the case."

He stepped over a fallen log and walked parallel to the river. "If you were in Chicago, would the plan be to keep teaching? Or is there something else calling to you?"

She stopped and leaned against a thick tree trunk; her attention was fixed on the rapids pushing the water downstream. "The last few years I've been wrapped up in caring for my mom, so I didn't have much time to think about my future. Then once she passed, I was lost in a sea of grief. Just getting out of bed was tough some days. Losing my grandfather was another blow, but one that provided me a new opportunity I jumped at." She glanced at him, and a shy smile spread across her lips. "That doesn't really answer your question, does it?"

Jamming his hands in the pockets of his jeans, he lifted a shoulder. "Kind of. Tells me you haven't had a chance to figure out your dreams. Did you have any before your mom got sick?"

"Silly ones, probably." She stared into the sky, as if searching for the right words.

"Why do you say that?" He took a step closer, pulled into her orbit by some unseen force.

"I was young."

"So. Tell me what little Vanessa wanted out of her life."

She kept her gaze glued heavenward but swished her mouth to the side. "I wanted to create a community. Use my hands and talents to make people happy. I wanted to make a space that was mine, a space that was sustainable and could also provide that same peace to others. I don't even know what that means or looks like. I guess I just want to find a way to give back to the world."

"That's not silly at all," he said, captivated. "Sounds like a cowboy, if you ask me—use what God gave you to leave the world a better place once you leave it. I bet if you really think about what you can do to make those dreams a reality, you'd be surprised by how you could achieve that here. You have the space. Now you need to figure out how to make it yours."

Her gaze finally met his. Her mouth was slightly open, cheeks flushed from the bite of the wind. "Well, in that case, maybe I need to buy myself a hat."

Laughing, he swept his hat off his head before placing it on hers. The wide brim sat low on her forehead but couldn't hide her amusement. "Phase one complete. Now let's keep looking. Who knows what's waiting to be discovered."

He could think of a hundred things she could do with this land that would accomplish what she'd always wanted, but this wasn't his dream—wasn't his life. She had to make the choices that would take her where she wanted to go. He was just along for the ride for as long as she hung around.

And he hated the feeling in his gut telling him if she cut ties and decided to leave, he'd spend an awful lot of time lost in his own grief—longing for a woman who'd captivated him in ways he'd never experienced.

In a way, that scared the hell out of him.

Chapter 9

After a call to the vet, who confirmed the goats were doing well, and finishing the tour of her property, Vanessa was invigorated. Dax's pep talk hadn't hurt. He had a way of building up her confidence and making her feel she could do whatever she wanted.

And she was really starting to believe him.

Hopping out of Dax's truck, she stared at the hardware store and secured her purse across her chest. The building looked more like a log cabin that would be found in the mountains than a store. Colorful flowers exploded from pots of all shapes and sizes, creating a homey atmosphere.

The attached nursery told her she could buy most of what she saw outside, down to the stone birdbaths and cute little benches. Excitement thumped along with her pulse.

Dax stood beside her, one brow hooked toward the black cowboy hat she'd returned before they'd left. "Ready?"

"You betcha."

Once inside, she followed Dax from aisle to aisle. He pointed out food she'd need for the animals and other supplies she should have on hand for emergencies. By the time they'd gone down every row, her cart was full.

"Good thing we brought your truck," she said. "I'm not sure this would fit in my car."

"We're not even done. Did you want to look in the nursery? They've got a lot of seeds for flowers and starters for gardens. There's that nice patch of land you could till. You'd just need to clear out some weeds and work the soil a bit."

She recalled the overgrown garden at the back of the house. When her mom was sick, she'd loved being surrounded by new life. Vanessa had packed as many plants as possible in their apartment, working diligently to keep them vibrant.

"I'd like that," she said. "My mom loved plants. She even had a rooftop garden where she grew tomatoes and peppers. Sometimes she'd get strawberries to grow and get so excited. She shared everything with our neighbors. It became a kind of community garden. Neighbors took turns tending the plants when Mom got too sick to do it herself."

Dax leaned against the cart and smiled. "That's really nice. Is the garden still there?"

"No," she said, the simple word hitting her like a punch in the gut. "I haven't done anything like that since she passed. Growing a garden here, in the place where she grew up, would be a beautiful way to honor her. Maybe I could do the same thing as she did and give what I grow to the people in town."

"Looks like things are falling into place. Let's see what they've got." Dax pushed the cart into the attached greenhouse.

The scent of dirt and flowers brought with them memories of her mom, which threatened to overwhelm her. She embraced the memories, played them over in her mind as she picked out plants and seeds then filled a second cart with dirt and other tools she may need.

By the time she paid and followed Dax out to his truck, she was brimming with anticipation.

"You almost bought out the store." Dax tossed the last bag of dirt into the bed of his truck. "You sure you don't want to head inside and grab the rest off the shelves?"

"I think I'm good. I'll return the carts." She pushed her cart into Dax's and maneuvered them to the front of the store. When she turned around, the sight of a familiar truck caught her attention and blocked her from where Dax stood waiting on the other side.

A man climbed out of the passenger side, and moments later, Chip rounded the hood and spied her. His frown deepened into a scowl. The other man's expression remained blank as they crossed the parking lot.

She stood her ground, refusing to let her uncle's gruffness intimidate her.

"What are you doing?" Chip barked the question.

"Same as you, I suspect. Buying supplies." She tried not to let her own words match his bite. Her initial impression of her uncle was anything but positive, but that didn't mean she had no hope for a better relationship with him in the future.

As long as he wasn't the one working so hard to run her out of town.

"And what would you know about supplies?"

Dax stomped past the back of Chip's extended cab until he reached her side. "Morning, Chip. Ethan."

The other man—Ethan she presumed—tipped his hat but kept his mouth shut.

Chip aimed his scowl at Dax. "What are you doing here?"

"You're awfully concerned with what everyone's doing at the hardware store," Dax said. He kept his voice even, but his clipped words made his irritation clear. "You've spent enough time at your pops's place. You'd know more than anyone what all needs to be purchased to keep it running."

Vanessa took note of the bulging vein at Chip's temple. His clenched jaw broadcast his anger loud and clear, and she couldn't help but wonder how tight of a leash he kept on his emotions. Would he let his outrage at not being given her grandfather's property lead him to harm innocent animals?

"Dax brought me to get more food for the goats since I had to throw most of it out." She studied his expression, but nothing chased away the irritation.

"Why the hell would you do that?" Chip asked.

"Because what I fed them this morning almost killed them," she said.

Chip's eyes widened for a beat, and he dragged a hand over his mouth. "Geez, you're in town less than twenty-four hours and already ruining everything. I told you before—go home. This isn't the place for you. Leave now before you destroy everything my father built. Hell, I'll pay you double what the place is worth."

Indignation burned her cheeks. "I'm not selling the property. My grandfather wanted me to have it."

"Crazy old man." Chip rolled his eyes skyward. "He almost ran everything into the ground and now you're here to finish the job."

Dax took a step forward, his fists clenched at his sides. "Watch yourself."

Ethan placed a hand on Chip's shoulder, but he shrugged it off. "I'm not going to coddle some city slicker who doesn't know the first thing about this place. She doesn't belong here. At least her mother had good enough sense to know that."

As much as she hated it, his words stung like a hundred angry bees. Tears threatened to fall, but she held them back. She refused to let this jerk see how much his disdain affected her.

"Enough," Ethan said. "This won't help a damn thing. Let's get what we came here for and go on with our day."

"Listen to your friend," Dax all but growled. "And I suggest the next time you run into Vanessa—and trust me, there will be a next time—you treat her with a little more respect."

Chip scoffed and shoved past Dax, making sure to avoid her as he stormed away and disappeared inside.

Ethan gave them both a tight-lipped smile and followed after his friend.

Vanessa wrapped her arms around her middle. "I don't know why he hates me so much."

Dax shook his head. "He doesn't hate you. He hates what he thinks you took from him. He's too stubborn and stupid to understand none of that's your fault. Come on. Let's get this stuff back to your place."

With all the excitement from earlier gone, she stayed quiet and walked back to the truck. Her uncle might have succeeded in dimming her shine, but he wouldn't keep her down. If nothing else, she was more determined than ever to prove herself. This was her town now, and she'd make sure everyone knew it.

After leaving the hardware store, Dax took Vanessa to the market to nab a few necessities then grabbed something quick to eat from a drive-thru. She'd been eager to return home to attack the weeds strangling the overgrown garden.

He scraped a hoe against the rough ground, his momentum interrupted by vibrating in his pocket. He yanked off his glove and snagged his phone. Madden's name flashed on the screen and a punch of annoyance broke through his contentment at working the land.

"I got to take this call," he called to Vanessa.

Her head shot up from where she kneeled, pulling weeds. "Take your time. I mean… I feel this goes above and beyond your responsibilities."

Grinning, he shrugged. "I like it. I'll grab us some water while I take a break."

"Thanks," she said then returned to work.

Dax answered the call before it went to voicemail then made his way toward the front of the house. "Hey."

Frankie trotted at his side, his labored breaths wheezing through his open mouth.

"Afternoon," Madden said, the stiffness in his voice raising Dax's hackles. "Where you at?"

"The Kemp place." He bit the words out. "What do you need?"

"Did something happen this morning?" Madden asked. "I didn't see any reports made that she had any more trouble."

"Her goats were poisoned. I think someone tampered with the food, but nothing showed on the security feed. It could have been done before the camera was installed." He jogged up the porch steps and walked inside, toeing off his boots before heading toward the kitchen.

Frankie scurried behind him, his nails clicking on the hardwood floors with each step.

Dax glanced at the floor and winced at the muddy paw prints Frankie left behind.

"Geez," Madden muttered. "Did you call that in? I know

you're taking the lead on this, but we all need to be aware of what's happening with our clients."

"I haven't had a chance," Dax snapped. "I helped her pick up more food for the animals after tossing most of it."

Silence stretched out on the other line.

Dax grabbed two bottles of water from the fridge then leaned against the counter. Frankie sat in front of him and panted. "Say it," he said.

"Say what?"

"Whatever it is you're thinking." Spying the dog's empty bowl, he filled it with water then placed it in front of Frankie.

The dog leapt to his feet and plunged most of his head in the dish. Water sloshed on the floor.

Great, another mess to clean.

"Nothing. Just didn't know taking clients on shopping trips was part of the job," Madden said. "Is this serious enough that she needs more one-on-one protection?"

Dax rolled his eyes. "I'm helping her out, man. Didn't know I needed your permission for that."

"You don't. Just making sure things are going okay and there's not something else we should be doing. But it sounds like you have everything under control. Any idea who could have tampered with her supplies?"

"Only one person comes to mind."

"Who?"

"Chip Kemp." Unscrewing the cap from his bottle, he took a long swig before setting it back on the counter. "Vanessa mentioned she'd never met him before coming to town, and they'd only communicated via email. He showed up at her place this morning. She said he wasn't very nice. We ran into him at the hardwood store, and the guy was a jerk."

Madden snorted. "The guy's always a jerk."

"True, and there appears to be some bitterness about not inheriting the property. He even offered to buy the place, and Vanessa refused. He could try to scare off his niece. Then he can swoop in and take what he wants."

"It's a good theory," Madden said. "I'll run it past Reid and Ben. There's not much we can do except keep an eye on the guy. Are you finished over there now?"

Dax debated how to answer. He didn't want to leave Vanessa, but that had more to do with enjoying her company than working. And he could only imagine Madden's reaction if he told his brother he was helping in the garden.

"Just about," he said. It wasn't a lie, and this way he could figure out why Madden even cared. He wasn't one to micromanage, but if he wanted to continue their earlier conversation, Dax wasn't about to head into the office for another lecture.

"I got a call from Valley Goods. They've had some issues with shoplifting and want some cameras installed. Can you take care of that this afternoon?"

Dax bit back a sigh. As much as he wanted to decline, he had no real reason. Vanessa wasn't in danger at the moment, and she could pull weeds on her own. Not to mention working for Sunrise Security was his job. One he needed if he wanted to keep helping his dad pay the bills.

"Yeah, I can handle that," he finally answered. "Let me finish a few things here then I'll head into town. Stop by and see exactly what I need before I grab the equipment."

After a few more words, he disconnected the call and watched Frankie lick the bowl clean. He filled it again, but apparently the little guy had had enough. He stood and stared at Dax.

"What is it?"

Frankie barked then turned in a circle before facing the front door.

"Outside it is."

Dax grabbed the bottles of water and followed behind Frankie. Frankie found a patch of sunlight and curled into a ball before closing his eyes.

Dax kept moving until he reached the edge of the garden. He stopped and watched Vanessa work. She focused on her tasks with intensity, yanking at weeds and tossing them in a growing pile. Strands of hair slipped from her braid and stuck to her face. Dirt covered her clothes.

And, by God, she was the most beautiful thing he'd ever laid eyes on.

As if sensing him, she glanced up and smiled. "Break time over?"

"Unfortunately, yes. That was my brother. I have another job in town. I gotta take off so I can get it done today."

Her smile fell for a beat before she forced it back into place. "Totally get it. You can't waste all your time here with me."

"Trust me, time with you is never wasted. Here," he said, tossing her the unopened bottle. "Call if anything else happens, okay? I'm just a phone call away."

She snagged the bottle from the air. "Thank you."

He hesitated, wishing for an excuse to stay—a reason to see her again. "Do you like baseball?"

She furrowed her brow. "Yeah, why?"

"I promised my pops I'd watch the game with him tonight. He's usually good for a laugh or two, and almost always has a pot of chili on the stove. Care to join us? I could pick you up around seven."

"Can I bring Frankie?"

He gave an exaggerated sigh but couldn't hide his grin. "I suppose. I mean I'm getting used to having him around."

"All right, then. Sounds lovely."

He grinned and decided to lay his cards on the table. Their friendship was new, and he didn't want to scare her or move too fast. But the last thing he wanted was to be put in the friend zone and never make it out. Better to set his intentions.

"Good, it's a date."

Chapter 10

Exhausted, Vanessa dropped from her knees to her bottom in the middle of the half-weeded garden. Her muscles screamed for mercy, but she was almost finished with the current section. If she could get a little more done, then she'd head inside and clean up for dinner.

For her date.

Giddiness swam in her stomach. Dax had been such a bright spot since the second she'd showed up in Cloud Valley. A part of her was unsure if dating him was a great idea. She didn't have any friends yet and would hate to lose him if things didn't work out.

But then he looked at her and her entire body turned to mush.

Sighing, she attacked the ground with the spade. Nope, no way she couldn't at least dip her toe in the dating pond and see what happened. She'd just make sure they both understood that no matter what, they'd maintain their friendship.

Frankie ambled her way and barked twice.

"I know," she said, wiping sweat off her forehead with back of her forearm. "We'll go inside soon. I'll feed you then shower. Just let me get this last weed. It's a big one."

Her pile of weeds had tripled in size in the hours she'd

worked, and a deep satisfaction settled in her bones. She may have underestimated how much work would go into transforming the large plot, but that was okay. She'd make sure the starters she'd purchased stayed alive until she could plant them in the ground. If the rain could hold off another day or two, she could finish this part of the project and start on the next.

Whatever that would be.

Spearing the tip of her tool into the ground again, she connected with something hard below the surface. Moving an inch to the side, she dug into the dirt and hit something hard again.

She frowned at Frankie. "Must be one hell of a rock under there."

Not wanting to waste time but needing to know what she'd hit, she used her gloved hands to break through the tough mud. She brushed away the clumps of dirt and revealed tarnished metal of some kind. "What the heck?"

Curiosity moved her faster until she'd uncovered an old, weathered hammer. The wooden handle was cracked and dirty, but it was the head of the hammer that puzzled her. The metal was a deep brown, bordering on red, with dark stains from the muddy earth.

Frankie growled.

"Why would someone bury a hammer in a garden?" She inspected the tool, hoping for some kind of sign or message that could clue her in to what had prompted the owner to do such a thing, when a spot of blue still in the ground caught her attention.

Eyebrows raised, she glanced at Frankie. "This keeps getting stranger."

He pawed at the ground, as if to tell her to keep going.

She did, shoveling away the muck until she unveiled

a T-shirt. She held it up to inspect it, and streaks of sun shone through the thin material. She studied the cartoon bull in the middle of the shirt and a hint of a memory flitted forward.

"Holy crap," she mumbled and shot to her feet.

Grabbing the hammer and shirt, she darted for the house. She yanked off her garden gloves and tossed them on the porch, along with her muddy boots. She debated carrying the tool and shirt inside but cringed at the thought of tracking dirt into the house. She set them beside her boots then ran inside.

Frankie stayed a step behind her.

She made a beeline for her mother's room, wincing at the dirt crumbling off her dirty clothes, and found the photo she'd tucked against the mirror. She resisted the urge to roll her eyes at the smiling face of her uncle, took a second to stare at her mother's youthful face, and forced herself to not dwell on the boy with the scratched-out eyes.

It was her uncle's shirt that sent her into a tailspin. A blue shirt with a cartoon bull, block lettering spelling out what she assumed was a local town or attraction.

Her mind raced as a hundred questions assaulted her. Why would her uncle bury one of his shirts in the garden, and what the heck was a hammer doing beside it? Maybe her cousin would have some answers. Autumn might have spent a lot of time at their grandfather's house and could be a wealth of knowledge. She'd appeared enthusiastic to become friends. Maybe Autumn could shed some light on a lot of different things she found odd since arriving.

Her mother would know some of those answers, but she'd been a vault with her secrets. Vanessa had learned from a young age not to pester her, but now she regretted giving her mom that space. She'd give anything to have her mother here. To pepper her with questions and demand the truth of what had forced her from her home.

A wave of grief crashed against her. She backed into the bed and sat on the edge. Questions regarding an old T-shirt and hammer were the least of the reasons she wanted her mom back. She squeezed her eyes shut against the heart-crushing pain, let herself feel the loss for the millionth time, then blew out a long breath before standing.

"Enough of that," she told Frankie, who sat near her feet. "I need to scrub off the mud then pour through a mountain of boxes to find something decent to wear for a first date at a man's house with his father."

Chuckling, she shook her head and padded down the hall to the primary bath. Her life had taken a lot of unexpected twists and turns over the last year, but this might be the strangest.

Nerves danced beneath the surface of Dax's body as he stood on Vanessa's porch and waited for her to answer the door. The skies had darkened, promising another storm soon. The rest of his day had moved at a snail's pace. Once done installing security cameras at Valley Goods, he'd seen to his evening chores and taken way too much care in getting ready to watch baseball.

With his dad.

He groaned. His first date with Vanessa should include a fancy dinner or romantic picnic at the foot of the mountains. Not eating a bowl of chili from a TV tray in his dad's living room.

But there was no changing plans now.

Before he could mentally berate himself any more, the door swung open and Vanessa greeted him with a beaming smile. Her long hair was curled into a flurry of dark waves. Her jeans molded against lean legs and the fitted T-shirt hugged her curves, the color the same shade as her olive-green eyes. "Hey."

His mouth went dry, and all his doubts fluttered away with the wind. He didn't care what he did with Vanessa, as long as he got to spend more time with her. "Hey," he echoed. "Ready?"

"Yep." She glanced down at Frankie. "What about you?"

Frankie barked.

Dax scooped up the dog and extended an arm toward his truck. "Ladies first."

She shot him a grin over her shoulder as she passed him on her way down the porch steps. Once she settled into the vehicle, he set Frankie on her lap and hurried to climb in behind the wheel.

"How was the rest of your day?" he asked as he motored down the country road.

"Good. I'm about halfway through the garden. I made an interesting discovery at the end."

"Oh really?"

"Yeah. Someone buried an old hammer and T-shirt."

Dax scratched the bottom of his chin. "That's weird."

"I swear the shirt matches one my uncle was wearing in a picture with my mom. I'm probably grasping at straws, but something's just off about the whole thing. I think I'll call my cousin tomorrow. She seemed sweet, and she might have some insight."

"I don't know Autumn very well," Dax said. "She's a few years younger than me. It'd be good for you to get to know her. Make some more friends in town, especially if she can help you connect with your roots. Not sure if she'll know why random stuff was buried in the garden, but it doesn't hurt to ask."

They filled the rest of the ride with small talk. When he drove under the rusty sign that announced McKay Ranch, his stomach muscles clenched. He hadn't brought a girl home in years. He hadn't given much thought to what Vanessa might think about his bringing her to meet his father.

Hell, he hadn't thought beyond wanting to have dinner with her and not wanting to cancel plans with his dad.

But maybe he should have.

"Oh my goodness," Vanessa said. "I love it here. You have actual horse stables, and how cute is that porch! Do you sit outside a lot? I think I'd be out there every single night."

Her enthusiasm relaxed his muscles, and he parked in his usual spot before shutting off the engine. "Pops and I usually do."

"That's nice. I love that you two are so close. Reminds me of me and my mom. I hate that she's not here."

Her words were like a knife twisting in his gut. "Losing a parent isn't easy. I was young when my mom died, but I remember it like it was yesterday. The pain is still there, even twenty years later."

She rested a hand on his. "I'm sorry. I didn't even think about that. I've lived my whole life only having one parent. Sometimes I forget people have both in their lives. Losing your mom so young had to be tough, but I'm glad you had your dad with you."

"Me, too. He's been my best friend for years." A question sat at the tip of his tongue, but he wasn't sure it was the right time to ask.

As if reading his mind, she said, "Go ahead. Say what's on your mind."

"Have you ever had contact with your father?"

She shook her head. "To be honest, I don't even know

who he is. My mother never told me. It used to piss me off. We'd fight about it, but she'd stand firm on the decision to keep his name from me. I finally realized she had her reasons, and as much as I hated her for it when I was a teenager, I knew she was protecting me. I figured I had plenty of time to get her to tell me about him one day. I was wrong." She shrugged as if it didn't matter, but the quiver in her voice told another story.

Flipping his hand over, he linked her fingers with his and gave a little squeeze. "If you really want to know, you may find something to point you in the right direction among all her boxes."

"Maybe."

The front door of the house swung open and Walter came into view. He threw his arms in the air in a what's-going-on gesture.

"We better head inside before he storms out here," Dax said. "He can be a bit of a pistol."

"Can't wait to meet him." She severed their connection and grabbed Frankie, then hopped out of the truck.

Dax inhaled a steadying breath and led her to the house.

"Well, what in the world is that wiggly little thing in your arms?" Walter asked.

"This is Frankie, and I'm Vanessa Kemp. Thank you for having us over." Vanessa sat Frankie on the worn wooden planks of the porch and extended a hand.

Walter took it and gave it a small shake. "Are you kidding? It's not every day I get to spend the evening with someone other than this rascal. You're giving me a real treat. Let's head in. The chili's hot and the game's about to start."

Frankie butted his head against Walter's legs.

"Are you a dog or a cat?" Walter chuckled and scratched

Frankie behind the ears before leading everyone inside. "I've got my stuff all ready. Dax, grab your girl a bowl and something to drink. Use those manners I tried to teach you."

Grinning, Vanessa raised her brows high and struggled not to laugh.

Dax just shook his head. "Told you. A pistol," he whispered and made a beeline for the kitchen.

"What can I do to help?" she asked.

Walter shooed her away. "Sit with me and keep an old man company. Dax can handle everything."

"I'll be right there," Dax said, watching the two of them step into the connected living room. He hurried to fill two bowls and grab two waters then met them there. "Water, okay?"

"Perfect."

His dad had already retreated to his recliner, his meal on the TV tray beside him. He fiddled with the remote until the baseball game took up the screen.

Dax made sure Vanessa had everything she needed then sat beside her.

Frankie chose to sit in front of Walter, staring at him with his big bug eyes.

"So, Vanessa…" Walter began. "I'm glad you're here, but I have one very important question. Do you like baseball?"

"I'm a Cubs fan, sir. Born and raised in Chicago. My mom and I tried to make it to Wrigley Field at least once a year." She spooned a little bit of beef and tomatoes and took a small bite. "This is delicious."

"She likes baseball and my chili. She's a keeper, even if her choice of team is a bit questionable."

"Pops." Dax mentally kicked himself for bringing Vanessa over.

"Excuse me? My team is a national treasure, and I have no reason to ever question my love of the Cubbies."

Walter let loose a hoot of laughter. "You're a spitfire. Just like your grandmother."

Vanessa's mouth curved into a small smile. "You knew my grandma?"

"Sure did. You remind me of her, which isn't surprising since your mama was the spitting image of Justine."

"You knew my mother, too?"

The lines in Walter's face softened. "Not well. But she was a sweet soul. I'm sorry you lost her, and Earl as well. I'm sure your grandpa would be thrilled you're here though. I wouldn't be surprised if you feel his presence in that old house. He was awfully proud of that land."

"I hope he'd be proud of what I plan to do with it."

"As long as you're doing what you love and respecting the land, he'd be proud. He was a good man. I was sorry to see him go."

Dax's nerves settled. More chatter filled the room as they ate and watched the game. The innings stretched on, and their bowls emptied. Frankie managed to claim a spot on Walter's lap, snoring away much to his dad's delight.

When the sound of Walter's snores matched Frankie's, Dax stood and carried all their dishes into the kitchen.

Vanessa leaned against the counter. "This was nice."

"Glad you thought so." Dax rinsed the dishes then left them in the sink. "I wasn't sure if this would turn out to be a big mistake."

Tilting her head to the side, her hair spilled over her shoulder and her eyes widened. "Why would it be?"

He shrugged and stood beside her. "You saw my dad. There's no telling what will come out of his mouth."

"He's great," she said, knocking her shoulder against his. "I really enjoyed him, and he got me thinking. Well, you both did, actually."

"Should I be scared?"

"No, but I should be."

He frowned down at her. "What do you mean?"

She let out a long breath. "Well, talking with your dad made me realize that so many people around here knew my grandpa, knew my mom. Yeah, I'll talk to Autumn, but there's only so much she'll be aware of, and all of that through stories. But there must be ways to learn more. To uncover more."

"Is this about what you found in the garden? I doubt the person who buried them told a bunch of people."

"Although that's going to bug me, it's not what I mean. I want to finally know what really made my mom leave town. Figure out why she never came back. A cloak of secrecy has always been wrapped around my family. Maybe it's time to finally unwrap it."

He was silent for a beat, thinking back to secrets that had held his own family hostage for so long. "In my experience, secrets always find a way out. And when they do, they can either heal you or inflict even more pain—sometimes both. You might not like what you find. Are you prepared to deal with that?"

"I think so."

"Then good luck. Where will you start? I doubt your uncle will be a wealth of knowledge."

"No, but my aunt might. And I can keep going through Mom's boxes, look for friends who may still be around."

"You can try the library, too," he said. "The local paper

has always kept close tabs on the happenings of the town. The library would have old articles to comb through. That could give you a glimpse of your grandparents as well."

"I love that idea! Is the library close?"

"It's right off Main Street. I can take you, if you want." He tried to keep the eagerness out of his voice, but damn, he liked having reasons to see her.

Her instant smile was enough to tell him he hadn't overstepped. "I'd like that. Thank you."

He wouldn't call it a date this time. Tonight had gone well, but the next time he took her out, he'd put forth a bit more effort—and his father wouldn't be an audience.

Frankie trotted into the kitchen and whined.

"I think that's our cue to head home," Vanessa said.

He hated to take her back to an empty house, to be away from her, but she was right. The announcers on the television had moved onto post-game talk. She'd had a long day and was probably exhausted. As much as he wanted her to stay, it made more sense to call it a night.

Peeling himself away from her side, he swept Frankie off the floor and ruffled the fur on the top of his head. "All right, you little weasel. Let's get going."

Chapter 11

Vanessa stood under the bright artificial light on her porch and told her stupid heart to stop beating so hard. Heavy rain pelted the tin roof and claps of thunder boomed across the sky.

Dax stood in front of her, his hands shoved in the front pockets of his jeans. He'd left his cowboy hat at his place, and his dark hair stuck out in a sexy way that made her want to run her fingers through it.

He rocked back on his heels. "Thanks again for having dinner with me. I know it wasn't the ideal first date, but Pops enjoyed your company as much as I did."

"I think he liked Frankie more than he liked me, but that's okay. I get that a lot."

Dax's lips curved up at the corners. "I doubt that. The dog's nice and all, but…"

"Good answer."

"Well, I guess I should get going." His tongue swiped his bottom lip, eyes locked on hers.

Oh dear Lord, anticipation made her batty. She didn't want to wait any longer to find out what he tasted like. Standing on her tiptoes, she rested her palms on his chest and pressed her lips to his. Excitement zipped up her spine, making her giddy.

She pulled back but kept her face close. “Was that okay?”

“Okay? More like great.” He wrapped his arm around the small of her back and molded her against him before capturing her mouth with this. His lips moved over hers until his tongue poked into her mouth.

She wrapped herself around him and her whole body tingled. Need built inside her, creating a dizziness that threatened to knock her off her feet.

Dax broke the kiss, his breath ragged. “Really, really great.”

Vanessa lowered back to flat feet and struggled to get herself under control. If he hadn’t stopped, she wasn’t sure she could have. Her pulse thundered and a part of her wanted to throw caution to the wind and invite him in to see where things went.

Hell, they both knew where things would go. And as much as the thought thrilled her, she still needed to claim a bedroom and turn it into a place she’d be comfortable bringing a man.

“I’ll see you tomorrow.” She kissed his cheek then forced herself to step inside the house. She gave him one last wave then closed the door. “I’m in trouble,” she said to Frankie.

Her dog barked then trotted into the kitchen.

A quick glance at her phone told her it wasn’t too late. She could follow Frankie into the kitchen to prattle on about her evening with Dax or she could call her cousin. Nothing like fawning over a guy to bond them. It might loosen her up to discuss more serious things.

Racing upstairs, she found the pants she’d worn earlier and dug out the paper with Autumn’s and her aunt’s numbers. She opted to sit on her mom’s old bed—something about being surrounded by all things pink and girly matched her mood—and punched in the numbers.

"Hello?"

"Hi, Autumn, it's Vanessa. I hope it's not too late to call." A pinch of nervousness took hold of her stomach. Maybe she should have waited until the morning.

"Oh my gosh, hi! No, it's never too late to call. How are you? Is everything okay? Do you need something?"

Just like when they'd met, words poured out of her cousin in rapid succession.

Vanessa smiled at her excitement. "I wondered if you had time to stop by the house tomorrow."

"Seriously?" Autumn asked. "I'd love to."

"Good. I need a few more friends in town." She debated saying more or sharing that she wanted to pick her cousin's brain for information about their family. But she was afraid Autumn would refuse to come if she understood Vanessa was searching for answers.

Besides, she wasn't lying. She did need more friends, and she wanted to get to know at least one person from her family.

"Have you met anyone else?"

"I went to Tilly's with Dax last night and met the owner—I think her name was Eve." She made a mental note to stop by the restaurant again soon. Eve seemed nice, and the food had been delicious. If she planned to stay in town, she needed to step out of her comfort zone and make an effort to ingratiate herself with the people of Cloud Valley.

And Eve might be a good resource for figuring out how to create a community garden. A woman who dealt with food for a living could have some ideas.

"Eve's the best," Autumn said. "And to have Dax take you for dinner. Lucky girl."

Vanessa tucked her bottom lip between her teeth as she caught Autumn's excitement like a virus. "I had dinner with him again tonight. At his house, with his dad. He called it a date."

Autumn's squeal threatened to split Vanessa's eardrum. "Lady! I need all the details."

As the reminder of her kiss with Dax attacked her senses, she pressed the tips of her fingers to her mouth. Flaps of butterfly wings beat against her stomach lining. "We had such a nice time. His dad was wonderful. I didn't want the evening to end."

"And how exactly did it end?" Autumn's singsong voice made Vanessa laugh.

She could be coy—could be a lady and not spill the details. But she wanted to scream what had happened from the rooftop, and the whole reason she'd called Autumn instead of a friend back in Chicago was that she knew her cousin would flip.

"With the best kiss of my life," she said, flattening a palm over her heart.

"No. Freaking. Way. Tell me everything."

Vanessa spent the next ten minutes pouring over the time spent with Dax and his father, ending with the moment their lips had touched on her front porch.

"I really like him," she said. "Which kind of scares me. Is it silly to jump into a relationship with someone I barely know right after I move to town?"

"Nah," Autumn said. "I mean do we ever truly know anyone until we peel back the layers? Sometimes the people we've known our whole lives turn out to be someone we'd never expect. Might as well yank those layers away from Dax now and find out if there's anything underneath that sexy surface. Because it might end up being something really special."

"Thanks. I needed to hear that."

They finished their conversation, Autumn promising to touch base in the morning about what time to come by, and Vanessa flopped back on the bed. She stared up at the ceiling, the same spot her mom probably saw when she was younger, maybe even feeling zips of excitement and happiness after a date with someone she cared for.

Maybe even with her father.

A familiar ache gnawed at her heart. She'd ignored it for so long, but something about being in this house among her mother's old things brought that ache back with such fierceness that it couldn't be shoved aside anymore.

One way or another, she'd find answers. She just prayed they brought her peace and didn't drown her in even more grief.

With a renewed sense of urgency, she jumped off the bed and walked over to the closet. She'd already dragged most of the boxes out. Photos and yearbooks might paint a picture of part of her mom she'd never know, but they wouldn't spill any secrets.

Staring into the closet, she studied the clothes hanging from the silver rod and shoes stuffed in one corner. Chances were high her mom had grabbed what she could when she'd left. She wouldn't have been the one to neatly store her things and stack them away to never be seen again. Her grandfather probably had done that.

That meant anything she'd want buried she would have taken with her or hidden somewhere that wouldn't be easily found.

A clap of thunder shook the house, quickly followed

by the patter of Frankie's claws on the floors. He skidded into the room barking like a maniac.

Crouching, she cuddled him close. "It's okay, buddy. It's just another storm. We're fine."

He trembled against her and buried his snout in the crook of her arm.

She plopped on the floor and pulled him onto her lap. Running her palm over his silky fur, she stared into the closet, and an idea took hold. "Sorry, little guy. I've got to put you down."

With Frankie beside her, she moved all the boxes from the closet then piled all the clothes on the bed. She shuffled the shoes out of the way and stared at the wood-paneled walls and spots of dust on the floor.

When she was a teenager, she'd found a loose floorboard in her closet to hide her diary. She might have shared most things with her mom, but there were still secrets she'd guarded. Boys she'd kissed or friends she'd snuck out with that she'd written about and never wanted her mom to discover. Maybe her mother had a similar spot.

She skimmed her hands over the walls first, then dropped to the ground. Dust bunnies rolled around like tumbleweeds. She brushed them away, dirt coating her palm. The boards were smooth and firmly planted.

Well, damn it.

Crawling out of the closet, she studied the rest of the room. She didn't have the energy to move the furniture, but if the room was kept the same, her mom wouldn't have wanted to move the bed or dresser anytime she needed her hiding spot. Easier to pull back the fuzzy white rug to get to the floorboards underneath.

Sighing, she replaced all the boxes in the closet, Frankie watching her with his buggy eyes. Then she folded back the soft rug, flipping the end up on the bed. She stared down at the floor. “All right, Mom. Is there something here or am I grasping at straws?”

Dropping to her knees, she roamed her palm over the worn boards. She searched for any divots or knicks in the wood that could clue her in to a loose board. She inched toward the bed, almost out of room, when a gap between two planks caught her eye. Her heart seized and she dug her fingernail between the space, lifting until the board popped up. The overhead light streamed down and highlighted a glimpse of something purple.

“Holy crap, Frankie.” She stared at the dark spot, shocked her instincts had proven correct. Hesitation stilled her hand over the newly discovered hiding spot. Her throat went dry, and a boom of thunder had her jumping out of her skin.

“Okay, I’m being stupid.” She dipped her hand into the opening, and it brushed against worn fabric. Curiosity moved her quicker, and she snatched out a tattered and stained T-shirt. Recognition turned her stomach, and she shot to her feet to snatch the photo from the mirror.

The bright purple T-shirt with an explosion of white daises stared back at her, the older and worn version in her hand.

More thunder combined with the dizzying reality crashing against her, leaving her jittery. Dread dried her throat as she flattened the T-shirt on the floor. The stains on the fabric deepened the purple and dark red splattered across the daisies.

Blood.

Fear hitched her breath higher in her throat. Scrubbing her hands over her face, her mind worked in overdrive.

What the hell had happened? Why was her uncle's shirt buried in the garden and Mom's hidden in her room?

And then there was the hammer.

A shiver ran down her spine. She wouldn't find any more answers tonight. What she needed was a warm bed and a good night's sleep.

But not in here. Surrounded by the ghost of her mother. She replaced the rug and tossed the T-shirt back in the closet.

Turmoil turned her stomach with each step she took to her grandfather's room. His things may remain, but at least the cozy space wasn't filled with gut-wrenching secrets—at least not any she'd uncovered. Removing her jeans, she opted to sleep in her long-sleeved shirt that rested at the tops of her thighs. She climbed into the king-sized bed and curled under the sheets, the smell of cedar and citrus clinging to the pillowcase.

She inhaled. Was this what her grandfather smelled like? Had his cologne lingered to greet her, to hold her with a promise that everything would be all right?

Frankie hopped onto the bed and cuddled in beside her. She wrapped him up tight, closed her eyes, and forced her thoughts on Dax. The sound of the storm was her constant companion as she finally drifted off to sleep.

The explosive blare of the alarm tore Vanessa out of a deep sleep. Her heart shot to her throat and fear thumped against her temples.

Frankie crouched beside her and growled.

Oh my God, someone was in the house. She jumped out of bed and searched around for her phone. The alarm should alert the police to an intruder, but she didn't want to take chances. She patted the bed then swiped her hand across the nightstand.

Shit, she'd left her phone in her mom's room. Terror stole her ability to think, to react to the nightmare storming back into her home. She rolled off the bed and curled into a ball on the floor, her mind refusing to work.

Frankie leapt to her side and barked, snapping her into attention.

She sucked in a deep breath and stayed low to the ground as she crept toward the door. The alarm continued to scream its warning. At the doorway, she peeked into the hall. She'd left the lights on upstairs when she'd retired for the night. No one waited to ambush her. No shadows lurked in the corners. She darted into her mom's room and waited for Frankie to follow before closing and locking the door. She found her phone and grabbed it with shaking hands.

Her fingers moved on autopilot, bringing up Dax's number. She hit Call and lifted the phone to her ear.

"Hey," Dax said, answering on the first ring.

She pressed the heel of her hand over one ear, blocking out the blaring alarm as much as she could. "Someone's in the house. I'm scared. Help me, please."

Chapter 12

Time slowed as Dax drove toward Vanessa, speeding down the country road. He reached her house before any law enforcement. He'd kept her on the phone while he drove, so as scared as he was, at least he knew she was all right. Parking, he jumped out of his truck and raced toward the front of the house.

"I'm here," he said into the phone. "The sheriff isn't, so stay put. I'm not sure if anyone is still in the house, but the door's wide open."

"Be careful," she whispered, fear making her voice thin and thready.

"I have to hang up now, okay? I need both hands on my gun." He hated to sever the connection, but he couldn't be distracted when he stepped inside.

"Okay."

"I'll see you soon," he said then slid his phone in his pocket.

Before he could head up the porch steps, Madden arrived and parked his truck next to Dax's. His dad must have sounded the alarm after he'd left him in the living room, but right now, he was happy to have his brother as back-up.

Dax secured his weapon as Madden approached. "Dad call you?"

"Yeah," Madden said. "Deputy Sanders is on his way. I told him we were working with Vanessa and wouldn't wait to enter the house."

"Good." Dax would have forced his way in regardless of if the deputy had said otherwise, but it was nice to know they weren't pissing off any law enforcement. "Vanessa's upstairs in one of the bedrooms. The alarm woke her. She hasn't seen anyone and is scared to death."

"Let's head in then."

As Dax fixed his weapon in front of him, sirens sounded in the distance. He stepped over the threshold with Madden at his back. The lights on the main floor were off, shrouding the house in darkness. As much as Dax wanted to rush upstairs to Vanessa, they needed to make sure no one lurked in the shadows.

Stepping quietly down the hallway, Dax led the way into the living room. Wind barreled in through a broken window. The moon bled in, creeping across the room. Dax flipped the switch to illuminate the room. He blinked against the sudden assault on his eyes.

"Room's clear," Madden said. "Let's go to the next."

They moved together, Dax's heart beating harder with every step. His desire to get to Vanessa quickened his pace. By the time they reached the stairs, Deputy Sanders was at the door.

Dax pounded up the steps, leaving any communication for Madden to handle. The sound of Frankie's soft whining turned him to the shut bedroom door. He knocked. "Vanessa? It's Dax."

The door swung open and Vanessa flung herself into his arms. "Oh…thank God."

He ushered her back into the room. "Madden, I've got Vanessa," he called over his shoulder as his brother and

Deputy Sanders got to the top of the steps. "The other two rooms need to be cleared."

"We're on it," Madden said.

Dax pulled back and smoothed his palms along Vanessa's jawline on either side of her face. "Are you all right?"

Her body shook but she nodded. "Just scared. Did you find anyone?"

"No, but the window was broken. I'm guessing they smashed the glass to get inside then ran out the front door when the alarm went off. Probably wasn't expecting that."

Frankie barked and jumped, resting his two front paws on Dax's leg.

Dax glanced down, and heat burned a hole in his gut. The dark green shirt Vanessa wore skimmed the top of her thighs. Nothing clothed her long, lean legs.

She followed his gaze then wide eyes shot back to his. "I was sleeping. I didn't want to go downstairs to put on pajamas."

"Do you need me to grab something for you?" It took every ounce of self-control he possessed to focus on the flecks of yellow in her eyes and not the smooth skin his fingers itched to touch.

"We're all clear," Madden called. "Whoever broke the window is long gone. Vanessa, the deputy will need you to make a statement."

"I need pants," she hissed, embarrassment flush on her cheeks.

"Give her a minute," Dax called over his shoulder then shut the bedroom door. "Where are they?"

"In the room across the hall, on the floor."

"Okay. I'll be right back." He pressed a kiss to her forehead then stepped into the hallway to find Madden and

Deputy Sanders's matching expressions of confusion. "I've got to grab something."

He didn't offer any more explanation but dipped into the room across the hall and found her pants in a heap. A ball of desire lodged in his throat as he picked them off the floor. He'd be lying if he said he hadn't envisioned Vanessa's clothes thrown across the bedroom floor, but this wasn't how he'd imagined it playing out.

And now was definitely not the time to get lost in that fantasy.

Shoving aside his misguided thoughts, he passed his brother and the deputy and ducked back into the room. He offered Vanessa the pants, forcing himself to spin away as she put them on. A light touch on his back turned him around, and he folded her against him once more.

Her arms wrapped around his middle.

He gave her a second to catch her breath then asked, "Are you ready to speak with the authorities? They'll need a statement and will want you to take a look to see if anything's missing."

Tears threatened to fall, but she sniffed them back. "As ready as I'll ever be. Better to get it over and done with."

"I'm right here with you, okay?"

A whisper of a smile touched her lips. "Okay."

Dax took hold of her hand and led her into the hall where the men waited.

Deputy Sanders dipped his chin. His heavyset frame was dressed in his firmly pressed deputy's uniform. "Hello, Ms. Kemp. I'm Deputy Sanders with the sheriff's department. Do you want to go downstairs and talk? I'll make this as quick and painless as possible. I promise."

Dax stayed close as they made their way downstairs

and into the kitchen. He pulled out a chair for her to sit then stood behind her.

Madden stayed in the doorway.

"Okay," Deputy Sanders said. "Can you give me a rundown of what happened?"

Dax reined in his temper as she gave a play-by-play of her night and what had led them all there. By the time she finished, he was on the chair beside her with an arm draped over her shoulders.

"I'm sorry this happened." Deputy Sanders scribbled notes as he spoke. "I took photos of the broken window. You'll want to do the same for insurances purposes. Do you need help securing everything?"

"Dax and I can help with that," Madden said.

Deputy Sanders stood. "Then all that's left is to take a look to see if anything's missing."

"Shouldn't be too hard," Vanessa said. "Most of my stuff is still in boxes."

Dax helped her to her feet. "Well, we know nothing was taken from your mom's old room since you were in there."

"And, honestly, I haven't spent enough time in the other two rooms to even know if anything had been stolen."

"That's okay," the deputy said. "Let's focus downstairs."

Vanessa glanced around and shrugged. "The kitchen seems to be in order, or at least as much in order as I'd expect it."

"Let's check the living room," Madden said. "I'll look at the security feed to see if the camera caught an image of the intruder, but my guess is whoever it was took off as fast as possible. Probably didn't have much time to look for valuables."

Vanessa snorted. "I don't have any of those anyway." She led the way to the living room. "It's impossible to tell if anything's gone. The boxes are all taped shut. Nothing else was really in here except..." Her eyes went wide, and she ran out the front door. "They're gone."

Dax hurried to her side. "What's gone?"

"The hammer and T-shirt I told you about." She spun to face him and pointed at a pile of dirty gardening gloves and boots. "I put them right here. I know I did. Someone stole them."

Vanessa huddled on the couch with Frankie and watched Dax and Madden temporarily fix her busted window. Fear clung to her like a cobweb, and unanswered questions plagued her.

She'd explained to the deputy what she'd found in the garden as well as her mother's bedroom. He, along with Madden, agreed it was an odd thing to find, and the fact someone took such a risk to steal them told an even more terrifying story.

A story in which no one knew the beginning or the end. But she couldn't help but feel like she was stuck smack-dab in the middle.

Dax smoothed a thick piece of duct tape along the bottom of the window, securing the cardboard even more. "This should hold you for a day or so. Luckily, it's not winter, or you'd have to combat the cold. Now we just need to make sure no one else tries to get through it."

"I'd feel better if we could pinpoint who broke in." She drew her knees up to her chest and replayed the video they'd watched moments before.

The security camera had caught someone running out of the house, stopping on the porch to grab the T-shirt and hammer, then running to the back of the house. The dark figure could easily have been the same person who'd ambushed her when she'd arrived, but there was no way to tell for sure.

Madden packed the tools he'd brought in from his truck. "The sheriff's department is on the lookout. There might not be much to go on, but they won't stop until they figure it out."

"They aren't the only ones who'll be looking," Dax said.

The steel in his voice comforted Vanessa in a way nothing else could.

Madden cast a curious glance Dax's way before focusing on her. "Sunrise Security can provide whatever you need to make you feel safe right now."

"Screw that," Dax said. "Someone's pissed she's here and wants her to know it. She doesn't have to pay me a dime to make sure she's protected."

"I understand where you're coming from, but this needs to be a discussion." Madden spoke through gritted teeth.

Tension crackled between them, and Vanessa didn't have the energy to figure out why. "Can we talk more tomorrow? It's late and I'm tired. All I want is sleep."

Madden nodded. "Sure. Call any time tomorrow." He arched a brow at Dax.

Dax crossed his arms over his chest. "Good night."

Madden flashed her a small smile then disappeared out the front door.

Dax waited for Madden to be gone before crossing the room and sitting beside her on the edge of the sofa. "Sorry about that, we have some issues." He scrubbed a palm over his face. "That doesn't matter now. How are you?"

She leaned against him, needing his sturdy form to anchor her—soothe her. "Overwhelmed. Scared, but not as much now that you're with me."

He secured an arm around her then scratched Frankie behind his ear. "I'm here as long as you want me to be."

"Could you stay here tonight?" She held her breath as she waited for an answer. She'd fantasized about inviting him into her home after they'd kissed earlier. Never would she imagine she'd be asking him over because she was too afraid to be alone.

"Absolutely," he said, placing a kiss on her forehead. "If you grab me a pillow and blanket, I'll sleep on the couch. That way I can keep an extra eye on things with the window being busted."

Glancing up, she bit the inside of her cheek. She hated being vulnerable, but her walls had been demolished with a sledgehammer. "Can you lay with me upstairs?"

He swallowed hard. "Are you sure? I don't mind staying down here."

"I don't think I can sleep if I'm alone." She rested a palm on his chest and locked her eyes on his. "I'm so tired, but I keep hearing those sirens, keep thinking about how things could have played out differently. If I'm in that bed with Frankie, I'll lay awake for the rest of the night. I just want to rest."

"Okay. Then that's what we'll do." He stood and held out his hand.

Relief cut through her terror and insecurities. She fit her palm in his and walked up the stairs, Frankie trailing behind them. Excitement pressed against her lungs, but she ignored it as best she could and led Dax into the bedroom she'd claimed as her own.

Dax stood in the doorway, the light from the hallway washing over him, and scratched the back of his neck. "Nice digs."

His joke loosened the anxiety in her gut, and she

grinned. "I decided this room made the most sense. I planned to spruce it up tomorrow, but for tonight, it's Grandpa's comforter and flannel sheets."

Dax wiggled his eyebrows. "Sexy."

She climbed under the thick blanket, opting to keep her pants on this time, then smoothed part of the covers back.

Frankie leapt up and claimed the spot.

"Not tonight, Fido," Dax said, stalking into the room to slide Frankie to the foot of the bed. He stared down at Vanessa, indecision in his pinched brow.

Her mouth went dry, and she struggled not to squirm under his scrutiny. "Is everything all right?"

He wrinkled his nose. "I'm not used to sleeping in jeans."

"Oh." Her gaze dropped to the dark jeans surrounding his thick thighs then back up to his handsome face. "We're both adults. Get comfortable. I'll even turn my back, so I don't sneak a peek."

He grinned, but she turned away to keep the playful banter going. Pretending like she wasn't interested in Dax McKay taking off his clothes before climbing into bed beside her was far better than reliving the past few hours of hell.

The mattress dipped alongside her and the heat of Dax's skin nearly scorched her. Dear Lord, maybe this wasn't her best idea, but there was no turning back now.

A strong arm hooked her middle and pulled her close. "Is this okay?" he asked, his breath tickling her ear.

She cleared the desire from her throat before she said, "Yes." She relaxed against him, feeling safe for the first time since the blasting alarm had ripped her out of a deep sleep. "Thank you."

His throaty chuckle skimmed her neck. "There might be

a lot of things you can thank me for some day, but holdin' you isn't one of them. Now close your eyes and go to sleep. Because if you keep me up much longer, I'll be tempted to do a whole lot more than snuggle."

She debated discovering how much more that would be but thought better of it. She was too tired and overwhelmed to let go and spend the night with Dax the way her body really wanted. Instead, she closed her eyes and fell into the deepest sleep she'd experienced in years.

Chapter 13

A warm body nestled against Dax's chest, and he wrapped his arm around soft curves. Fatigue kept his eyelids shut, but he couldn't argue with waking up slowly in bed with a beautiful woman. Even if being a gentleman all night was one of the hardest things he'd ever done.

But morning had dawned, and he could indulge in bed for a few minutes with Vanessa in his arms.

Moist breath hit his face seconds before a wet tongue slid across his cheek.

"What the hell?" He reared his head back and found big brown eyes staring back at him.

Frankie whimpered then lunged forward, landing another good-morning kiss before hopping out of the bed and barking.

Dax groaned and wiped the puppy slobber off his face. "Dude, not cool."

Frankie responded with another bark then trotted into the hallway.

Stretching into a sitting position, disappointment pressed down on Dax's lungs to find the room empty. Alarm moved him out of bed. He grabbed his clothes and hurried to dress. He'd slept so well beside Vanessa, he'd never forgive himself if something happened to her while he'd slept.

He pounded down the steps and followed the sounds of sizzling bacon. His heart rate slowed along with his pace. He spotted Vanessa in front of the stove with her long black hair tied on the top of her head. She still wore the same clothes as the night before. Her feet were bare as she swayed along with the notes of classic rock coming from her phone.

A part of him didn't want to interrupt her. He could stand there all day and watch her move along with the music. But the magnetic force that had existed since the moment he'd met her drew him across the room. He stopped short of pulling her against him and nuzzling her neck. They might have spent the night together, but he hadn't earned that type of intimacy with her.

Not yet anyway.

He laid a gentle hand at the small of her back and kissed her cheek. "Good morning."

She turned around, a smile wide on her face. "You ruined my plan. I wanted to bring breakfast up to you as a thank-you."

"You can thank your dog for that," he said, resting his hands on her hips. "I woke to a faceful of Frankie tongue. Not exactly what I was expecting."

Giggling, she wrinkled her nose. "Been there. Not a good way to start your day." Raising on her tiptoes, she pressed her lips to his. "Better?"

"Not sure. Maybe we need to try it again."

Rolling her eyes, she obliged, circling her arms around his neck.

He held her closer. Heat ignited in his core as his hands skimmed down her back toward her bottom.

The doorbell blasted into the room, and he groaned. "Can't catch a break."

She smoothed her palms on his chest and frowned. "Autumn's stopping by today, but she won't be here for at least another hour."

"Any chance she decided to come earlier?"

Vanessa shrugged. "Maybe, but I bet she'd call or text to let me know."

"I'll grab the door, you watch the bacon." Dragging himself away from her, Dax walked to the front of the house. A quick peek out the window had his irritation growing at being torn away from Vanessa.

He opened the door to Ben Besler, his coworker at Sunrise Security and a Marine who'd served with his brother and Reid overseas. Madden and Reid Sommers had left the service with their fair share of scars—both mentally and physically—but war had taken a bigger toll on Ben.

For reasons Dax didn't know or understand.

"Morning," Dax said. "What brings you out here?"

Ben twisted the bill of his baseball cap and grunted. "Madden gave me measurements for the window that was busted last night. I got my hands on a replacement. More rain's coming and this temporary fix won't hold—not to mention it isn't safe. I can install it if she wants."

Appreciation beat back the annoyance at the interruption. He swept his hand inside, allowing Ben to step past him and into the house. "Go ahead and ask her, but I'm sure she'd be thrilled."

As he followed Ben, he called out, "Vanessa, you got a visitor," not wanting her to be alarmed by seeing a man she didn't know preceding him into the kitchen.

Vanessa scooped bacon onto a plate then set it on the counter before wiping her hands on a dish towel. Curiosity widened her eyes, but she kept a pleasant smile on her face. "Hello," she said then glanced at Dax.

"This is Ben," Dax said. "We work together. He brought you a new window, if you're interested."

Her mouth fell open. "Are you serious? That's amazing." She closed the gap between her and Ben and squeezed him in a big hug.

Ben stiffened, his discomfort palpable. "No big deal. I just ordered new ones for my place. If Dax can give me a hand, we can install it pretty quick."

Dax spotted the time from a clock on the wall and winced. "I have to tend the horses at my place. Can you wait a little bit?"

"Would rather not." Ben worked his jaw back and forth.

Dax resisted the urge to argue. Ben wasn't a bad guy; he just happened to be as prickly as a damn cactus.

"Besides," Ben continued, "Madden said he'd handle your chores. He figured you'd rather stay here than tend the horses."

Okay, so Madden might be right, but that didn't mean Dax wanted his decisions made for him, but he wouldn't drag Ben or Vanessa into that drama.

"Fine, but I'm eating this bacon and drinking some coffee first. Wait," Dax said, directing his attention to Vanessa. "You do have coffee, don't you?" He'd taken Vanessa to the grocery store the day before, but she'd only picked up a handful of items. He hadn't planned on staying the night with her, so hadn't paid attention to whether she'd have any caffeine at her place.

"Yeah, I just need to find the coffeepot." The horror etched on her face mirrored his thoughts. "Oh God, what if Grandpa doesn't have one? I didn't even think of that.

Mine's in a box somewhere, but that could take forever to find."

Ben grumbled something under his breath and turned and walked out of the room.

"Is he all right?" Vanessa asked.

"He's really into his coffee," Dax said, struggling to keep a straight face.

Laughing, she playfully slapped his chest. "I doubt that. But seriously, he seems upset. He doesn't need to help with the window if he doesn't want to."

Dax trapped her hand with his, keeping it in place on his pec. "He's a good guy. He wouldn't have showed up first thing in the morning if he didn't want to help. I don't know the details of what he survived while serving in the Marine Corps with my brother, but I know it was rough. He's still trying to figure his stuff out—he just doesn't hide it like the rest of us."

The side of her mouth trailed down. "That's admirable."

"What is?"

"Not pretending to have everything together." She lifted one slender shoulder. "I like that better than someone who puts on a happy face to make everyone else more comfortable."

He tossed her words around. "I never thought of it that way."

She kissed the tip of his nose. "You're not the only one who has some wisdom. Now help me find the coffeepot."

He snatched a piece of bacon from the plate then helped her rummage through the cabinets. Something in his soul settled, calmed in a way he'd never experienced. Starting his day with a beautiful woman and falling into step with simple domestic tasks just felt right.

And he hoped he'd have more mornings like this to come.

* * *

The sound of the guys installing the new window floated upstairs while Vanessa and Autumn sat on the floor in her mother's old bedroom. Vanessa stretched her legs out in front of her and leaned against the bed while Autumn poked inside one of the boxes they'd pulled out of the closet.

Frankie slept on the bed, soft snores competing with the banging downstairs.

"This is wild," Autumn said, pulling out a framed photo. She stared down at it for a second then flashed the front toward Vanessa. "This is my dad and your mom as kids."

Vanessa took the metal frame and grinned down at the children playing on the banks of a river. "Every single photo I've seen of the two of them broadcasts happiness. How had things changed so drastically?"

Autumn screwed her lips to the side. "I wish I knew. I learned at a young age not to ask questions. They made Dad mad, Grandpa sad and Mom nervous."

"So, nobody ever talked about my mom? Never shared memories? Never wondered about me?" Vanessa hated how small her voice sounded, but it broke her heart to think that as soon as her mom had left town, she'd been scrubbed clean from everyone's lives.

Not to mention that Vanessa didn't appear to be a blip on anyone's radar, even as she'd sat in Chicago and wished to know the family she'd never met.

Frowning, Autumn shook her head. "Sorry. I know that must be hurtful. I always wanted to know my aunt, to meet you. The only time I heard my dad speak about your mom, I overhead a fight with Grandpa. I'd been outside and when I came in, they were yelling."

"About what?"

Autumn scrunched her nose and looked away. "I'm not sure you want to know."

"Tell me," Vanessa said, bracing herself. "Please."

Autumn sighed. "It was about a year ago. Gramps told my dad your mom was dying and that you needed us—you needed family. Dad said you were the reason this family fell apart. That your mom brought shame on the Kemp name because she wouldn't listen to reason. She was ungrateful and selfish, and running away was the best decision she'd ever made."

Anger fisted Vanessa's hands in her lap. Sensing her turmoil, Frankie leapt onto the floor and cuddled beside her. She ran her palm over his silky fur until her heart rate slowed, sadness flooding in to smother the anger.

"I don't understand," Vanessa said. "It's not like they grew up in the 1920s when getting pregnant while unmarried was the end of the world. And why would her brother be so much more upset than her own father? Grandpa and I started writing letters when I was a teenager. He was so happy I reached out. He didn't see me as this stain on the family name, why would my uncle?"

Autumn shrugged and tucked a strand of her long, dark hair behind her ear. "He's always been a pious prick."

Vanessa stared down at the photo again. "Doesn't look like it. At one point, our parents weren't just siblings. They were friends. Something changed that, and it has to be bigger than my mom getting pregnant."

"Any idea what else it could be?" Autumn asked.

She debated telling her about the buried shirt and hammer that were taken, along with what she'd found in her mother's room. As much as she'd love her cousin's insight, she didn't know her well yet. Trust had to be earned, and at this point someone was sending a clear message that Vanessa wasn't wanted here. She needed to hold some cards close to the vest for now.

Standing, Vanessa scooped the picture with the unknown boy from the dresser and passed it to her cousin. "Do you know who that guy is?"

"Yikes," Autumn said. "I don't but looks like someone didn't like him."

"But look at my mom's smile," Vanessa said. "And your dad is happy, too. I can't help but think this guy might know something. Any chance your dad would tell you who it is?"

Autumn snorted. "Yeah, right. He'd flip if he knew I was here. If I come home asking questions about his past with your mom, the bulging vein on his neck will explode. But wait—" She dipped back into a box and pulled out a yearbook. "Did you look for him in here? Might be hard to figure out his identity, but we could narrow it down."

"I looked at it a little bit, but mostly to see pictures of my mom. There's no harm in trying again."

"Good. I love seeing all the old clothes and hairstyles. My parents should be in here, too."

Vanessa plopped down on the ground beside Autumn and they poured over the pages. They giggled over the fashion choices and Autumn explained silly traditions that she'd participated in high school as well.

"And you graduated three years ago?" Vanessa asked.

Autumn nodded. "Yeah. I wanted to go off to a big college and really get that experience, but my parents wanted me to stay closer to town."

A pang of sympathy echoed inside Vanessa. She'd had dreams that had been put on hold because of her parent as well. She just hoped Autumn was happy with the choices that would affect her life and not her parents'.

"So, are you going to school closer to home?" she asked.

"Yeah. I'm taking classes while living with my folks. I'm not sure what I want to do now. My plans have kind of changed a little." Autumn shifted, her body a bit tense, as if the discussion made her uncomfortable.

Vanessa searched for the right thing to say to bring back the positive energy between them. "I understand that more than anyone. I never thought Cloud Valley, in my grandfather's house, is where I'd end up. But I'm really excited about where I'm heading."

Unease skittered across Autumn's face and she buried her focus in the yearbook.

"What is it?"

"Dad always thought he'd inherit this place. We talked about how we'd change things, what we'd add, and how to make it a profitable ranch again. I planned to take classes focusing on agriculture science, but now that doesn't seem too useful. I'm just taking business classes for now until I figure out what I really want to do."

The admission sat like a heavy rock in the pit of Vanessa's stomach. She'd been so excited about her new adventure in her new home, she hadn't stopped to think about what other people lost because of her gain. She searched for words but came up empty.

"Oh look! There's my mom," Autumn said, pointing at the page. "She's with my dad and Ethan. This is when they went on a class trip, senior year. I can't believe the school's been making kids go to Typhoon Ranch for so many years."

Vanessa found the photo and her heart dropped to the shaggy rug. Her aunt, uncle and the man she'd met at the hardware store all grinned at the camera and held up blue shirts with cartoon bulls in the center.

Just like the one she'd found buried in the garden.

Chapter 14

The muscles in Dax's arm quivered. He held the window steady while Ben finished caulking the frame.

"Damn, these projects always take so much longer than I think they will," he said, shaking out his noodled arms as soon as the window was steady.

Ben grunted and returned his tools to the rusted red box at his feet. "At least it's done."

Footsteps padding down the stairs turned Dax toward the front of the house.

Vanessa and Autumn appeared with Frankie behind them.

Autumn gave a little wave then opened the door, giving Vanessa a quick hug before hurrying outside.

Vanessa stood in the doorway. "This place is Grand Central Station this morning," she said. "Someone else just pulled in."

Dax crossed the living room to her side then swallowed a sigh. "Madden," he said, seconds before his brother hopped out of the driver's side and rounded the hood to open the passenger door for his fiancée. "And Lily."

"Who's Lily?"

"His bride-to-be. You'll like her. She's much more enjoyable than my brother."

Ben stomped forward and snorted. “As much as I’d love to stay for this little family gathering, I’ve got to go.” He tapped the tip of his baseball cap and wedged himself past Dax to get outside.

“Thanks again,” Vanessa said.

Another grunt came from Ben as he continued to his vehicle.

Madden passed Ben, clapping a shoulder on his back, then continued to the house with Lily beside him. He carried two cloth tote bags while Lily held a casserole dish in her hands.

“Hello, there,” Lily said. “I hope you guys don’t mind my stopping by with Madden. I couldn’t wait to come and meet Vanessa.”

Vanessa flashed a bright smile. “Same to you. Please, come inside.”

Dax took a step back along with Vanessa to allow the visitors in.

Frankie pranced between them all.

“How cute is this little guy?” Lily said on a chuckle.

“Sorry to drop by like this,” Madden said. “But I wanted to sit and speak with you in more depth after everything that happened last night. Lily suggested we bring along some food to make our visit less intrusive.”

“I made chicken-and-noodle casserole.” Lily offered the glass dish to Vanessa. “We also brought along some other snacks for your pantry. I hope you don’t mind?”

“This is amazing. Thank you,” Vanessa said. “Everyone around here keeps feeding me.”

Lily shot a questioning look at Dax. “Oh really?”

Dax squeezed the back of his neck. “She watched baseball with me and Pops. He made his famous chili.”

"I talked to him this morning when I was at the house," Madden said. "He had a hell of a good time."

"I did, too," Vanessa said, smiling. "How about we take this stuff into the kitchen before we discuss the break-in?"

Lily grabbed the tote bags from Madden and followed Vanessa into the kitchen, Frankie right behind them.

Dax stayed in the hallway, watching them go. He hated the weird tension lingering between him and Madden. Maybe if he ignored it, it'd go away. "Thanks for taking care of the horses this morning so I could give Ben a hand. Vanessa really appreciated the window."

He led Madden into the living room. Ben had collected all the tools, but bits of debris sat on the floor. He made a mental note to clean it up once Madden and Lily left.

"No problem." Madden inspected the new window. "You and Ben do good work."

Dax snorted. "You sound surprised."

Sighing, Madden rubbed a hand over his face. "You gonna keep taking everything I say as an insult? Because, honestly, it's exhausting."

"You're right," Dax said, holding up his palms. "I'm a little on edge."

"I get it. It's been an interesting couple of days. How'd things go after everyone left last night?"

Just the thought of the night before curled his toes, and damn it, he hadn't even kissed her. "Quiet. We were both exhausted."

"I spoke with Deputy Sanders, and they have no suspects. He talked to Chip Kemp, but he had an alibi."

"And what was that?" Dax asked.

"Sanders wouldn't tell me," Madden said. "But he did say the sheriff's department will keep asking questions. They're as concerned about everything that's happened since Vanessa got into town as we are. Sanders was curious if we plan to increase our security."

Vanessa and Lily reappeared.

Vanessa wrapped her arms around her middle and crossed the room to stand beside Dax. "What else can you do? I mean I installed the security system and cameras. Dax put up motion-censored lights on the barns."

"We can have someone with you until whoever is causing trouble is stopped," Madden said.

"Like a bodyguard?" Vanessa asked.

Madden nodded.

Dax rested a hand on the small of her back. "It wouldn't be much different. I'd be here with you, just like I have been."

"Well, one of us would be at least," Madden said. "We can also look into the case. Help try to figure out what's going on around here."

Irritation started ticking through Dax. He struggled to rein it in, knowing Madden was right. He was so used to taking everything his brother said as a personal attack, even if it wasn't meant that way. But did Madden think he was just sitting around, not helping Vanessa with her problems?

"Again," he said, voice tight. "Pretty much the same thing as we've been doing."

Lily cleared her throat, drawing all eyes her way. "What these two are trying to say is they can do whatever you're comfortable with, in whatever way you want, to offer you peace of mind. They just have to annoy each other before they make their point. It's been like this since we were kids."

Dax struggled against a grin. "I don't know what you're talking about."

Lily rolled her eyes. "Don't let them fool you. They really do love each other, and they want to help. No one in town is better."

Vanessa glanced up at Dax then over to Madden. "I'd be lying if I said I wasn't scared. The thought of being in the house alone makes me nervous. I don't know if the person who broke in got what they wanted, or if they plan to return to find something else I don't even know is in here."

"Then Sunrise Security will be here for you," Madden said.

Dax kept his gaze fixed on her. "I'll be here for you. I won't let anyone hurt you. I promise."

Vanessa yanked the sheets off the full-sized bed in her uncle's old bedroom. Dax had left to grab some of his stuff, which gave her the perfect opportunity to see to her own chores. Starting with making a spot for him to stay the night.

Not like she wanted him across the hall. Sleeping beside him had made her feel more at home than she'd felt since her mother's passing. The apartment they'd shared had turned cold and sterile the moment she died.

But lying in the comfort of Dax's arms had felt like a missing puzzle piece clicking into place. As much as she wanted to repeat that tonight, she didn't want him to feel obligated. Especially if he was sticking close in order to do a job.

Nothing sexy about that.

Lily pulled a pale blue fitted sheet from one of the boxes she'd helped carry up. "This the right one?"

"Perfect. You don't have to help me make the bed."

"Nonsense." Lily whipped the end of the sheet in the air then let it settle over the mattress. "Madden's walking around the property to make sure everything's in order. Since I don't have any intention of traipsing in this rain, I might as well make myself useful."

Vanessa tucked the corners of the sheet in place on her side of the bed while Lily did the same on the other. "I appreciate it. I'm so overwhelmed with everything I need to do. Instead of diving in, all I want is to sit in a corner and do nothing."

"That's understandable." Lily smoothed down the sheet then pointed at the discarded comforter on the ground. "Are we putting this back on?"

Vanessa peeked into the opened box where she'd found the sheets and sighed. "Yeah, for now anyway. I must have been drunk when I packed. I don't see any other blankets in here. I'll find everything eventually."

"It will take time, but once you have everything where you want it, all the time and stress will be worth it."

Once the comforter was situated, Vanessa plopped the pillows by the headboard and sat on the edge of the bed. "I know you're right, but I have to admit, nothing has gone as I expected since stepping into town."

Lily climbed on the mattress and tucked her feet beneath her. "What did you expect?"

Frankie leapt up and cuddled in Lily's lap.

Vanessa couldn't help but smile at the easiness at which she found talking with Lily. The blond-haired beauty was kind and sweet, with empathy shining through her blue eyes. "Well, for one, I didn't expect someone to keep breaking into the house."

"Fair point," Vanessa said, scrunching her nose.

"I guess I thought I'd get here, work at making it my own while getting to know my grandfather a little more. Maybe dig into my mom's past and discover new things about her. But now that I'm here, it's as if I'm uncovering all these layers of people who are from a completely different planet—like I'm watching a foreign film play out but don't speak the language."

"I get that. You've been thrown into a bit of a mess since day one. I went through my own storm and know how terrifying it can be when you feel like some unknown force is attacking you and you don't know why or how to stop it."

Vanessa hooked a brow. "You do?"

"It wasn't that long ago a mess found me when I least expected it. Someone else's mistakes finally caught up with them and I was stuck in the crossfire. I won't go into details right now, but just know that as scary as things got, getting to the bottom of the problem offered a freedom—and happiness—I never imagined. Freedom to create the life I wanted with the man I love."

"I don't know how to get to the bottom of things. I don't even know what's the root of the issue."

Lily shrugged. "Neither did I. I just kept asking questions."

"I have plenty of those," Vanessa said. "Dax is taking me to the library when he gets back. We're going to search through old news articles. See if there are any reports about my family that could tell me something I don't know."

"That's a good idea. You could also ask around town. Dax knows everyone, so he could help you there. And you met Walter. He has a group over once a week for poker. They've all lived in Cloud Valley their whole lives. They might have some answers or at least could point you in a certain direction."

"You don't think Dax would mind taking me to talk to his dad?"

Lily grinned. "Girl, I've known Dax a long time. He's

always worn his emotions on his sleeve, and from where I'm sitting, I think he'd do just about anything to help you."

Talking with Autumn earlier about Dax had been fun, but her cousin was too young to really know Dax. She'd giggled like a schoolgirl but hadn't offered any real insight. Lily was different. She had a friendship with Dax and apparently had known him for a long time. Her opinion on the situation held merit.

Besides, Vanessa didn't exactly know anyone else in town she could coax information from. She picked at a loose thread on the blanket, striving for casualness she didn't feel where Dax was concerned. "So, uh, does he date a lot of women?"

Lily scratched behind Frankie's ear and shook her head. "Not really. He's pretty busy. He lives for training horses as well as helping with their dad."

The way Lily dropped her gaze when she spoke told Vanessa there was more she wasn't saying, but she didn't want to pry. She'd pick a different approach. "When I mentioned his name to my uncle, he made a comment about finding trouble as soon as I got into town. Don't get me wrong, my uncle seems like a bully, but his comment struck me as odd. Especially with how great Dax has been."

"Dax and his family haven't had the easiest time the last few years," Lily said. "Walter sold part of their land to a developer, which brought in a ton of tourists. Something folks around here weren't too happy about."

"And because of that, Dax is looked at as trouble?"

Frowning, Lily nodded. "They all were. No one understood why they'd sell, an unforgiveable sin to most. People still don't know the whole story. Things have turned around since Sunrise Security opened, but it's hard to change some people's minds once they're set. Your uncle is one of those people."

"Yeah, I got that impression of him." She continued picking at the thread as she thought about what Lily had said. "Do you think my uncle looks at my getting the land where he grew up the same way he sees Dax's family selling their property?"

The lines on Lily's face softened. "Maybe, but if he does, he's wrong. People make decisions every day that others don't understand. But it's not up to you or anyone else to make your uncle understand your grandfather's choices. I'm sure your grandfather did what he thought was best, just like Dax's family did what was best for them."

She chewed that over for a beat. "I doubt my grandfather knew that leaving me his property would be like kicking a hornet's nest."

"You're probably right," Lily said. "Your grandfather was a good man who loved his family. Maybe he wanted to give you and your uncle a chance to reconnect."

Vanessa couldn't stop the derisive snort from coming out her nose. "I don't think that will happen anytime soon."

"Maybe not, but weirder things have happened."

"Weirder than buried hammers, break-ins and poisoned farm animals?"

Lily cringed. "Okay, you've had a rough road. But one day I'll tell you my whole story. We can commiserate about the effect of other people's bad decisions."

"Only if we do it over a glass of wine."

Lily held out her hand, waiting for Vanessa to shake it before she said, "Deal."

Chapter 15

Rain poured down in buckets in the late afternoon. Dark clouds smothered the sky. Dax held open the door to the library and waited for Vanessa to step inside before following her into the quiet space.

Vanessa ran a hand through her long locks. "Man, I think this whole town's about to float away if it doesn't let up soon."

"Tell me about it," Dax grumbled. "The roads are a mess. The sheriff's department will have to close some soon. We should hurry so we can make it back to your place."

"You really think it could cause issues with the roads?"

"More likely it will affect the hillsides and mountain highways. We don't want to be driving if a landslide crashes down."

Vanessa shuddered. "That's something I never had to worry about in Chicago."

Dax couldn't help but chuckle at her wide-eyed bewilderment. "You've run into a lot of things you've never had to worry about before."

"True," she said, scrunching her nose. "But I've found some good surprises, too."

Before he kissed her in the entryway of the town library, he swiped his cowboy hat off his head then nodded in the direction of the circulation desk. "Let's ask for help. Can't say I've spent much time in here before. Not quite sure where to go."

Vanessa stared around her as she fell into step beside him. "I love this place. The library in Chicago is beautiful, but it's so grand and cold. This is warm and cozy, like being in a grandmother's living room."

"Seeing how this was a house decades ago, I understand how you could think that." He stopped in front of the desk and a young woman with shoulder-length brown hair and a nice smile greeted them. "Do you have old newspaper articles here?"

"We sure do," she said. "Are you looking for a certain date? Year?"

"What do you think?" he asked Vanessa. "Do you want to go way back to when your grandparents were young, or something more recent?"

Vanessa bit her thumbnail. "Um, probably around the time when my mom was in high school. Before she left."

She rattled off a range of dates.

"That won't be a problem," the woman said. "Follow me."

Dax waited for Vanessa to pass him before taking up the rear. They walked by shelves of books and a line of computers with a few teenagers hunched over the screens until they reached the back corner.

"You two can take this computer. It's a little more private, and it has more sophisticated software. I'll pull up what you need and show you how to use the filters." The woman's fingers flew across the keyboard then she stepped aside, gesturing with her arm for one of them to take a seat.

He pressed a hand to the small of Vanessa's back to encourage her to sit.

"You click on these two lines here to refine your search." The woman pointed to the side of the screen and waited for Vanessa to navigate to the spot she'd indicated before continuing. "I recommend sticking with one year, but you can refine the results further if needed. The articles will appear one page at a time, just scroll down, and once one edition is finished, another will pop right up. Let me know if you have any questions."

Dax waited until the librarian walked away then dragged over another chair. He settled in beside Vanessa. "Well, seems easy enough. What's the plan?"

Vanessa blew out a long breath. "I think we should pull up the year before my mom left town. I can't help this feeling that something besides getting pregnant made her run away. Beyond prying that information out of my uncle, I don't know where else to look."

"Then let's get started."

He let her take the lead and put in the year, then watched as the screen filled with the front page of the *Cloud Valley Gazette*. They sat in silence and scanned page after page. He chuckled at stories with names he recognized, reliving town festivals and sharing local victories.

"I've seen some of these photos," Vanessa said, stopping to read about the high school's win at the state championship. A picture of the team surrounded by cheerleaders showed a celebration for the ages. "It's so strange to think about my uncle as a football star and my mom a cheerleader. I'm glad she experienced this. Looks like fun."

The comment made him wonder what she'd been like in high school. "Were you in sports when you were in school?"

"I danced, but not for my school," she said. "That's what got me into yoga. I was never the most flexible kid and had to really work hard to get better. Yoga helped with that and uncovered a passion. What about you? Were you a big handsome athlete?" she asked, bumping his shoulder with hers.

He snorted out a laugh. "Not at all. I didn't have the time. I tried to get out of school as much as I could, something that was easy enough with just my dad to outsmart. I've always wanted to be outside. Felt like there was more to learn about life in the mountains than in a classroom."

She smiled at him. "I'm starting to see that."

"Keep scrolling," he said, nodding toward the screen. "Maybe we'll find out some more about your mom."

Vanessa kept the articles moving, commenting on a photo of his dad and mentions of Tilly's weekly line dancing. "Does Eve still do that?"

"She sure does."

"Will you take me?"

He grinned. "You know how to line dance?"

Her growing smile matched his. "Not even a little bit."

He couldn't help but laugh. "I'll teach ya. Sounds like a much better date than the first."

"I don't know, I thought the first one was pretty darn great." She winked then returned her focus to the task at hand.

The sound of a clock ticking in the background competed with the raindrops hitting the roof. The words on the screen started to blur together and Dax blinked to keep his focus. A headline flashed that caught his attention and he straightened in his seat. "Stop."

Vanessa's hand stilled. "Holy crap. That boy died in the river behind my house."

Dax read the article, his lips moving along with each word. "Wow. Only eighteen years old. Looks like he fell, hit his head and drowned. Is there another page?"

She pressed the down arrow until the second page appeared. Another picture of the boy who'd died—Garrison Steele—accompanied the article; he was flanked by a girl and a second boy.

"Oh my God," Vanessa said on a gasp. "That's the same picture I found in my mom's room. The only difference is someone scratched the boy's eyes out in my mom's photo. This doesn't make any sense."

He studied the picture, anxiousness crawling over his skin like an army of red ants. "Look at how your mom's looking at him."

"I noticed that, too," Vanessa said. "She's staring up at him like he hung the freaking moon."

"If the newspaper used this photo, your uncle and mom must have been pretty close with Garrison," Dax said. "Makes me wonder how close to his death this was taken."

"Can't be too soon before. My cousin said the shirt my uncle's wearing is from a senior trip. If I can look in the yearbook for when that was, it can create more of a timeline. Something had to have happened between then and when this kid died in March for my mom to change her opinion of him. The question is, does it matter?"

Dax shrugged, wishing he had more answers. "We won't know until we get to the bottom of things, I'm just not sure how to do that."

Vanessa ducked her head to escape the rain and ran past Dax into the café. The scent of strong coffee assaulted her senses and made her mouth water.

"Do you want anything to eat?" Dax asked as he led her

to the back of the line. "Cloud 9 Café has the best pastries in town, just so you know."

She wrinkled her nose. "I love a good pastry, but I'll stick to herbal tea. I don't think my stomach can handle anything much stronger."

"How about I get a couple to take back to the house?"

She nodded, appreciating his thoughtfulness.

While they waited, she glanced around the quaint café. Dark blues blended with metallic accents, creating an industrial vibe. Dark wood tables sat in the middle of the room and golden letters scrawled across the front window boasted the clever name.

During her perusal of the scarred wooden floors and framed artwork, she spotted Diane sitting alone at a table with an oversized mug and a book. She poked Dax with her elbow. "My aunt's sitting over there. Should I go say hello?"

He shrugged. "Why not? Looks like she's alone. Could be a good time to ask her some questions. She might be the only one who can give you answers, and we both know she'll have tighter lips with Chip around."

Vanessa's stomach fluttered but she agreed. Noticing Diane by herself as soon she'd uncovered the disturbing article seemed to be some cosmic doing. She couldn't let this moment pass without at least trying to talk to her aunt.

She blew out a long breath. "I'll be right back."

"Take your time," he said. "If I order before you're done, I'll just bring your tea to you then keep myself busy until you're finished."

"Thanks." She flashed him a tight smile then weaved through the tables until she stood in front of Diane. "Hi," she said, hoping she didn't sound as nervous as she felt.

Diane glanced up from her book. Recognition dawned

and she jumped to her feet. "Well, hello there! How are you? I'm so happy to run into you. Come, sit, sit."

Her aunt's enthusiasm melted away her nerves, and she settled in the seat across from her at the round table.

"Are you hungry? Thirsty? I can grab you something really quick," Diane said.

Vanessa flicked her wrist toward where Dax stood, now in the middle of the line. "Dax is getting me some tea, but thanks."

"I'm glad you're making friends. Autumn was thrilled you invited her over earlier. Did you two have a nice visit?"

"We did. She's very sweet. I hope to get to know her better, and you as well."

Diane patted her hand. "I'd like that, too."

She debated how to continue with the conversation. Just like with her cousin earlier, it didn't seem right to just blurt out what she really wanted to know. "I'm also enjoying getting to know my mother better."

A sad smile curved the ends of Diane's mouth. "Your grandfather never could be talked into doing anything with her room. With Chip's either, really. But I always felt like Earl was holding on to your mama, hoping she'd come home and life could return to the way it once was."

The description made Vanessa's heart heavy. "Grandpa wrote me a lot of letters. He'd ask about my mom but never gave much detail about his feelings. Never talked about the past. Neither did my mom."

Diane clicked her tongue. "Such a shame. An avoidable tragedy, if you ask me."

"Speaking of tragedies," Vanessa said, taking hold of the opportunity to steer the conversation. "I read about a local boy who drowned on the property. His name was Garrison Steele. Did you know him?"

"Oh my." Diane's hand fluttered to her heart. "I haven't heard that name in years. He was good friends with your uncle. He, Chip and Ethan were together all the time. Everyone was devastated when he died. The kind of shock that people don't really recover from."

"I bet," Vanessa said, studying her aunt's face for any emotions or opinions she wasn't sharing on the subject. "Loss is never easy, but it had to be especially tough with someone so young. I'm sure the whole town had trouble dealing with it."

"Absolutely," Diane said, nodding her head in an exaggerated motion. "His poor parents went through hell. Then his father passed away a few years later, leaving his poor mama all alone."

"Was my mom friends with him?"

A softness settled over Diane's features as if she thought back on something from long ago. "Mindy was always following the trio around. I didn't blame her, I was, too," she said with a laugh. "I had such a crush on your uncle, and your mama had it bad for Garrison. When he died, she was never the same. A light went out in her eyes that I never saw come back. I hope it returned eventually."

The news struck a chord deep within Vanessa's soul that she wasn't sure what to do with. "Did he return her feelings?"

"Not that I know of," Diane said. "At that time, I wasn't dating your uncle yet. And I'm ashamed to say I was young and only into what was affecting me and my world. If Garrison liked your mama, I wasn't aware."

A stab of disappointment pierced her lungs, but she couldn't let it show. "Do you remember when my mom left town?"

Clearing her throat, Diane shifted in her seat. "Yes, I do. Another devastating blow to your family."

She swallowed a retort about how her uncle seemed more upset about not inheriting the family's property than losing his sister—not getting to know his niece. "How long after Garrison died did she leave?"

Diane picked up her cup and took a sip, her gaze settling everywhere but on Vanessa. "I mean I don't think I could recall the exact day."

Vanessa struggled to cover her impatience with a smile. "I'd be surprised if you did. But do you remember what time of year it was?"

Diane finally met her eyes. "It was summer. Chip and I started dating right before he graduated. Your mother left a month or so after he and I got together. It was a tough time. For all of us."

"It's hard to imagine Chip struggling with my mom leaving. There doesn't seem to be any love lost there." She cringed, regretting the words as soon as they came out of her mouth. "Sorry, I don't mean to speak ill of your husband. His attitude has thrown me. I was excited to meet him, to meet all of you. The fact he has no desire to know me stings, and it's hard to imagine him being any nicer to my mom."

Diane frowned, sadness hovering over her like the dark clouds outside the window. "Your mom and Chip were close once. Best friends. His heart was broken when Garrison died, and it completely shattered him when he lost your mom. He changed after she left town. A part of him never recovered. I still see the glimpses of the boy he used to be. He's a good man, even if he doesn't always show it."

"I'm sure you're right. Hopefully one day I get to meet that side of him."

Dax arrived at the table with his hands full. "Sorry to interrupt, but I wanted to bring you the tea you wanted."

Diane beamed up at him. "No interruptions at all. I've got to get going. Honey, it was lovely catching up. Let's do it again soon. Maybe you, me and Autumn can get together for a girls' day. Manicures on me." She gathered her things and hurried out the door.

Vanessa took the warm paper cup and took a sip. She sighed, repositioning all the new pieces she'd just been given as she put together a timeline in her mind. Garrison drowned in March and her mother left town, pregnant, four to five months later.

And she was born in November.

Chapter 16

Rain continued to fall as Dax held open the door for Vanessa then jogged around the front of the truck to climb inside. Water dripped from the rim of his hat. He took it off, giving it a gentle shake before setting it back on his head. "Hope the rain didn't ruin your tea. Good thing I tucked the pastry bag inside my jacket."

She flashed him a half-hearted smile then snapped her seat belt into place. "I'm definitely going to need that chocolate when we get back to the house."

He squeezed her knee then backed from the parking spot. "Honey, you can have anything you want."

His windshield wipers flew across the window, working in overdrive to clear the heavy drops of rain from his view. Dax squinted, his muscles tight as he maneuvered out of town. Silence settled between them. He wanted to help her process whatever she'd learned from her aunt, but he also needed to focus. Thunder boomed, and he crawled forward, his hands tight on the steering wheel.

Vanessa's brow puckered as she stared outside. "I hope Frankie's okay. Storms make him nervous."

"I'm sure he'll be fine, but we'll be back shortly. How are you?"

She let out a long, shaky breath. "My aunt told me

my mom had a thing for the boy who drowned. That she changed after he died, then left town a few months later. Do you think he could be my father?"

"Holy shit," he said, trying to wrap his mind around the question. "I mean, I don't know. I'm not even sure how you'd find out." He cast a quick glance her way before returning his focus to the road. "Do you want to know?"

"Yes." Her voice was so quiet it was nearly drowned out by the constant pinging on the roof. "But you're right. How do I even begin to tackle that question? Besides, I think there are more pressing issues at hand."

He hated the quiver in her voice and wished he could gather her close. "It's all important. Yes, finding out who's messing with you is crucial, but you said you wanted to find out who your dad is. This is a lead you didn't have before. We just need to figure out how to follow it."

"I wonder if my uncle's friend, Ethan, would talk to me. He was with him at the hardware store, and he didn't seem so bad. Diane said the three of them were together all the time. He might know something."

"I don't know much about the guy, but Madden might. We can call him and ask his thoughts. He and Lily are both seven years older than me, so they have connections with people in town I don't. They might even remember the events surrounding this kid's death."

Beams of light flashed through the mist and cut into the back window. A vehicle came up fast behind them.

Dax flicked his gaze to the rearview mirror. "This clown needs to slow down. There's too much water on the road. I'm not speeding up to make him happy or I'll hydroplane."

Vanessa twisted around and scrunched her nose. "He's getting closer. What's his problem?"

"Who the hell knows?" Dax said. "I swear, people don't make the best decisions when they're behind the wheel. It's probably some teenager." He flashed his hazard lights twice as a warning.

The vehicle sped up until the front bumper tapped the back of Dax's truck.

His body lurched forward, and he shot an arm out to brace against Vanessa's middle. "What the hell?"

She gripped his forearm. "Is he doing that on purpose?"

Gritting his teeth, Dax pressed down harder on the gas pedal. A little space separated him from the truck. "I'm not sure. Maybe whoever it is got distracted for a minute."

"I hope you're right."

Tense seconds ticked by when the vehicle surged forward until it appeared beside the driver's-side window. It lingered in the other lane, keeping pace with Dax, until it veered to the side. Confusion and fear battled in Dax's gut, but he blocked it out, intent on keeping him and Vanessa safe.

"Oh my God!" Vanessa screeched. "What is he doing?"

Dax sped up, but the other truck stayed right beside him before ramming against the driver's side door. The truck jerked to the side, the tires skidding over a large puddle. Terror clutched his heart and sweat slicked his palms. He fought for a calm he didn't feel.

He pulled his arm out of Vanessa's death grip and steered the truck back on the road. "Sorry, honey, but I need both hands on the wheel. Call the police. Tell them we're on County Road 281, about two miles south of your place."

His heart thundered in his ears, and he swallowed the panic rising in his throat. He struggled to keep his voice from belaying the mixture of terror and anger flooding through his veins. Vanessa didn't need him to heighten her own fear.

The black truck smashed against his, sending the back end of his vehicle fishtailing off the road. The sound of metal against metal vibrated his bones. Vanessa's screams and pleas for help as she spoke into the phone combined with the dizzying sensation in his head as his neck jostled with the sudden motion.

The truck swiped against him again, and Dax slammed his foot on the brake. The tires glided on the pool of water swallowing the road, taking control of the vehicle as it spun toward the edge of the road. He wrangled with the steering wheel, straining to keep it straight so they didn't flip over.

Skidding to a stop, he glanced up just as the asshole in the black truck flew by. He caught a glimpse of a black ballcap, broad shoulders and nothing else. Adrenaline coiled his muscles, and the urge to run after the bastard who'd tried to kill them almost had him jumping outside and sprinting after him in the damn rain.

"He's gone," Vanessa said. "We're on the side of the road. Okay. Thank you." She disconnected the call and squeezed her eyes shut.

Dax unhooked his seat belt and slid across the seat to gather her in her arms. He smoothed his hand over her hair, needing to know she wasn't injured. "Are you hurt?"

She burrowed against him, her whole body shaking. "I can't…why…it's just…"

"Shh," he said. "You're safe now. He's gone. Coming back wouldn't make sense. He's got to know we've called the sheriff's department."

She fisted the neck of his T-shirt in her hands and shook her head. "He might not come back this time, but there will be a next time. I don't understand any of this. I'm a good person. I'm here because my grandfather left me his home. Why is this happening?"

He held her tight, wishing he could absorb her pain. "I don't know, honey. But this person is extremely dangerous, which tells me he has a lot at stake. I think this goes beyond wanting your family's land. Anyone willing to act this way has a lot to lose and is scared as hell to lose it."

"But what do I have to do with any of that?" she asked, throwing her hands in the air. "I'm running around town, chasing my tail like a dog, and keep coming up empty. Each hour leads to more questions, more confusion. I'm not a threat to anyone."

He might not have all the answers, but one thing was clear. Someone didn't just want to run Vanessa out of town, they wanted to hurt her. To quiet her. To make her stop whatever crusade she'd started.

And they were willing to kill.

The deafening noise of raindrops pelting the top of the truck heightened Vanessa's anxiety. Her teeth chattered despite the heat pumping from the vents. She stayed tucked against Dax's side until blue and red lights flashed through the haze behind them and came to a stop.

Dax kissed the top of her head. "As soon as we speak with the deputy, we'll go back to your place. You all right?"

She nodded even though she was far from okay. She'd thought watching cancer take away her mother would be the hardest thing she ever experienced. Being hunted down by some unknown assailant for a reason she didn't even know was a close second.

Dax rolled the window down a crack and water sprayed inside.

"Afternoon, Dax," Deputy Sanders said. "Sorry to be seeing you like this again. How you two doing?"

"You the only one who works at that station?" Dax asked.

"Nah. I was on patrol when the call came through. Figured it'd be best to come myself since I was the one who spoke with you both after the break-in. Want to give me a rundown of what happened?"

As Dax spoke, Vanessa squeezed her eyes shut and tried to block out the memories. Since coming to town, a lot of scary things had happened. But other than surprising an intruder when she'd first arrived, none had been direct attacks on her—even the break-in seemed more about grabbing something and not hurting her.

This was different. Someone had tried to run them off the road. Smashed their truck against Dax's in an attempt to hurt them both. Thank God, Dax had managed the situation so well.

"Are either of you hurt? Do I need to call an ambulance?"

The deputy's question snapped her back to the moment.

"I'm fine," Dax said. "Vanessa?"

She took mental stock of her body. An ache throbbed in the middle of her forehead and the muscles in the back of her neck were a little tight. Other than that, nothing else seemed affected. "I don't need an ambulance. Just a few aches and still shaken. Nothing a hot bath can't fix."

Rivulets of water continued to snake down the side of the door and splatter across Dax.

"Either of you get a good look at who was behind the wheel?"

"It was a man," Dax said. "He wore a baseball hat, but I couldn't tell you much else. With the rain coming down so hard, and trying not to roll the truck, I couldn't get more details."

"I didn't see any more than Dax did," Vanessa said.

"And the vehicle?" Sanders asked.

"Black truck. Full-sized cab," Dax said. "Again, not sure of make and model. The bastard caught me off guard."

"Don't be too hard on yourself, son. You did good, as far as I can tell. Neither of you has a scratch on you, and that's the most important part."

She closed her eyes again and tried to remember anything else. "Wait," she said, opening her eyes. "There was an animal on the back of the tailgate."

The deputy frowned. "You mean like a decal or sticker of some kind?"

"No," she said, shaking her head. "Like a logo."

"A ram?"

"Yes! It was black, like the rest of the truck. And I noticed the first three letters of the license plate were JMK. It stuck out because they were my grandmother's initials. I don't remember the rest, though."

"That's okay." Deputy Sanders wrote down the information. "This is great. You gave us the make and partial plate number. And with how bad your truck looks, this guy's probably driving around with quite a bit of damage."

Dax nodded in her direction, a whisper of a smile on his lips. "You did good."

"One more thing and then I'll let you go before I wash away with the rain. Did you notice anyone following you before the incident? Anyone know where you were?"

"I didn't notice anything out of the ordinary," Dax said. "We went to the library and were there for a while. Then we stopped by Cloud 9 for coffee. If this guy was following us, it didn't stand out to me."

Her stomach twisted into a knot. "I talked to my aunt."

Deputy Sanders frowned. "Excuse me?"

"At the café. My aunt was there. We had a conversation then she got up and left. She seemed a little upset by where the conversation ended."

"And where did it end?"

"She was telling me about how my uncle changed after my mom left town. Before that she told me about Garrison Steele. The boy who died in the river."

Deputy Sanders let out a low whistle. "Heavy conversation. Do you think your aunt had anything to do with the man who ran you off the road?"

She shrugged, hating that she couldn't say absolutely not. "I have no idea. A man was behind the wheel, but that doesn't mean a woman didn't tell him where we were. She could have called my uncle and told him about the conversation. Even if she didn't mean to put a target on our backs, she could have." She didn't want to think that her aunt would play a part in tormenting her, but she didn't know the woman well enough to say for certain.

"I'll talk to her and Chip. As of now, there's no one else on our radar. But if you were at Cloud 9, we can pull up security footage from them and other businesses downtown. See if anyone followed you out of town."

"Talk to Madden. Sunrise Security is a couple doors down. We've got cameras out front. And maybe check to see if Chip Kemp owns a black RAM truck."

"That'd be pretty dumb of him to use his truck if it's him," Vanessa said.

"Criminals aren't usually very smart. That's why they get caught," Deputy Sanders said.

"Then let's hope this guy's the dumbest criminal out there," she said.

The deputy offered her a tight smile. "I'm going to go dry out then make those calls about watching the video. I'll place some calls to the local autobody shops, too. On the off chance this guy takes his truck in to get fixed. I can get some quotes for you, if you want." He tossed out the last sentence in jest.

Dax snorted a quick laugh. "So nice of you, but I'll see to it later. This thing's so old, it might not be worth pouring any more money into. I've been wanting a new one anyway."

Vanessa waved and thanked the deputy before he walked back to his cruiser and Dax rolled up the window.

A shiver shook her shoulders. "Sorry about your truck."

Dax faced her, mouth slightly agape. "You're kidding, right?"

She shrugged even though guilt at the destruction of his vehicle rolled around inside her. He wouldn't be in this position if it wasn't for her.

He grabbed her hand and squeezed. "You have absolutely nothing to apologize for."

Tears blurred her vision, and she sniffed back her emotions. She hated falling apart in front of this man who'd been so strong since the day they'd met. "None of this would be happening if it wasn't for me. I've turned your life upside down since I came into town, and now your truck's ruined."

"Hey," he said, cupping her jaw with his palm. "You're right. You've turned everything upside down, but in the best way possible. Don't you dare think otherwise."

"You're the best part of moving here," she said, meaning it in her core.

He grinned. "And meeting Frankie's the best part of having you here."

She threw her head back and laughed. "All right, smart-ass. Then we better get back home to see him and you can be the one to take him out in the rain."

Chapter 17

The shaking in Vanessa's hands refused to stop even after she and Dax spoke with the sheriff's deputy and were safely back in her home. She sat in the living room with a throw blanket wrapped around her shoulders.

Frankie stayed glued to her side, as if sensing her turmoil and wanting to comfort her. She loved the little guy, but even he couldn't take away her anxiety.

Dax returned from the kitchen with two coffee mugs.

She scrunched her nose. "I don't want any coffee, but thanks."

"Good, because this is whiskey. Don't worry, I just poured a little bit. I just couldn't find any other glasses." He offered her the cup then sat beside her. He took a sip. "Your grandpa had some good stuff in there."

Bringing the mug close to her face, she sniffed the pungent alcohol before taking a small sip. The liquid burned her throat all the way down until it settled in the pit of her stomach. She coughed, clearing the bitter taste as much as she could. "If this is good, I'd hate to try what you think is bad."

He took another swig. "Not a whiskey girl, huh?"

"No," she said, shaking her head. "Give me a margarita any day of the week."

"Well, if I knew how to make one, I would."

"Mom and I used to just buy it premade and pour it from a bottle. Easy peasy." She fell back against the soft sofa. "That seems like a lifetime ago. Hell, my entire existence in Chicago feels like it took place in another dimension."

"And what would you be doing in Chicago right now?"

She considered the question and a wave of homesickness washed over her. She glanced at the old grandfather clock in the corner. "I'd be finishing a yoga class. Probably planning on grabbing coffee or making dinner plans with Alicia."

"Who's Alicia?" Dax settled in beside her, casually draping an arm over her shoulders.

She tucked her feet under her and leaned against him. "My best friend. I taught at her studio, and she was a lifesaver when my mom was sick. She'd stop by the apartment with food or card games or anything else she could think of. And since Mom passed, she's made sure to drag me out and stay a part of the living. Reminding me that my mom would want me to be happy."

A longing to hear her best friend's voice tightened her chest. She made a mental note to call her in the morning to check in. With so much happening, she'd barely had time to catch her breath let alone fill her friend in on the crazy details consuming her life.

"She sounds great," Dax said. "I hope I get a chance to meet her someday." A beat of silence passed before he asked, "Have you considered teaching yoga in Cloud Valley? I mean, I can't say for sure, but I don't think there's anyone doing that around here."

Sighing, she ran through the logistics in her head. "I'd love to, but that actually makes it a little harder."

Dax frowned. "What do you mean? I'm not a business

expert, but wouldn't it be better if the market wasn't saturated with the service you're providing?"

She grinned up at him. "You sound pretty savvy to me, and usually, yes. Providing a service no one else is would be a positive. But in this case, if someone already had a yoga studio, I could be hired as a teacher. Make the money without the overhead of renting a space and all the start-up costs."

"Then do it here," he said with a shrug. "I've heard of some crazy fad where people use goats while taking a class or something."

"Oh my gosh." She sat up straight. "How did I not think of that? Goat yoga! I wonder if people would actually come out here for something like that."

"Why wouldn't they? You wanted a place for the community to come. Lure them here with goat yoga and whatever other wacky practices you provide."

Laughing, she playfully slapped his arm. "Yoga isn't wacky. It's good for you."

"But then you add the goats and the wackiness kind of follows, doesn't it?"

She rolled her eyes. "Sure, whatever you want to tell yourself. If I can figure out a way to teach here, I'll make you be my first client."

"Deal. But honestly, I think it could be cool. There's a large section of the barn that's not being used. We could spruce it up a bit. I'm pretty handy with a hammer." He gestured at the new window as if to make his point. "And I know a few people who always love to lend a hand."

"You really think something like that could work?"

"I do. You should talk to Lily. She transformed her family's dude ranch into one of the most coveted wedding venues in the area. She might have some good ideas."

The chill clinging to her bones since being forced off the road by some brute behind a steering wheel finally melted away, and it had nothing to do with the whiskey. "I'd love that, and focusing on the positive will help keep me from going crazy with everything else happening. As scared as I am, I don't want to put my life on hold. I was forced to do that once. I won't do it again."

Dax's face pinched with an emotion she couldn't quite put her finger on, but he chose not to add anything else to the conversation.

Disappointment pressed down on her shoulders. Since meeting him, the door to her life had been forced open. She'd confided so much in such a short time, but she'd be lying if she said she would have been so forthcoming with him under normal circumstances. She couldn't expect him to be as open with her about whatever put that look in his eyes.

Dax's phone rang and he shifted to fish the device from his pocket. "It's Madden," he said before answering.

She fixed her attention on Frankie and let her mind wander over the possibilities of creating a studio at her new home. The barn would provide an amazing atmosphere, but the portion she'd use for classes would need a complete overhaul. Insulation and heat for winter classes, windows to let in the mountain views, air-conditioning for the warm summers. And what about parking? Could the driveaway hold enough spots for clients?

Then there was the big issue of how much a remodel would cost. The inheritance she'd received from both her mother and her grandfather was enough to provide her a hefty safety net, but she wasn't sure spending it all on one big dream was a wise decision.

But if now wasn't the time to take a risk, she wasn't sure when was.

Lowering the phone, Dax studied her. "Everything all right?"

"Sorry, I'm just running through some thoughts in my head. It's a big decision and one I'm not equipped to make right now. Especially when there's so much I don't even know to consider. I've always taught yoga. I've never planned on owning my own business. I think I'll take your suggestion and speak with Lily about some ideas. I think it'd help."

"How about tonight?"

Her mouth fell open. "Tonight?"

He nodded. "Madden wanted an update on what happened earlier. He asked us to meet him and Lily for dinner at Tilly's. We can chat while we eat, then you can ask Lily questions about her business. What do you think?"

A flutter of excitement blossomed in her chest, one that screamed at her to take the next step with this new idea. Tonight might not be the best time to broach her new idea to Lily, but it was a good idea to get to know the other woman better before pelting her with questions. "Count me in."

The dinner crowd at Tilly's filled the bar and grill, creating the sounds of Dax's adolescence. Pool balls bouncing off each other in the corner, country music blaring from the jukebox, and a chorus of voices caught up in conversation. His stomach growled, and he hoped the kitchen wasn't too backed up.

Either that, or Eve would give them special treatment. Too bad Reid wasn't with them, or no doubt they'd get their food fast—or she'd make Reid wait longer to serve her other customers quicker.

They'd take their chances with Nellie as their server.

"You guys know what you want?" Nellie asked. Her brown hair hung in tight curls around her shoulders, half of it pulled back and out of her young face.

Vanessa studied the menu while everyone else placed their usual orders. When it was her turn, she smiled up at Nellie. "I'm new in town. What do you recommend?"

"First off, welcome," Nellie said with a returning smile. "Second, you can't go wrong with anything on the menu. Fried pickles are my personal favorite for a side. Burgers are always good, but we've got a great chicken club sandwich, too."

"Then a chicken club sandwich with fried pickles it is. A cola as well, please."

Nellie collected the menus. "All right. I'll have this out to you guys as quick as I can."

Madden waited for Nellie to walk away before asking, "So you're both okay?"

The question reminded Dax of the tension in his neck that hadn't quite left and the ache in his head, but he nodded. "Could have been a lot worse. If he'd waited until we were closer to Vanessa's place, there's a drop-off on the side of the road. Landing in that ravine could have been a disaster."

"So scary," Lily said. "Any idea who's behind these attacks?"

Dax glanced at Madden, hoping for more news.

Madden sighed. "I spoke with Sanders. No luck on the autobody shops, and the video footage he got his hands on didn't show much. Flashes of a truck similar to what you described leaving town shortly after you, but nothing to tell us more than we already knew."

"So, no way to be certain if he followed us from the library or just happened upon us in town?" Dax asked.

Madden shook his head.

"How do we know he's not outside waiting for us right now?" Vanessa leaned back in her chair and glanced around the crowded restaurant. "Or if he's in here watching us?"

Dax reached under the table and rested a hand on her leg. "You've got a lot of people around to protect you. If anyone came after you, they'd regret it."

"Did the deputy speak with my aunt?" Vanessa wrinkled her nose, as if hating to even ask the question.

"Last we spoke, he couldn't reach her or your uncle," Madden said.

Dax frowned. "That's weird, right?"

Madden shrugged.

Nellie hustled over with a tray filled with drinks. She set them down then hurried away, disappearing among the throng of tables.

Vanessa took a sip of her cola then bobbed her straw up and down in the glass. "I can't help thinking that what we found about Garrison Steele plays a role in all of this."

"The boy who died years ago?" Lily asked.

"Did you know him?" Dax asked. "I was too young. I wondered if you two had any memories of the time around his death."

"He was about ten years older than us," Madden said. "So, when he died, we would have only been about seven or eight. I don't even recall when he passed, but that's probably because I was just a kid caught up in my own life."

"Same," Lily said. "Sorry. But at that age, I went to

school and played at either our ranch or the McKays'. I wasn't exactly aware of much else outside that world. But why would you think his death would be connected to someone harassing you all these years later?"

Vanessa gave a brief rundown of everything she'd uncovered since moving into her grandpa's house.

Dax followed along, mentally trying to make sense of the jumble of information. He agreed with her that something fishy had happened to set everything in motion, and he wasn't convinced it was all because her mom got pregnant. But even he had to admit it all sounded like a mashup of events that seemed unrelated.

They had to be missing something.

Vanessa sighed. "I wish my mother was here. I'd pry everything out of her. My uncle's made it clear he wants nothing to do with me, and my aunt was like a nervous little bird who flew away the minute I ventured into territory she wanted untouched. I don't know if it's because she was afraid of my uncle or scared she'd say something she shouldn't."

"Ethan Scott is the other person who might know something," Dax said, picking up the story thread. "He was close with Chip and Garrison, and is still close with Chip. Just depends on if he'll actually talk to us or not."

"Ethan's a much nicer guy than Chip," Lily said. "I used to deal with him when my place was a Dude Ranch. He owns the butcher shop in town, raises a small herd of cattle. When we'd have guests, we'd place bulk orders for meat. If you catch him away from Chip, he might open up."

Nellie and Eve wove through the crowd, loaded down with plates of food.

"Hey, guys." Eve set plates on the table. "Thought I'd help Nellie and come say a quick hello while I had a chance. We're packed tonight. Vanessa, nice to see you again."

"Same to you," Vanessa said. She inhaled a deep breath as Nellie slid her sandwich in front of her. "Everything smells amazing."

Madden picked up his burger. "Perfect timing. We can take a break before diving back in to figuring out how Garrison Steele could play a hand in messing with Vanessa from beyond the grave."

Eve let out a low whistle. "Haven't heard his name in a long time."

"Did you know him?" Dax asked.

Eve rested one hand on the back of Lily's chair and anchored her other on her hip. "Not really, but my folks had his wake here. Wanted to help his parents and take that burden off their shoulders. I was young, so I don't recall everything that happened, but I remember it was a real disaster."

Dax straightened in his seat. "What do you mean?"

"A fight broke out, I think. Shouting and broken glasses. My parents and some other adults had to step in and settle things down. I was shuffled into the kitchen, but I peeked out the door to keep an eye on what was happening. It was a nightmare. Everyone was already on edge after such a tragedy. The disruption at the wake just made everyone even more upset."

"Any idea who was fighting?" Vanessa asked.

"I can call my parents and find out for sure, but I think your mom and uncle had a hand in things. Went off on each other before your mom stormed out. I'm pretty sure Ethan was there, too, trying to calm them both."

"Wow," Vanessa said. "I guess it's not uncommon for emotions to run away from people at funerals. Grief can make us do crazy things. But up until then, it seemed like my mom and Chip got along so well."

Dax popped a fry in his mouth and considered the new information. "You thought something happened between the time Garrison died and your mom left town to put a rift between her and your uncle. Looks like you have another event to place in your timeline. Now we have to figure out if she was just upset about losing a friend or something else had pushed her to her breaking point."

Chapter 18

"Are you sure you want to do this now?" Dax asked, standing in front of the butcher shop. The stand-alone white building had a pitched red roof with matching red door, the sign flipped to Open in the front window.

The rain had finally stopped—for now—and he'd driven them to Choice Cuts as soon as they'd left Tilly's. He still needed to check on the horses before heading back to Vanessa's place, but she'd wanted to attempt to speak with Ethan while she had the nerve.

Vanessa nodded. "I need to get this over with. Besides, the sooner we talk to him, the better. This way I'll either have more important information or know if we should move on and find a different thread to pull."

"All right then. After you." He swept his arm forward and followed her into the store.

The metallic scent of blood and meat greeted them, along with an older woman behind a counter. Encased in the glass were slabs of beef, homemade sausages and stuffed chicken breasts that were enough to make his mouth water despite his full stomach.

"Evening," the woman said. "You made it just in time. We're about to close for the night. Can I help you with something?"

Dax spied a nametag attached to her white apron and approached her with a smile. “We’ll try not to keep you, Nancy. We were actually looking for Ethan. Is he around?”

“He should be. Give me a second and I’ll check in his office.”

Vanessa stood with her back to the arrangement of meat. “This place kind of gives me the creeps.”

He couldn’t help but chuckle. “Not used to visiting the local butcher in the big city?”

“More like the corner market. I’m all for respecting where my food comes from but seeing it all laid out like this is a little disconcerting.”

He stifled the urge to tease her. Not everyone was raised the way he’d been—taught from a young age exactly where his meat came from. Farm to table in every sense of the word.

Ethan Scott emerged from the doorway where Nancy had disappeared. He darted his gaze from Vanessa to Dax, confusion rippling his forehead. “Can I help you?”

Vanessa spun around. “Hi. I’m Vanessa Kemp. We kind of met yesterday.”

The corner of his mouth ticked up. “Yes, I remember. What can I do for you? In the market for some grade A beef?”

“No, sir. I came hoping you could give me some answers.”

The ripples increased along the top of his head. “About cattle?”

“Nah, I’ve got her covered about anything she may need to know in that area,” Dax said. “She has some more personal things she’d like to discuss.”

Ethan rubbed the back of his neck. “Not quite sure how I can help since we just met, but go ahead and fire away.”

"I'm sorry to be so blunt, but I don't want to take up more of your time than necessary. Basically, is there anything you can tell me about when my mom left town? Anything strange that occurred after your friend Garrison died that led to my mom and uncle's estrangement?"

Sighing, Ethan palmed the dark whiskers covering his jawline. "I don't know what you want me to tell you. I know the same thing as everyone else around here. Your mom left because she was pregnant. Her relationships with both your uncle and grandpa were nonexistent after that."

Vanessa's shoulders drooped. "Are you sure it was nothing else? I don't see how two people could go from a loving relationship to such animosity just because she was knocked up. It might not have been ideal, but that stuff happens all the time. Even my grandfather wanted them to reconcile."

"Look, I'm sorry I can't tell you what you want to hear. Chip wanted your mom to tell him and your grandfather who the father was so they could talk to him. Make him do the right thing and marry her. When she refused and left town, she gutted them. Left them confused and brokenhearted."

"Then why did they fight at Garrison Steele's wake?" Dax asked.

Blood drained from Ethan's face for a brief second before his composure slipped back in place. "That was a rough day for all of us. Garrison was like a brother to me and Chip. Not everyone handles losing someone so close to them well. Anything that happened after his funeral came from grief and sadness."

"Did Garrison have feelings for my mother? Could he be the one who got my mom pregnant?"

Ethan's jaw dropped and he blinked his brown eyes in rapid succession. "What?"

"Is Garrison Steele my father?"

"Man," Ethan said on a long breath. "I know your mom had a thing for him, but Garrison never mentioned returning those feelings. That doesn't mean it's not a possibility. Like I said, we all spent a lot of time together. Hold on, I need a second." He braced a large palm against the glass case.

"You never considered it before?" Dax asked.

"No. I mean, hell, that would mean he would have gotten her pregnant right before he died. But if that's true, why wouldn't she tell someone? Garrison's folks would have been thrilled to have a little piece of him to hold on to, and so would the rest of us. We would have done everything we could for both you and your mama."

"One more thing," Dax said, remembering the photo Vanessa had described. "Did Garrison and Vanessa's mom ever get into an argument of some kind?"

"Sure," Ethan said with a small laugh. "Those two were always teasing each other. Sometimes one of them would take things a little too far and piss the other one off. Garrison treated her like a little sister most the time—we both did, which she didn't like. But never anything serious. Like I said, we all knew she had a thing for him."

"Even Garrison?" Vanessa asked.

Ethan nodded. "He never talked about it, but there's no way he wasn't aware. She wasn't exactly subtle. But we both knew Chip's little sister was off-limits, no matter what."

"Bro code," Dax said.

Ethan finally smiled. "Exactly. Above all else, you've got to honor the code. Is there anything else I can do for you? I don't want to be rude, but I need to close the store and get home before my wife thinks the worst. She's always worrying when I don't show up on time."

"We won't keep you any longer," Vanessa said. "Thank you for speaking with me. I really appreciate it."

"No problem. I hope you find what you're looking for."

"Me, too."

Dax lifted his hand in a wave then led Vanessa back into the gray, dreary evening. Once in the truck, he hooked an arm on the seatback. "How do you feel about that conversation?"

She stared ahead. "He said more than I thought he would, I just don't know what to do with it yet."

"Do you think he was being honest?"

She frowned. "I have no reason to believe that he wasn't. Why? Do you think he lied about something?"

He put the truck in Reverse and backed out of the empty lot. "It's hard to tell. But someone is hiding a hell of a secret. One that might be worth killing over."

With another conversation to dissect, Vanessa feared her head might explode on the drive to Dax's place. She kept her thoughts to herself until Dax parked his truck and she jumped out, meeting him at the hood before heading to the barn.

"I want to talk to Garrison's mom," she said. "My aunt mentioned she still lives nearby. She's the last person I can think of who could give me answers. Maybe she'll know if Garrison is my father."

"Do you think he would have told his mother?"

She shrugged. "I hope not, or that means she never cared enough to find me. But maybe she'll just know by looking at me, even if I am the spitting image of my mother. It's a long shot, but one I need to take."

He gave a decisive nod. "Okay, we'll find her number and give her a call."

"Thank you." She wasn't sure what she'd done to have a man like Dax walk into her life, but she was eternally grateful for his unwavering support. "Now let's get these chores done."

"You can wait in the house if you want," he said. "I'll be as quick as I can. I need to work one of the horses a little before I feed him. There's a break in the rain, and I need to take advantage of it."

"I'd like to watch, if you don't mind."

"Not at all. Maybe I'll put you to work so I can finish a little faster."

"With everything you've done for me, I'd say I owe you." She hesitated on her way to the barn. "But I've never even touched a horse before. Bessie's the biggest animal I've been around, and she's pretty much a giant puppy."

Dax slid open the barn door. "No need to do anything you're not comfortable with. They're well trained, but if you're afraid, they'll sense it."

She stopped and stared at the massive heads poking through the metal slats of their pens. "Will it help if I just follow you and tell them how pretty they are?"

His soft chuckle was like cashmere on her skin. "Sure. I'll work the Thoroughbred first. He's feisty, so you might want to stand back. Once I get him out of his stall, I'll lead him to the back door and out to the paddock. You'll want to stay on the outside of the fence. He wouldn't hurt you on purpose, but sometimes he doesn't react the way you'd expect. Best to give him some space."

A shiver of trepidation shot through her center. Horses

were beautiful creatures, but that didn't make them less dangerous. "Okay. I'll head there now."

She opted to walk outside to reach the pasture instead of getting in the way. She rounded the side of the barn and stopped to take in the surrounding view. Mountains rose in the distance, twilight causing a haze of purple clouds to surround the steep peaks. Lush green land rolled away from her and disappeared in a sea of trees. Something shifted inside her, settled into a contentedness she barely recognized.

Continuing toward the paddock, drops of water clinging to the grass seeped into her pant legs. A chill in the air announced more rain to come, but she was happy for the brief reprieve. Happy to lift her head toward the sky and feel the breeze on her face. To enjoy the landscape without worrying about escaping a downpour or—at least in the moment—an unknown assailant sneaking from the shadows to scare her.

Once she reached the split rail fence, she spied Dax leading a giant black horse from the back door of the barn. He'd shed his jacket, and his navy-blue shirt molded against his muscled chest. He ran a large palm over the animal's neck, whispering something in his ear, then took a few steps back with his grip firm on a rope of some kind.

She watched him work, watched the horse refuse to obey, until finally relenting. Dax had a singular focus on what he did. The lines on his handsome face tight and his gaze directly on the animal. She had no idea what he was doing or why, but it was clear man and beast worked in unison—like a synchronized dance they'd done a hundred times before.

Desire stirred deep within her. Something about the way Dax handled the animal. The way he spoke softly yet firmly—his ability to use a tiny bit of force then a gentle touch to get the horse to obey. To comply. To give himself over with full trust to the man before him.

Saliva pooled in her mouth. She wanted those hands on her, those words whispered in her ears as Dax took control of her body. Excitement rippled over her skin as she stood transfixed, anticipation beating inside her with every command Dax shouted.

"It's a sight to see, isn't it?"

Walter's booming voice broke into the trance she'd fallen into and set her heart thundering faster than the horse's hooves. She slapped a hand to her chest and laughed. A flash of embarrassment heated her cheeks. Dear Lord, if Dax's dad only knew where her mind had wandered, she'd die on the spot. "So sorry. You startled me. I guess I was a little caught up in watching Dax work."

"I can see that." Walter chuckled and hooked his forearms on the fence beside her. "You like horses?"

Tilting her head to the side, she continued studying the duo. "I do, yes. Not enough to get in there with them though."

"Hell, I wouldn't step foot in the arena while Dax is training that young thing. That horse has a wild spirit. One that doesn't want to be broken."

She frowned and considered the expression. "Is that a bad thing? I mean we all need a little extra spirit to get us through the hard times, don't we?"

"I suppose we do. Spirit. Grit. Gumption. Whatever you want to call it," Walter said. "But that's not always true with an animal the size of that Thoroughbred. If he has a job, you want to make sure he can do it safely. That he knows what's expected of him and can do it without hurting nobody."

"I guess I never thought about it like that."

"Probably because you've never had to."

She smiled at Walter. "I see where Dax got all his wisdom."

One gray, wiry eyebrow shot up. "I've heard a lot of words used to describe the two of us, not sure *wise* has ever been one of them."

She opened her mouth to dive deeper, but Dax walked over, leading the horse behind him.

"This guy giving you trouble?" Dax asked.

"Nah," she said, grinning. "Just keeping me company and teaching me about horses."

Dax snorted. "You better come to me about that. He's better with cattle. Do you want to pet this guy?"

Nerves tightened her stomach, but she nodded.

He led the horse closer. "This is Cliff. He likes to be scratched right on the nose."

The animal leaned his head down, and she smoothed her palm over the wide bridge. "Hey there, big guy. How was your workout?"

Dax patted Cliff's side. "He did good today. I think he was showing off for you."

"He probably wasn't the only one," Walter said, grinning.

Dax rolled his eyes. "I was doing my job, nothing more."

"Sure. I'm heading inside. Vanessa, nice to see you again. Don't be a stranger." Walter pivoted toward the house.

"You okay alone tonight?" Dax asked.

Walter waved a hand through the air and grumbled something under his breath as he continued on his way. He used a cane to help him navigate over the uneven terrain.

"You want to help me feed them? Then we can get back

to your place and take care of your crew before we call it a night."

Words stuck in her throat, so she simply nodded. She wanted more than anything to get back to her house, but she didn't plan on ending their evening any time soon. It didn't matter that she'd only met him a few days ago. This man did something to her—made her feel things—no one before him ever had.

And she had no intention of waiting longer than necessary to see exactly what Dax McKay could do with those magnificent hands.

Chapter 19

Dax kicked out of his muddy boots and left them on the porch before walking through the front door. With his business complete, Frankie pranced past him then found a spot to curl up on the floor, his eyes closing as soon as he was settled.

Vanessa chuckled. "You'd think he was the one feeding animals and mucking stalls."

"I'm sure he had a rough day of napping," Dax said.

Vanessa snorted. "Poor guy. Any chance you found some wine earlier when you stumbled upon my grandpa's whiskey? After today, I could use a drink, but I don't think I can handle anything that strong."

He grinned down at her. "There might have been a few bottles of red in the cabinet. A drink sounds great, but can I grab a shower first? After working with the horses and taking care of your flock out there, I smell a little."

"That's cute that you think it's just a little."

He wrapped an arm around her waist. "Oh really?"

Laughing, she playfully shoved him away with one hand while plugging her nose with the other. "Seriously, it's too much. Go wash off that stink."

Letting her go, he lifted his palms in surrender. "Okay,

okay. I'm sorry. But I hope you don't think you smell like a fresh flower."

She opened her mouth wide in mock outrage. "You better get up those stairs before I hurt you."

Pulling her close again, he lowered his mouth to give her a quick kiss. He kept his face close to hers. "Don't worry. A little stink won't scare me away."

"You really know how to sweet-talk a lady, don't you?"

His grin widened. "I try my hardest."

"Try harder," she said on a laugh. "Use the bathroom off my room. I haven't checked on the other bathroom to see if the shower has any toiletries. I'll find that wine."

"I'll be quick." He gave her another kiss then jogged up the stairs.

His smile stayed in place as he hurried through her grandpa's old room to the bathroom. Slipping back into the easy banter with Vanessa had loosened the tension wrapped around his neck since their earlier accident. Between the danger and the mass of information they'd uncovered, the day had been heavy. Knowing they could unwind and decompress, even joke around with one another, lightened his mental load more than he thought possible.

Turning on the shower, he adjusted the knobs so warm water rained down. He shed his dirty clothes and tossed them aside before stepping under the spray. He let out a long breath and stood for a few minutes, appreciating the rising steam enveloping him into its comforting cocoon.

He closed his eyes and images of Vanessa overwhelmed him, causing an inferno of heat to spark to life in his core. Damn, she was something. He wasn't sure if she was more beautiful covered in dirt and taking care of a damn cow or standing in the kitchen with messy hair and wearing pajamas. Hell, he'd take her any way he could get her.

He gritted his teeth. If he went down this path, he'd be in the shower a lot longer than he'd planned—and he'd have to douse himself in cold water. Instead, he summoned all his self-control and focused on what needed to be done. He squirted shampoo in his hand, the floral notes tightening his gut.

Damn, he had a problem if he couldn't even wash his hair without being turned on by reminders of Vanessa.

Rushing through the rest of the process, he rinsed off and stepped out of the shower. He grabbed the towel hung on the rod and dried himself off then stared down at the dirty pile of clothes on the floor.

Well, damn.

He'd forgotten to grab the bag he'd brought from home. He'd wrap the towel around his waist and dash across the hall to find clean clothes from where he'd left them in the other room. Stepping into the bedroom, he found himself staring into Vanessa's wide eyes and his world stopped.

Her gaze dropped to his abs then shot back up to his face. Pink tinged her cheeks, and she swiped her tongue across her lips. "I…um. Sorry. I brought you this." She extended her arm, offering him his duffel.

He swallowed past the lust burning his throat and shoved a hand through his wet hair. "Thanks. Appreciate it."

He grabbed the handle, and when she didn't let go, he gave a gentle tug to pull her closer.

She kept her gaze locked on his and finally dropped the strap. She lifted her hand and tentatively placed it on his chest.

Trapping her hand under his, he studied her slightly parted lips and heavy-lidded eyes. Fire shot across his skin. Words stuck in his dry mouth. He wanted to hold her close, to feel her soft skin and taste every inch of her body.

But he didn't want to scare her or move too fast. What they were building could be different. Could be special. He didn't want to mess anything up.

"Well?" she asked, eyes wide.

The side of his mouth inched up. "Well, what?"

"Aren't you going to kiss me?"

Her directness turned the heat building inside him into a raging inferno. "I want to. Damn, I want to more than I want my next breath. But I don't want to make the wrong move."

"Kissing me could be the wrong move?" she asked, frowning.

"Never." His voice was soft, cracking with desire. "It's what would come after. My self-control is on a very thin leash right now. If I kiss you, that leash will tear in two. If you want to take this slow, I better throw some clothes on before things go too far."

She tucked her bottom lip between her teeth and roamed her hand to rest on his abdomen. "What if I don't want you to do that?"

His heart pounded and he dropped the bag, curling his arm around her waist. If this is what she wanted, he was all in. And not just for tonight. This was a woman he could see his whole future with. Tonight would be the beginning of something beautiful, and he'd make sure to show her all he had to give.

Pinning her against him, he felt every inch of her against his body—memorized every curve. "Then we're in for one hell of a night."

* * *

Vanessa's breath caught in her throat. She couldn't stand one more second without her mouth on Dax's. Rising on her toes, she sealed his lips with hers and circled her arms around his neck. The hard wall of his chest pressed against hers and his palm slid down to cup her butt.

The cotton towel did little to hide what lay beneath, and her belly tingled in anticipation. It'd been so long since she'd been with a man—since before her mom got sick. She'd dedicated so much of her life to caring for her mom that she'd closed the door to anything else. Since then, no one had sparked her interest.

No one but Dax.

Dear Lord. This man was protective and caring, sweet and supportive, and damn was he sexy as hell. In only a few days he'd been there for her in a way that no one ever had, and even if she was a little scared at the intensity of her feelings so quickly, she wanted nothing more than to be with him. To show him how much she already cared.

Deepening the kiss, her tongue dueled with his as she took tiny steps backward toward the bed.

A husky laugh rumbled from his throat. "I feel like I'm chasing you down."

"Just trying to get us to a better location," she said, pressing her lips along his jawline. His skin was still warm from the shower. The subtle scent of soap invaded her senses.

He skimmed his hands down to the backs of her thighs, lifting her off her feet.

Squealing, she wrapped her legs around him as they fell onto the bed. "Well, that's another way to do it."

He hovered over her with his forearms anchored on either side of her head. "In this situation, I thought it'd be better to pick up the pace."

She struggled to keep her face straight. "I hope that's not your outlook on the rest of this adventure."

He grinned, dimples flashing, and her heart melted into a puddle. "Don't you worry, darling. I plan on taking my sweet time with you the rest of the night."

He swooped down to take her mouth in his, and her body arched up to meet his—demanding his attention. She roamed her palms over his broad shoulders then inched them lower, reveling in the feel of every muscle.

When she reached the top of his towel, he lifted away from her and shook his head. "Not yet."

She faked a pout as disappointment ebbed with a thrill to see the impressive bulge tempting her from under the cotton.

His grin widened and he pressed his lips to hers then trailed them down the side of her neck. He stopped at her collarbone and traced his finger along the sensitive skin. "I've wanted to kiss this spot since I saw it."

She smiled as heat swirled in her belly. "I never thought I'd be so excited about my birthmark." Her pulse slammed against her veins as he moved lower, his kisses smattering her warm skin. When the neckline of her T-shirt stopped his progress, he grabbed her hemline and lifted a brow, as if seeking permission.

Wanting to take away any doubt lingering in his mind, she yanked the shirt over her head. She settled back on the bed, resting on her forearms as she put herself on display for his benefit.

Dax sat up on his knees, the towel rising high on his thighs, and sucked in a sharp breath. "You don't play fair.

No way to control myself when you're looking at me like that."

"I don't know what you're talking about."

He growled and nipped her bottom lip then continued his lazy trail down the side of her neck. Each second, each tender kiss, raised her heart rate and heat inside her body. When his tongue dipped into the black lacy bra and circled her nipple, a moan caught in her throat.

He groaned. "You're killing me."

"Let's make this a little easier," she said, reaching around to unclasp her bra. The lace fell away, and she shimmied the straps down her arms then tossed it on the floor.

"Much appreciated." His tongue found her puckered nub again as his hand molded around the other breast, flicking his thumb around her sensitive spot for double the pleasure.

Leaning back, she closed her eyes and got lost in the moment. She savored his touch, the difference between his moist tongue and callused skin causing shivers of anticipation to ripple through her body.

His hand stayed in place as his head moved south. He bit the top of her pants and, my God, if it wasn't the sexiest thing she'd ever experienced. She lifted her ass off the bed to help him glide her pants and panties down her legs, exposing all of herself to him.

He rested both his palms on her hips and pressed his lips to the insides of her thighs.

She sucked in a breath, her body voluntarily squirming from his attention.

But she wanted more.

"Now you're the one killing me," she said on a small moan. "Forget what I said about not going too fast."

He blew hot breath in the apex of her legs as his thumb

stroked her slippery folds. "Oh, trust me. It's worth the wait."

He took her center in his mouth, and her hips bucked up as shimmers of pleasure made her see stars behind her eyelids. Pressure built in her core as his tongue licked inside her in a steady rhythm, his finger joining his thumb as he wound her up, taking her higher and higher until ecstasy exploded, making her body shake with her release.

She threaded her fingers through his hair, fisting the strands then yanking them up. Needing his mouth, his body, his entire being on hers. He hovered over her and his towel finally fell away, revealing nothing but his raw masculine glory.

She reached for his erection. Her fingers brushed against the velvety skin at the head, and he climbed over the bed, staying out of her reach

Frowning, she sat up. "What's wrong?"

"Not a damn thing. I just need to grab something."

She couldn't complain about the view as she watched him walk across the room to his bag.

He rummaged through the contents then stalked toward her with a foil packet in his hand.

"You were that certain you'd get lucky, huh?"

"Honey, never in a million years did I think I'd ever get lucky enough to find a woman like you."

The words hit her square in the chest like a missile, and she held her arms open for him. She swallowed words of devotion and commitment, but his statement was enough to reassure her that they were on the same page. That what they'd found went beyond logic and words.

Dax ripped open the package and slid the condom over his impressive member before falling back into her arms.

His mouth found hers and he brushed the hair off her face to stare into her eyes. "Ready?"

"I've been waiting a lifetime for you," she whispered.

"You don't have to wait any longer, baby." He pushed inside her, filling her completely until she stretched around him. Fitting him like a glove. He moved in a steady rhythm, her hips rocking with the motion as he went deeper and deeper. Took her further and further to the precipice of blinding pleasure.

Before she exploded, he captured her hands and pinned them above her head. Smirking, she shook her head. "Two can play at that game."

In one swift motion, she yanked her hands free and shoved at his chest. Without severing their connection, she rolled on top of him. She ground against him, creating a new sensation that threatened to undo her. She moved her hips back and forth then leaned over his body, trapping his hands with hers. The tips of her breasts brushed against the hair on his chest, causing a tingling sensation to shoot from her core. Another orgasm ripped through her and sweat dotted her brow.

Dax groaned and gripped her hips. He locked his gaze with hers and the lust burning the blue of his eyes threatened to singe her. He moved her back and forth, fast and faster, pummeling inside her until he gritted his teeth and gripped the back of her neck. He pulled her to him and moaned into her mouth until his body went lax.

"Holy hell, woman," he said between labored breaths.

She smiled down at him, her hair spilling over her shoulders brushing against his arms. "That was pretty amazing."

He spun her to lie beside him on the bed then slid an

arm around her shoulders, holding her against him before pressing a kiss to her temple. "You can say that again."

She curled against him and struggled to steady the frantic beating of her heart. Joy filled her to the brim, spreading her smile. She was happier than she'd been in a long time and Dax was a large part of the reason why. No matter what other chaos held her hostage, he held her in his arms.

And she never wanted to be anywhere else.

Chapter 20

Peeling himself away from Vanessa was akin to torture, but it couldn't be helped. He escaped into the bathroom and cleaned himself as quickly as possible before returning to her with a warm washcloth. "I wasn't sure if you needed to clean up or not."

She sat to take the offering, and her full breasts jiggled with the motion.

Desire stirred in his gut, preparing for round two. He'd give his right arm to climb into bed and repeat what they'd just finished—maybe with a few different moves—but he didn't want to place expectations on her.

And, hell, he was just as happy to hold her for the rest of the night.

"Thanks," she said. "I appreciate it, but I think I'll use the bathroom."

"Take your time." He debated putting his boxer briefs back on but opted to climb under the covers without them. He might not want to make Vanessa feel uncomfortable or obliged to continue with more sexy time, but he also didn't want to encourage her to put on her own clothes. If it were up to him, he'd keep her naked all the time.

Emerging from the bathroom, she hesitated in the doorway.

"Is something wrong?"

She glanced toward the closed door and twisted her lips. "Frankie's in the hall. If we fall asleep without letting him in, I'm not sure what we'll wake up to in the morning."

He fought not to cringe. He understood her dilemma but damn it to hell and back if he ever thought a dog would end up being a potential cock block. "Go ahead and let him in. But do me a favor first."

"What's that?"

"Toss me my boxers." Snuggling naked with Vanessa sounded like heaven. Snuggling naked with Vanessa while her dog was in the bed sounded like a disaster waiting to happen.

She threw him his things then put on her T-shirt before opening the door.

Frankie bounded in, barking twice as if to tell them what he thought of being locked out of the room, then leapt onto the bed.

Dax rubbed the top of his furry head. "Okay, boy. Nice to see you, too, but you're in your mama's spot. Move your little butt."

"No way he'll move by himself." Vanessa rounded the bed and climbed in. She picked up the dog, giving him a little squeeze, then set Frankie on the edge of the bed.

Sliding into his boxers, he rested one arm around Vanessa and the other behind his head. He skimmed his fingertips along her biceps. "I have to say, this is the best damn job I've ever had."

Giggling, she shifted to her side and gave his arm a little pinch. "Hey now. What we just did better be more than part of your job or I have some reconsidering to do."

"Don't you dare." He stared down at her and any sarcastic comment he had flew right out the window. He tucked his thumb and forefinger under chin, lifting enough so their faces were inches away. "What we just did was unlike anything I've ever experienced. It was special in a way I don't even know how to explain. I'm not sure what I did to deserve you walking into my life, but I'll be grateful every day you did."

Her lips parted in a small O before the corners of her mouth lifted. "I agree. I know this is moving fast, but it just feels…"

"Right," he said, finishing her thought.

"Yeah," she agreed. "Right."

He wound a long strand of her silky hair through his fingers, struggling to put his thoughts into words. "You have a lot on your plate. I want to lighten that load, not add any stress. I don't want to put pressure on you. We can take this at whatever speed you're comfortable."

She snorted. "I'm clearly pretty darn comfortable with lightning speed, but I am looking forward to getting to know you better. I want to understand your past and learn more about what makes you who you are. You've gotten a crash course in my life. I'm excited to see more into yours."

A familiar punch of anxiety slammed against his gut. His past wasn't something that was easy to remember let alone discuss. But she was right. He'd learned so much about her in such a short time, and he hadn't offered her much about what had shaped him into the man he was today.

He was so used to covering his scars with sarcasm, he'd forgotten sometimes he had to shine a light on them for the people he cared about. At least, if he wanted to deepen their relationship.

"My life's had its ups and downs," he said, continuing to play with her hair. He kept his gaze fixed on the ceiling.

He didn't want to drag down the moment by bringing up all his former issues but wanted her to see he'd get there eventually. "Things got bad when my brother was injured while serving overseas and my dad sold a large part of our land. I'd always planned on running the ranch then, all of a sudden I found my future sold right out from under me."

Vanessa propped her head up on her hand and frowned. "That had to be difficult."

"Yeah." He scratched the whiskers that needed shaving on his chin. "And confusing. Pops and Madden made all these decisions without me, destroying my plans and pissing off the whole town in the process."

"Is that why my uncle called you trouble?"

"Probably. Tons of rumors swirled around about why the McKays betrayed our family name. I spent a lot of time being angry. Not always making the best choices. But it forced me to grow up fast and develop a low tolerance for other people's bullshit. Madden and I have worked through a lot of our issues, but as I'm sure you can see, we can still rub each other the wrong way. But we're trying, and that's more than we've done in a long time."

"And what made you start trying?"

"He finally told me the truth." Dax sucked in a steadying breath, hating the emotion sweeping in to clog his throat. "Pops has Parkinson's. I didn't know until last year. He wanted to sell the land before it was clear he couldn't manage it any longer. He doesn't want everyone he knows pitying him or treating him any different. I might not agree with what they did, but I respect why they did it."

She traced her fingertips along the side of his arm. "I'm sorry to hear about your dad. I know those words don't really mean anything and they change nothing, but I understand what it's like to watch someone you love decline."

"I want to be there for him. Take care of him as his health deteriorates. He deserves that." He cleared his throat, needing to shift gears. "When I found out you took care of your mom, there was this instant connection."

The prettiest smile touched her lips. "I felt it, too. And if you need someone to talk to about what's happening with your dad, I'm here. Taking care of someone you love can take a toll."

"I'm not worried about me, and he's fine. A little shaky and some little slip-ups, but he's the same pain in the butt he's always been." He winked, softening his words with a little chuckle.

"He's lucky to have you, and so am I." She kissed his forehead then snuggled back in beside him. "I'm also exhausted. I think I could sleep for a week straight."

"Go for it. I won't stop you."

Sighing, she closed her eyes. "I wish I could. I actually tracked down Garrison's mom's information through Lily while you were in the shower. I left her a message. I'll be on pins and needles until I hear from her."

He shifted to gather her even closer against the curve of his body. "I bet, but let's wait to worry about that tomorrow."

"Sounds like a plan. Good night."

"Good night." He let his eyelids drift shut as he reveled in the feel of her in his arms and fell asleep to the sound of Frankie's soft snores.

Sunlight poured through the window and forced Vanessa awake. She'd rather snuggle up against Dax and stay in bed for the morning, but Frankie had a sixth sense about when she woke and would soon whine to be let outside.

She allowed herself one more second to rest in the comfort of Dax's embrace then opened her eyes.

She found herself staring into his blue eyes and smiled.

"Morning," he said.

"Morning," she parroted back.

"This is a much better way to start the day than yesterday. Frankie's sweet and all, but I'd much rather be looking at you than his ugly snout."

Frankie barked then jumped over Vanessa to land on Dax's chest.

She laughed, not knowing which was funnier—the wide-eyed horror etched on Dax's face or the sound he made when the solid ball of fur caught him off guard. "Frankie!"

Dax rubbed the top of the dog's head. "My fault. I deserved it."

She opened her mouth to tell Frankie to get up when the blast of the doorbell broke into the moment. Frowning, she glanced at the clock on the nightstand. "Who'd be here before eight a.m.? Are you expecting anyone?"

"No," he said. "But we can open the app and see who it is."

Sitting up, she scooped her phone off the nightstand. She spotted a new text message, and her breath caught in her throat. "Mrs. Steele said she'd talk to me later this morning, but that she's headed out of town in the afternoon."

He rested a hand on her knee. "Then we'll see her today. But first we need to figure out who's making such an annoyingly early house call."

She inhaled a large breath, steadying her nerves as she pressed the buttons to bring the doorbell camera up on her screen. Dread tightened her stomach. "It's my uncle."

Dax glanced over her shoulder, his whiskers scraping against her skin. "What the hell does he want?"

"There's only one way to find out, although a conversation with Chip isn't the ideal way to start my day." She climbed out of bed and threw on her clothes. By the time she was ready to head downstairs, Dax and Frankie were both out the door ahead of her.

Insistent banging hurried her pace down the steps. When she reached the foyer, Dax stood with his expression pinched and hands fisted at his sides. She leveled him with her stare. "I can handle this, okay? Don't let him get you all riled up. He's not worth it."

Ignoring his response, she opened the door and aimed her no-nonsense look at Chip. As much as she wanted to throw in a snarky comment or two, she held herself back. "Good morning. I wasn't expecting you. Can I help you with something?"

"Yeah. You can stop telling the police to talk to me and my wife. I don't know what the hell your problem is, or why you're dragging my family into your mess, but it needs to stop."

Frankie growled and pushed his way in front of Vanessa. He stood over the threshold, baring his teeth.

Chip snorted. "What? This little mutt supposed to intimidate me?"

"No," Dax said, taking a step so he stood beside Vanessa. "But if that's what's needed, I will."

Disgust twisted Chip's lips. "Didn't take you long to make a move. I shouldn't be surprised, but who my niece chooses to spend time with isn't my concern. What I *am* concerned with is how she's moved into town and is trying to smear my good name."

Vanessa lifted her nose. "I haven't smeared anything.

It's not my fault that you've done nothing but put a target on your back as far as the sheriff's department is concerned. No one else has bullied, threatened and yelled at me. No one else has made it clear, over and over, that they want me to leave town. Someone has attacked me multiple times. I can't think of anyone who hates me as much as you."

His eyes widened for a beat, and he worked his jaw back and forth. "I don't hate you. You just don't belong here. This," he said, throwing his arm wide, "shouldn't be yours. All I'm doing is trying to right another wrong and you're standing in the way of that."

She tilted her head, studying the stiff set of his shoulders and defeated tone of his voice. For the first time, the defensiveness he carried around like a shield slipped away. "What do you mean 'another wrong'?"

The shield snapped back into place. "Never mind. Just do me a favor and stop sending deputies to my house."

Snorting, Dax shook his head. "Do you think she's the one pulling the strings? That she likes knowing someone out there is plotting against her? If you're not behind this mess, maybe you could stop being a total ass and try figuring out who the hell is."

Chip aimed his narrowed gaze at Dax. "Is that why you're here? Helping? You might have fooled her, but I know all about you and your kind. You don't care about anyone else's well-being but your own."

Dax stiffened and took a step forward.

Vanessa rested a hand on Dax's arm. She appreciated knowing he was there, but she could handle Chip herself. She wouldn't stand by and let him insult the man who'd been there in every way since she stepped into town.

"Enough," she said. "Get off my porch. Now. I don't care if you think me being here is a mistake or not. This is my house, my property. I won't let you stand here and treat someone I care about like garbage. You've made your point, now leave."

Red climbed up Chip's neck and consumed his face. "I'll be watching both of you. I won't let you ruin this family." He stormed away and climbed into his truck.

When his taillights disappeared into the hazy drizzle, she sighed and sagged against Dax. "I'm sorry for what he said. He was just trying to get a reaction out of you."

Dax circled an arm around her shoulders and dropped his chin on the top of her head. "I'm used to it. Trust me, I didn't take any of it personally. All I care about is what you think of me."

She turned into him and wrapped him in a hug. "I hope I've made that clear."

"Abundantly."

Frankie whined and stared up at them.

"Go ahead, buddy," she said. "Do your business. We'll wait right here."

She'd have to head into another dreary morning soon enough and officially start her day. But first, she'd soak up a few more minutes of being held by Dax to combat the icky feeling her uncle had left in the pit of her stomach.

His parting words stuck in her brain. Were they a threat to start watching her now that he'd been pushed over the edge, or had he been keeping an eye on her since she'd arrived in Cloud Valley?

Chapter 21

With the animals fed and taken care of, Dax washed his hands at the kitchen sink then prepped the ancient coffee machine. After he made a stop at his place to tend the horses and Vanessa spoke with Mrs. Steele, they needed to carve out time for her to unpack. Living out of boxes had to be a pain.

The machine wheezed to life. He wrinkled his nose at the smell of burnt coffee, but beggars couldn't be choosers. He filled a mug then sat at the kitchen table to choke down the bitter liquid.

The clicking of Frankie's claws on the hardwood floor reached him moments before the little dog pranced into the kitchen ahead of Vanessa.

She'd dried and curled her long dark hair and applied just enough makeup to enhance her natural beauty. Dark-washed jeans covered her lean legs, and she'd tucked in a long-sleeved, caramel-colored shirt. The neckline scooped low enough to show off the birthmark he'd enjoyed kissing the night before. He'd engage in a repeat if he wasn't a mess.

"You look really nice." Okay, so that might be an understatement. He'd almost swallowed his tongue when she'd stepped into the room. "Do you want some coffee?"

She pressed her hands to her stomach. "No, thanks. My nerves are a wreck. How much longer before we leave?"

"After I finish this cup, we can head to my place. I'll feed and turn out the horses before we go to Mrs. Steele's. What time did you tell her to expect us?"

"Ten thirty."

"We have plenty of time." He took a big sip of coffee. They might still have over an hour before they needed to meet Mrs. Steele, but he didn't want to make Vanessa stand around and wait any longer than necessary.

"Thank you for taking care of things this morning so I could have more time to get ready. Luckily, I labeled the boxes with my clothes, so it didn't take me forever to find something decent to wear." She smoothed her palms over her sleeves. "Does this look okay? Is it too much?"

"You look perfect."

She beamed. "Thanks. Oh, and Dr. Hatcher called after I got out of the shower. She said the goats can come home tomorrow. She'll drop them off after we arrange a good time. I'm so relieved they're all okay. One disaster averted."

"Good news. Hopefully, only the first of many to come."

Pulling out a chair, she sat beside him and propped her elbows on the table. "Fingers crossed. I knew the day could only get better after such an eventful start. I still can't believe Chip showed up like that. He was really mad."

A flash of anger tightened Dax's expression. "I texted Madden to let him know about it. A grown man going to a young woman's house to bark orders. What the hell was he thinking?"

"That he could bully me out of here. Same as always. Either he's so angry he doesn't see how guilty he makes himself look, or he just doesn't care. Something tells me he'd risk about anything to get what he wants."

"And he has a lot to lose," Dax said.

"What do you mean?" she asked.

He scratched the back of his neck. "Trust me, I understand his frustration."

"Excuse me?" Her eyes almost bugged out of her head.

"Hear me out," he said before she lunged across the table and slapped him. "Chip thought this land would be his one day, and for some reason seems to be caught unaware by it ending up in your hands. I've been there, and it sucks."

She reached under the table to rest her hand on his knee. "I never thought of it like that."

"Probably because I figured out a different path and didn't drag other people through hell when I didn't get my way. The thing about Chip that bugs me, besides his attitude, is the fact he has a job. He has a wife and daughter. He's built a business. If he's the one terrorizing you, he could lose everything. Why?"

"You said it yourself. People around here don't take kindly to their land being sold. He wants to keep the property in the family."

"But you are family," Dax insisted.

"Not to him." She slumped back in her chair. "He doesn't care that we have the same blood in our veins, or that this is what his father wanted. After my mother left town, she and I were both dead to him. Heck, I don't think he ever thought of me as a person. Just a problem to solve. And now that problem is in his face, causing more issues, and he's not happy about it. The question that still remains is, exactly how far will he go to get what he wants?"

Dax let the question roll around in his head as he finished his coffee. Caffeine buzzed in his veins, giving him the extra jolt he needed to get through the day.

His phone rang and he spotted Madden's name on the screen. "Well, that's my brother. Maybe he has some insight."

He answered as he made his way to the sink to rinse his mug. "Hey. What's up?"

"Where are you?"

"Where do you think? I'm with Vanessa. We were just about to head home so I can handle the horses and check on Pops."

"Skip the house, you need to get to the hospital."

The words created an instant haze around his brain. "What are you talking about? Why would I need to go to the hospital?"

"I'm with Pops right now. At the house. We think he fell and is unconscious. He's being transported to the county hospital. You need to meet me and Lily there."

The mug slipped from his fingers and clattered into the sink.

Vanessa hurried to his side while Frankie spun in circles at his feet.

"Are you all right?" she asked.

"I…uh… I need…" He couldn't think, couldn't compute what Madden said on the other end of the line. His dad was found, unconscious, and he hadn't been there to help. Hadn't taken care of the person he loved more than anything else in this world.

She smoothed a hand on his back. "Do you need me to take the call?"

Clearing his throat, he regained control of his slipping composure and shook his head. "Is he going to be okay?" he asked Madden, ignoring Vanessa's worried eyes.

Silence stretched over the line for a few seconds. "I really hope so. We'll know more once we get to the hospital. I'll see you there."

Dax disconnected then tossed his phone on the counter. He gripped the edge of the sink and hung his head. Pressure built at the bridge of his nose, and he sniffed back his emotions. Now wasn't the time to fall apart. He had to get to his dad. Be by his side the way he should have been last night.

"Dax?"

He flinched then stepped away from her. "I've got to go. My dad's hurt. Madden found him this morning."

"Oh no. Do you want me to drive?"

Blinking, he stared at her as he struggled to keep up with all the things running through his mind. "No, I'll drive. Um, I'll call Reid or Ben on the way. They can pick you up at the hospital so they can take you to see Mrs. Steele. I know how excited you are to meet her."

He walked past her without waiting for a response. His heart thundered in his ears. Right now, all that mattered was getting to his dad. He found his keys in his pocket, swiped his cowboy hat off the hook by the door, and jogged to his truck. Only one thought ran on repeat—if his dad didn't pull through, he'd never forgive himself.

A weird tension crackled in the air between Vanessa and Dax all the way to the hospital. She yearned to reach out, to comfort him, but instinct held her back. An icy exterior covered the warm, openhearted man she'd come to know and care for.

She tried not to take it personally. She, more than most, understood the terror that accompanied the news of a loved one in danger. Hell, she'd been a shell of herself during the entire time her mother battled cancer. She couldn't fault him for retreating into himself, no matter how bad it stung.

Once he found a parking spot, he hopped out of the truck and waited for her to meet him at the hood of the vehicle before heading for the doors to the emergency room. She hurried after him, hating the sinking feeling in the pit of her stomach. Instead of dwelling on it, she focused all her energy on sending positive vibes into the universe for Walter.

The doors whooshed open and she hung back while Dax made a beeline for the desk.

"Vanessa, over here."

Relief overcame her once she spotted Lily standing in the corner with Ben, who dipped his head in a silent greeting.

Lily waved Vanessa over and offered her a small smile. "How's Dax holding up?"

Vanessa kept her gaze glued on Dax as he spoke in hushed tones with the middle-aged man behind the desk. "He's quiet. Upset. Barely said a word since he hung up with Madden. Where is Madden?" She glanced around the waiting room but only saw a line of mostly empty chairs on worn carpet and a messy coffee station in the corner.

"He's with Walter," Ben said.

"That's good, right?" Vanessa asked. "The doctors wouldn't let anyone with him if he wasn't stable."

"I'm not sure," Lily said. "I hope so."

Dax stalked toward them, his cowboy hat stuffed in his hands. "They won't let me back there. Said only one person can be with Pops at a time. Damn it, I don't even know what happened, and that guy's treating me like I don't deserve any information."

The crack in his voice splintered Vanessa's heart. Red

tape in the medical field was enough to drive anyone crazy. Especially a loved one searching for reassurance. "I'm sure he can't tell you anything. Doctors are usually the only ones who can give updates on patients."

"Dax, just sit down for a minute." Lily smoothed a hand over his arm, but he yanked it away.

"I don't want to sit. I want to see my dad."

Ben took a step forward. "Sit. Now. And shut up."

Dax worked his jaw back and forth. "Excuse me?"

"You're being a jackass." Ben pointed at a nearby chair. "Sit," he repeated.

Dax scowled and crossed his arms over his chest. "I don't take orders from you or anyone else."

Lily cupped Dax's elbow and steered him toward the chair. "No one is giving orders. We understand you're upset, but we can't help when you're acting like a jerk. Now take a seat, text Madden to let him know that you're here, and I'll tell you as much as I know."

Vanessa hated the pinch of jealousy that accompanied watching Dax give in to Lily's gentle prodding. It was stupid to feel anything other than relief that he'd calmed down a little, but she wished he'd let her support him. Let her in and be there for him the way he'd been there for her.

Instead, she was like an outsider. Standing by while everyone else handled the situation.

Once Dax sent off his text, Lily sat beside him. "Madden and I stopped by the house this morning. He wanted to have coffee with your dad before getting to work. When we got inside, we found him on the kitchen floor. There was no way to know how long he'd been there or what caused the fall. There were no apparent injuries, but he never regained consciousness while we were with him."

Dax scrubbed a hand over his face. "He gets hungry at

night. I usually set a snack on the TV tray he keeps beside the recliner. On the rare occasions he'll actually let me help him to his room, I'll put something on his nightstand. He must have woken up and needed something to eat. I wasn't there. I didn't leave him anything. He fell because of me."

Vanessa swallowed the urge to tell him he hadn't done anything wrong. But as much as she wanted to comfort him, he'd made it clear she wasn't the one he wanted right now.

"Don't be ridiculous," Lily said. "You didn't push him. Didn't leave water or a stupid banana peel on the floor so he'd trip. Things happen. People have accidents all the time. This is not your fault."

"I wasn't there," he repeated, and dropped his head in his hand. "I haven't been there in days. I just left him alone. Madden saw it. He even came out to tell me we should hire some help, but I was too stubborn to listen. Now Pops is lying in a hospital bed, and I put him there."

Hurried footsteps down the hallway paused the conversation. Madden arrived, his lips turned down in a frown and worry clear in the bags under his eyes.

Dax shot to his feet. "Is he awake?"

Madden shook his head. "Not yet. They're hopin' with a little time, he'll wake. Tests didn't show anything they should be concerned about. But with his age and the Parkinson's..." His voice trailed off and he wiped his eyes.

"I want to see him."

Madden nodded. "Of course. I'll take you back. Ben, can you stay with Vanessa for a while?"

"That's why I'm here."

Vanessa struggled against the jolt of disappointment. Yes, Dax needed to be with his father, but she didn't want to just be passed off to the next man to protect her. She was safe waiting with Lily at the hospital. "I don't need a babysitter. I'm fine."

"You should go," Dax said, finally meeting her eyes. "You have places to be this morning. You shouldn't put that off, and I need to be with my dad right now. We'll talk later, but until then Ben will keep you safe." He lifted a hand as if to reach for her then shoved that hand through his hair and walked away.

Madden offered her a stiff smile then followed his brother.

Disappointment melted into bitter rejection. True she hadn't known Dax for that long, but she'd really thought what they'd found was special. Was different. Could turn into a future she'd always wanted.

But now one thing was abundantly clear. Dax might blame himself for his father's accident, but she was the reason he hadn't been home. And if Walter didn't survive, Dax might never look at her the same.

Chapter 22

The anticipation of speaking with Mrs. Steele had diminished the second Vanessa heard about Walter's accident. But after Dax's chilly behavior, it had completely vanished. A part of her wished she had stayed in the waiting room with Lily, showing Dax she'd stand beside him even when he pushed her away.

Another part of her didn't want to be in the way. Hell, maybe even believed she'd been wrong to dive in headfirst with Dax. Maybe she didn't know him as well as she thought.

Either way, she had to get out of her head and focus on what lay in front of her. She stared out the window as Ben drove her up the mountain road. Her time in Cloud Valley had been so consumed with drama, she hadn't ventured outside of town or off her property.

The wilderness around her was mesmerizing. The narrow road hugged the rockface with a smattering of trees climbing heavenward. Pops of green broke through the grayness of the day as spring continued to lay claim to all it touched.

It was what loomed below that tightened her stomach muscles. A large guardrail wrapped around the side of the narrow road, separating Ben's truck from the sharp drop-off on the other side. Growing up in the Midwest hadn't provided a lot of opportunities for time spent in the mountains. She couldn't wait to explore this part of her new world but wasn't sure if she'd ever get used to the staggering heights—or potential drops.

"Don't let him bother you."

Ben's gruff voice snapped her back to the moment. "Excuse me?"

"Dax. He was upset and stupid. He's not usually like that. He was shaken up."

Sighing, she fidgeted with her purse strap sitting on her lap. "I get that, but his shift in personality shocked me."

Ben snorted. "People don't always respond the best when they get bad news. I don't know Dax that well, but he's a good dude. Usually."

As much as she appreciated Ben's attempt to smooth over what had happened with Dax, she wasn't really in the mood to discuss it.

"How long have you lived in Cloud Valley?" she asked, attempting to steer the conversation away from Dax and the conflicting emotions battling in her gut.

"Not long."

She waited for more, but when nothing came, she pressed on. "Do you like it?"

He shrugged.

"Anyone ever tell you that you talk too much?"

Chuckling, he glanced her way for a beat with a smirk then returned his focus out the windshield. "Nope."

He took the next turn off the main road and wound even higher up the mountain. "Where the hell are we going?"

"To visit a woman who I hope has some answers. I was told she lived off the beaten path, but I never expected this."

"You might want to get those answers before it starts raining again. It'd be a bitch to make this drive in a storm."

A log cabin tucked in a cluster of trees came into view, and she swallowed any promise of hurrying. She didn't want to put them in a bad situation on the way home, but she also didn't want to rush an old woman willing to speak with her.

He parked as close as he could to the small stoop. "I'll be right here."

"Thank you," she said then hopped out of the truck and zipped her jacket.

The air was chillier this high in the mountains and smelled like wet earth. Birds chirped overhead and a duo of squirrels fought over an acorn. As much as she enjoyed the scenery, she couldn't stop the bite of disappointment at taking this next step alone. Dax had been beside her for every leg of this journey. Not having him with her now was a tough pill to swallow. But she didn't have a choice.

Summoning her courage, she strolled up the sidewalk to the front door and rang the bell.

The door swung open to a petite woman with long gray hair that hung in loose waves around her shoulders. Her eyes were the color of the fresh grass outside and filled with kindness. She wore tan baggy overalls with a white long-sleeved shirt underneath. Her wrinkled face was free of makeup.

"Mrs. Steele?"

A warm smile lifted her lips. "That's me. Please, come inside. Don't mind the mess."

Vanessa stepped inside and if it was possible for a room to hug her, this one would. Warm colors splashed across the walls and furniture. Framed photos and knickknacks crowded wooden stands. Stacks of books lined the floor and shelves.

"Thank you for agreeing to see me," Vanessa said. "I'm sure my message came as a surprise."

Mrs. Steele settled into an armchair and flicked her wrist toward the brown-suede sofa beside her. "Have a seat. And yes, I have to admit, I was shocked. But when I heard Mindy Kemp's daughter was in town and wanted to talk to me, I had to find out why. And, my goodness, do you look like your mother. She was such a pretty girl, and always so sweet."

"Did you know her well?"

"Well enough. My boy, Garrison…he was always with her brother—your uncle. Your mama would follow along. Is that why you wanted to see me? For stories about your mother? I wish I had more, but she spent time with my boy more at her own place or in town. Football games and dances. I'd see her on the periphery, hear a few tidbits of information here and there as she was growing up, but I didn't know her that well. It wasn't until closer to Garrison's accident that she started coming around a little more."

"As in coming to your home?" She followed the thread of the conversation, searching for anything that could lead to something new.

"Yes. We lived in town back then. She'd come over after school. Just her and Garrison. She was very polite. A nice girl."

"Were they dating?"

A whisper of a smile lifted the side of her mouth. "I think something might have been burning between the two of them. He never mentioned it, but a mother knows these things. They'd whisper or sit close with their heads ducked together. I often wondered if that spark could have grown into something more if things had been different."

The emotion in Mrs. Steele's voice squeezed Vanessa's heart. She hated pressing on but decided to just rip off the Band-Aid. "I heard my mom and uncle got into a fight at Garrison's wake. Do you know what happened?"

"That was a rough day. My body was numb even as my heart shattered over and over again. I remember the argument, but I'm sorry, I can't put my finger on what caused it. I think everyone was just worked up." She jumped to her feet. "Where are my manners? Would you like something to drink? Take your jacket off and make yourself comfortable while I get us some tea."

She didn't have the heart to decline so she shrugged out of her jacket then crossed the room to glance out the window. Ben sat in his truck, looking at his phone. Rain hadn't started falling yet. She could spare a few more minutes before making her excuses to leave.

While she waited for Mrs. Steele to return, she circled the living room. Photos of who she assumed was Garrison as a young kid were hung besides family pictures showing off a happy unit through the years. Sadness pressed on her lungs. Mrs. Steele seemed like such a nice person, and she'd experienced so much loss.

Maybe that was why she'd felt such a kinship with the older woman. She understood losing her family, being alone in the world. Mrs. Steele might not have information for her, but at least she'd met a new friend.

"Here we are, dear." Mrs. Steele carried a teacup placed on a dainty saucer. Two feet away, she stilled, her shaky hand causing drips of tea to spill over the side of the cup.

"Oh goodness, are you all right?" Vanessa took the

saucer and set it down on the end table by the sofa. "Do you need to sit?"

Mrs. Steele rested her fingertips just above her collarbone. "You have a birthmark."

"I do, yes."

"It's just… Garrison had the same one. In the same spot. It took me by surprise." Mrs. Steele took another step closer.

The statement stole Vanessa's breath. She touched the mark on her neck. Having the same birthmark as Garrison wasn't a definitive answer. Maybe it meant nothing at all. But something in the way this woman stared at her, the connection she felt, had her believing she'd found something she'd been searching for.

Clearing her throat, Vanessa decided to lay all her cards on the table. "My mother never told me who my father is. All I know is that she left town when she was around three or four months pregnant. Since I've been in Cloud Valley, the only person I've heard she had feelings for was your son. She had a crush on him, but no one mentioned him returning those feelings. Or the two of them spending time together. Until now."

Mrs. Steele pressed her shaking hand to her mouth. "Oh my. I… I don't know what to say. Do you really think it's possible?"

She didn't know if the hope beating inside her was a deep desire to want to find the missing piece from her past or something more. "I do," she said.

"My dear girl." Mrs. Steele flattened her palm along Vanessa's jawline. Tears shimmered in her eyes. "Nothing would make me happier. How do we find out?"

Water filled her own eyes. "I guess we could do a DNA test. If you'd be willing?"

"I'll do whatever I can, but it'll have to wait a few days. I'm leaving soon to visit my sister."

Vanessa smiled. "I've waited twenty-five years to find out who my father is. I can wait a few more days."

Mrs. Steele drew in a shuddering breath. "Well, what a surprising turn of events. I still have some time before I have to go. Do you want to sit and chat over that tea? I'd love to get to know you."

A lump wedged in her throat. She'd love to settle in and talk, but the rain would start again any minute. "That sounds lovely, but I should get going. My friend is waiting to drive me home, and we'd like to get back to town before the weather turns."

"Yes, that's probably a good idea." Mrs. Steele grabbed her hands and squeezed. "As soon as I'm back, we'll figure out exactly what we need to do. I promise." She gave her a peck on the cheek then hugged her tight.

Vanessa melted into the embrace. She'd never had the opportunity to know any of her grandparents. If she had to go through hell to finally find one, all the fear and frustration would be worth it. "I look forward to it."

She gave her one more quick hug then walked back into the gray day. Her steps were lighter. She couldn't help but feel like something had clicked into place. She might not know how this possible life-altering news was tied to what was happening now, but she didn't care.

Jumping into the running truck, she grinned at Ben. "Hope I wasn't too long."

He grunted and shifted the truck into Reverse. "Get what you need?"

"I did." Excitement thrummed through her until she thought she might explode. She wanted to tell someone, to share this potential new discovery with someone.

To share it with Dax.

She slumped against the seat. "Any word about Walter?"

Ben shook his head.

Her heat sank.

"Where to next?" Ben asked.

Sighing, she leaned her head back and stared out the window. They could go back to her place. Lord knew she had enough to do to keep her busy for days. But the thought of being there without Dax was like a dagger in the gut. "Frankie will be fine for a while longer without me. Let's go back to the hospital."

He flicked her a quick glance. "You sure?"

"Yeah." She took Ben's lead and didn't elaborate. He didn't want to hear her rambling, and she didn't know how to put her thoughts into words. Dax might see her as clingy for sticking around when he'd made it clear she wasn't needed, but she wanted to show him she was there. That she'd support him through the hard stuff, even if he didn't make it easy.

And if he had a problem with that, maybe they'd rushed into things too quickly. The thought that Dax might not be who she thought he was made her heart ache, but she didn't want to waste her time on someone who pushed her away when things were tough.

"I'll give Dax a head's-up we're on our way," she said, grabbing her phone from her jacket pocket.

Rain drizzled from the sky and Ben mumbled under his breath. He tightened his grip on the wheel. "Damn weather. Should be better when we get back on the highway."

She glanced out the window and winced. The raindrops grew thicker, heavier, as they bounced off the windshield. Unease slithered down her spine as she punched in a message for Dax. She hit Send, and a sudden jolt rocked the truck. "What the hell?"

"We've got to get out of here," Ben said. The truck flew forward, the tires spinning on water and loose gravel.

"What's going on?" She peered past him out the driver's-side window and fear stole her breath. A stream of rocks and mud slid down the side of the mountain, swallowing everything in its way. "Oh my God. It's coming straight at us!"

Ben gritted his teeth, his focus fixed ahead as he sped forward.

Rocks and debris bounced off the glass, splintering the windshield. The tail end of the truck fishtailed off the road and the tires spun, searching for traction. Mud spit up, sprinkling the window and blocking her view.

"Are we stuck? Should we run?"

"I don't know." He slammed his foot against the gas pedal. "Come on," he urged.

"Maybe we—" Another blast shook the vehicle, rolling it onto its side. The impact knocked her forward and her phone flew out of her fingers. A scream ripped from her mouth. The seat belt trapped her in place, and she struggled to unhook the strap as momentum plunged the truck down the mountain. "Ben, we need to get out of here."

The only reply was the constant pinging of debris against metal as Ben hunched over the steering wheel, eyes closed and body limp.

Chapter 23

Dax sat on the edge of the chair in his father's hospital room. Leaning forward, he rested his forearms on his knees and kept his gaze fixed on Walter's pale face. A machine beeped beside him, announcing his steady heartbeat and stable vitals.

But he still hadn't opened his eyes.

Guilt burrowed into his stomach lining and refused to budge. Pops looked so small in the big bed, the thin blanket tucked around his slim frame. A small bump on his forehead showed where he'd hit his head, probably when he'd fallen at some point during the night.

While he'd been alone with no one to come to his aid.

Shoving his hand through his hair, he leaned back in the chair and rested his head against the wall. He'd become so consumed with Vanessa that he'd lost sight of his father's needs. How could he be so selfish?

"How's he doing?" Madden stood in the hallway with his arms crossed over his chest.

"About the same. He's still not awake." Dax sat up and rubbed his hands down his face. "I hate seeing him like this."

Madden dropped into the chair beside him. He kicked

out his legs and hooked them at the ankles. "You want to talk about it?"

"About what? How I messed up? How you were right, and I couldn't handle things on my own? Sorry, but I feel bad enough already. I don't need you shoving my mistakes in my face right now."

"I meant how you were a dick to everyone when you got here."

Irritation rippled through him. "Seriously? Dad's lying right in front of us and you want to talk to me about how I spoke to your fiancée."

"No, I want to discuss how you treated yours."

The hair on the back of his neck stood on end, and Dax shoved to his feet. He glowered down at Madden. All the resentment and anger he hadn't been able to let go of simmered at the surface. "I don't see how that's any of your business."

Madden shrugged. "Maybe not, but I can't help but think part of your bad attitude is my fault."

"I don't know what the hell you're talking about." Needing to move, he stalked back and forth across the shiny linoleum floor. "And screw you. I was upset. I needed to find out what happened, and no one would tell me. Sorry if how I handled things ruffled a few feathers."

"Sounds like you did more than that."

"Maybe I did, but what does that have to do with you? Why do you care?" Stopping, he faced his brother.

"Because you're taking on too much, including blame for Dad's fall. And it sounds like you took it out on everyone around you."

"I should take the blame," he said, pounding the heel of his hand against his chest. "I told you I didn't need help. I told you I could handle it. I told you I was fine. Then I left him. All alone in that house. Who knows how long he laid there? If he was awake for a while, waiting for me to come back? It makes sick to my stomach to think about."

Madden stood and rested a hand on Dax's shoulder. "And I bought into the bullshit. I told myself you were fine, and I wasn't being a horrible son and brother. I didn't recommend help taking care of Pops because I didn't think you could do it. It was because I've been so busy with the business and planning for the wedding, I've neglected him. Neglected you both. I wanted to help the only way I could without cloning myself."

"But I *was* fine. Pops and I were getting along just fine until..." He swallowed Vanessa's name before he said something he'd regret. Pressure increased in his chest, threatening to split him in two.

"Until you were needed somewhere else," Madden said, dropping his arm to his side. "You had a job to do, and you met someone. Someone special, from what it looks like. Pops was happy you were spending time with Vanessa. He likes her—likes you two together. You didn't do anything wrong by spending time with her."

"But if I'd been home, I could have stopped this from happening."

"Maybe. Maybe not. But one thing I've learned over the past few years is you can't stop living your own life. Can't put things on hold for other people. No matter how well-intentioned."

"So, I'm just supposed to abandon him?"

"Is that what you think I did?" Madden asked.

"No. You're busy. You're building a life, a business. But it's different. You've been gone for years."

Madden winced. "Does that make it better?"

"Damn it," Dax said, squeezing the bridge of his nose.

"That's not what I meant. It's just, Pops and I got into a good routine while you were overseas. When you came back to Cloud Valley, you never moved back in with us. It's been him and me against the world for a long time."

"Do you think that's what he wants? For you to give up happiness with Vanessa—or anyone else—so you're home with him every night?"

He squirmed under Madden's unflinching stare, hating the mirror being held in front of his face. "No."

"Do you think he wants to feel like a burden to his kids?" Madden pressed on.

"No, but he's not. I love spending time with the old geezer."

The side of Madden's mouth lifted. "That doesn't mean he's the only one you should spend time with. And, honestly, even without Vanessa, you've been busier than usual. Your horse training has picked up and you're taking on more responsibility at Sunrise Security. He's home alone quite a bit. He needs someone there. A friend. Someone to keep him company and just to look out for him a little."

"I guess I never looked at it like that."

"Maybe that's because you never gave me the chance to actually have this conversation."

Dax reclaimed the seat he'd abandoned and stared at Walter. "Let's hope we didn't have it too late."

"He's a tough old bird," Madden said, sitting back down beside Dax. "No way he's done with us yet. When he's out of here, we'll all discuss the best way to move forward. That's what we should have done all along. I'm sorry I put such a burden on your shoulders."

A little of the guilt eating away at him dissipated, replaced by shame and regret. "You were right about me acting like a dick earlier. I don't know what came over me. I was drowning in self-blame and fear and… I really made a mess of things."

"Yeah, Lily said it was pretty bad. You need to talk to Vanessa."

"If she'll talk to me after how I acted. Damn it. I just sent her with Ben and didn't even tell her good luck. She must think I'm a total jerk."

"Well, now she's like the rest of us, but we all still love ya."

The gravelly sound of his father's voice shot him and Madden out of their seats.

Relief loosened the tension tying Dax up in knots. "Pops, you're awake."

Walter coughed, cringing with his eyes closed another beat before opening them again. "From the sound of it, good thing I am. Now I can slap you upside the head for screwing up already with that nice Kemp girl."

Emotion pressed against Dax's sinus cavity, and he struggled to keep from crying. If his dad could already joke, he'd be just fine. "Madden already did that. I'll fix it. I promise."

"What are you waiting for?" Walter asked. "Call the girl."

Chuckling, he grabbed his phone and saw the text message he'd missed from her. He let out a long breath. She must be willing to at least hear him out. Either that or she wanted to give him a piece of her mind, which he more than deserved. "She and Ben are on their way here. I'll let them know you're awake."

He brought up her contact information and hit the call button. The line rang in his ear until her voicemail message picked up.

"Weird. She didn't answer."

"I'll try Ben," Madden said.

Dax double-checked the time stamp on the text message. They should have arrived by now. While Madden dialed Ben, he tried Vanessa again. When voicemail picked up, he disconnected. "Still nothing."

"Ben's not answering either," Madden said. "That's unlike him. Especially when he's on the job."

Dax cringed. Vanessa was more than just a job. She was the woman he cared about, who he'd fallen head over heels for then tossed aside as soon as another hardship swept in to demand his attention.

"Something's wrong. I can feel it. No way they both wouldn't answer their phones."

Madden frowned. "Maybe they're in the waiting room. They could have arrived when I walked back here."

"Pops, I'll be back." Praying his brother was right, Dax sprinted down the wide hall to the waiting area.

Lily stood when she saw him. "Is everything okay?"

"No, I can't get ahead of Vanessa, and Ben's not answering his phone. Have you seen them? She texted to let me know they were on their way. They should be here by now."

Lily shook her head. "No. They're not here."

Dread curdled in his stomach, and he fought the urge to be sick. Vanessa had been in danger since the minute she'd driven into town, and he'd sent her away without hesitation. He might accept that his father's fall wasn't his fault, but if something happened to Vanessa, there was no way to escape the blame.

Mud smothered the windows, blocking Vanessa's view as the vehicle continued sliding. Her body jostled with each bounce, each bump, as it barreled downward. With the truck on its side, she hung in the air, tossed around like a rag doll. Images of the steep drop-off she'd viewed on the way up the mountain nearly paralyzed her with fear.

"Ben!" she yelled again.

Nothing.

A sudden thud stopped the vehicle and sent her flying forward. The seat belt cut into her skin. She braced herself against the dashboard as her bones rattled. The truck stopped, but the sound of raining rocks and mud beating against the outside of the vehicle continued. She couldn't see what had pinned them in place, but it didn't matter. She had to get out of there and find help.

The seat belt still hooked across her chest kept her from tumbling toward Ben. She tried the handle. The door didn't budge. Frustrated tears filled her eyes. She slammed her shoulder against the hard barrier over and over.

"No," she said under breath. "I can't be stuck. I have to get out."

Remembering her phone, she reached down to the footwell. Her fingers brushed against the hard pink case.

The door flung open, and bits of dirt and rock rained down on her. She covered her face with her arms.

"Are you okay?" a familiar voice asked.

Lowering her arms, she blinked against the grainy bits of mud in her eyes and spotted Ethan. Relief blossomed in her chest.

"Vanessa? Is that you? You need to get out of the truck, okay? Nice and slow." Ethan extended a hand, like a lifeline.

Her phone rang at her feet. She made a move to grab it, and Ethan squeezed her hand.

"I already called for help," he said. "And I don't want to alarm you, but the truck isn't in the safest position. Any sudden movements could end badly."

She swallowed the terror inching up her body and fit her hand in his. “What about Ben?”

“Let’s get you out first then I’ll worry about him.”

She clung to the steady calmness of his voice as she unhooked her seat belt. Ethan cupped a palm under her elbow as he helped maneuver her from her seat. She climbed through the open door, and the truck teetered under her. Stopping, she held her breath until the movement stopped.

“Almost there,” Ethan said. “Just keep moving. Nice and steady.” He hooked an arm around her waist and kept her upright.

Her feet hit the ground, and she released a shuddering breath that had been trapped in her throat. Shock tightened her muscles. Thick mud covered the forest floor, the ground sloping down toward a jagged ravine. A towering pine tree blocked the back of the truck from plummeting over the edge.

“Oh my God, we have to get Ben out. He was knocked unconscious. We’ll have to drag him out before the tree falls over or the truck shifts.”

Ethan hauled a hand through his hair. “I’m not sure how to get to him. His door is blocked by the ground and hauling him out through the passenger door poses a lot of issues. Emergency responders should be here soon. They’ll know how to rescue him.”

“No,” she said, shaking her head. Adrenaline shot through her veins and the urge to act had her ducking her head for a better view of Ben. “I can climb in and unbuckle him. If we both grab an arm, we can pull him out.”

The thick tree trunk groaned, and a branch snapped as if in protest to her plan.

“It’s too risky. I have some rope in my truck. I’d feel better if I go in after him. You can stand up at the road and flag down help. I told the responders our location, but it's a real mess out there. I don't want them to miss us." He started jogging up the hill.

Indecision bounced inside her like a ping-pong ball. They were far enough down the side of the mountain that it could be easy to overlook them. And what Ethan said made sense. Ben was a big man, and it would be near impossible to drag his deadweight to safety. If Ethan had a plan, far be it for her to argue.

Ethan stopped and turned to face her. "Come on. We can't waste time. His life depends on it."

The terrifying reminder snapped her into motion. She ignored all her aches and pains as she followed him up the incline. Mud swallowed her feet and tried to keep her stuck to the earth. Each step was harder than the last, the edge of the road farther than she'd expected.

Ethan reached the top and stared down at her. "Almost there. I'll grab the rope."

Gratitude washed over her like the drops of cool rain falling from the sky. She fought the fatigue dragging her down and pushed forward to the top of the hill. Muck coated the road, but it wasn't as thick where she emerged.

"Are you okay?" Ethan asked.

"I will be once we get Ben out." She glanced down the road. "How much longer before the rescue team arrives? I don't even hear any sirens."

"Should be any minute, as long as there weren't other accidents and the roads are clear. Let's grab that rope."

She jogged to catch up to him, when the sight of his black truck stopped her in her tracks. A large dent folded in the passenger side and scratches ran from the headlight to the cab. Her heart caught in her throat. "What happened to your truck?"

"I ran into a little trouble as well. The same landslide caught me off guard, but I was able to get away from it before it took me out. Lucky for you, huh?"

"I'm surprised you were up here at all," she said. "Not much around."

He stopped beside the hood and shrugged. "Best hiking spots are up this mountain. You should wait in the truck, get out of this weather, while I get your friend."

"Can I use your phone to call Dax? He'll be worried and I want to let him know what happened."

"Sure." He grabbed his phone and held it forward.

Swallowing the fear climbing up her throat, she reached for it. Her finger curled around the phone just as he clamped his hand around her wrist.

"Get in the truck. Now."

Instinct had her yanking away, but she couldn't escape the hard grip on her arm. "Let me go. What are you doing?"

"No more games. I won't tell you again. Get in the truck before you make me do something we'll both regret." Still clasping her wrist, he glanced down the edge of the mountain. "I'd hate to hurt your friend more than he already is."

Terror drizzled through her system, drowning her from the inside out. Ben was already in a precarious situation. She couldn't make it worse and had no idea what Ethan was capable of.

"Fine," she said, lifting her chin. "I'll go with you. Just leave Ben alone."

"Good girl." He pulled her toward the truck, waiting until she was in the passenger seat to lift the flap of his jacket to expose a gun. "Don't do anything stupid. I'd hate to use this on your pretty face."

Her brain went into overdrive as he rounded the hood,

his eyes on her the whole time, and climbed in behind the wheel. As he drove away, she glanced over her shoulder. Headlights shone through the sheet of rain. Hopefully whoever had stumbled upon this disaster could get Ben the help he needed before it was too late.

But now she had an even bigger problem—she had to escape Ethan before he finished what he'd started.

Chapter 24

Dax's mind spun and he lowered himself into a chair beside Lily in the waiting room. Vanessa had planned to go to Mrs. Steele's house. She could still be there, but that wouldn't explain why she or Ben couldn't be reached.

Or why she'd texted to let him know they were on their way to the hospital.

"Where's your phone?" Dax asked Madden.

"What?"

"Your phone. Get it."

Madden fished it from his back pocket. "I can try calling Ben again, but I don't think he'll answer."

"Don't you have some app that includes everyone from work? To keep tabs on everyone?"

Madden glowered. "I don't keep tabs on anyone. It's just to keep an eye on where the guys are. In case we need to find them." The light bulb finally went off and Madden fiddled with his phone. "Okay. We've got a location."

Dax shot up and glanced at the screen. "The little dot isn't moving. Why isn't it moving?"

"I don't know, but we're going to find out. Lily, can you stay here with Dad? He woke up and shouldn't be alone. I'll text you where we're going. Call Deputy Sanders and let him know we think something's wrong and could use some help."

Dax didn't wait to hear Lily's response before dashing outside. Rain splashed down and thunder rumbled in the distance. He made a beeline for his truck when a hard hand on his shoulder locked him in place. He spun around, irritation fisting his hands at his sides. "What the hell, man?"

"My truck."

Not wanting to waste time arguing, Dax followed him to his vehicle and jumped inside.

"Hold this," Madden said, handing over his phone as soon as he got behind the wheel.

The tracking app was still on the screen. Dax stared at the dot that represented Ben and urged it to move. "Still nothing. What if they were in an accident?"

"Then we need to get to them quickly. Try calling Vanessa again."

He did, but with the same results. A kind of fear he'd never experienced hummed in his veins. "Nothing. I should have never let her visit Mrs. Steele without me."

"Don't jump to conclusions," Madden said. "It won't get us anywhere. Stay calm and focused."

Dax snorted. "Seriously? That's your great advice? This is my fault. I screwed up and Vanessa could be hurt."

"Dude, you don't know anything is even wrong. Shut up and stop focusing on the worst-case scenario." A few tense moments of silence lingered between them as Madden drove toward the location he'd plugged into his GPS.

Dax kept a firm grip on the phone and his gaze latched on the screen. They got closer and closer to the little dot. Rain splashed down, slowing their progress.

"Roads are a mess." Madden slapped the steering wheel.

Dax's stomach muscles clenched. "They'll be worse up

where it says Ben and Vanessa are. I'm going to jump out of my damn skin."

Madden flicked a quick glance his way before maneuvering off the highway and onto the narrow road that wound up the mountain. "You've got it bad."

"What the hell are you talking about?" He didn't have the patience to deal with his brother's cryptic comments right now.·

"Lily told me. I should have listened. That woman's always right." He shook his head, the slightest smile lifting one corner of his mouth.

Dax had to fight not to smack the look right off his face. "Stop blabbing over there. You don't know what you're talking about."

"I've never seen you like this over a woman before. Lily said she could tell you'd fallen hard by the way you looked at Vanessa."

He could keep arguing but there wasn't a point. Madden was right. He'd never experienced such intense feelings for anyone as he did for Vanessa. She was sweet and kind. Caring and compassionate. Strong and funny. She was perfection tied up in a beautiful package and he might have blown it.

Madden's phone rang, sending his heart galloping until he spied Lily's name. "Can I answer?"

"Go for it. The roads are in rough shape, and I need to stay focused."

"Hey, Lil. It's Dax. You find out anything?"

"I just got off with the phone with Deputy Sanders. I gave him the location Madden told me, and he said emergency responders are already there. An accident was called in. Apparently, it's pretty bad. I thought you should know."

His stomach dropped just as flashing lights came into

view and blocked the way. "We're here. We'll call you when we know more."

Madden muttered under his breath. "Looks like a landslide came through."

Bile shot up his throat. He thought the roads might become a problem with the constant rain and storms. Ben wouldn't have known what to look out for while traveling up the mountain. He searched for Ben's truck, but only the emergency vehicles were parked among the river of mud and rocks cascading down the jagged rockface.

Madden parked, and Dax catapulted himself from the vehicle. He jogged to the back of an ambulance. The back door was flung open, but no one was inside. "Vanessa!"

Madden came up beside him and pointed down the ravine. "Looks like they're down there."

Horror fisted his heart. Ben's truck sat on top a sea of debris that had been caught in the landslide, knocked onto its side and held in place by a giant pine tree. Two firefighters worked to get someone out the passenger side that looked up to the gray sky.

"We should give them room to work," Madden said. "We don't want to get in the way."

"Like hell I'm staying up here." He moved as quickly as he could, picking his way past upturned roots and boulders. Dirt caked onto his jeans and mud attached to his shoes with each step. Rain continued to fall, soaking through his clothes. Time crawled by and he kept his gaze fixed on the rescue, praying to see Vanessa's face.

One of the firefighters spotted him and held up a hand. "Stay where you are. The scene is a mess and disturbing it more might cause everything to shift. We don't want this truck to plummet past this tree before we get this guy to safety." He returned his attention to the rescue mission before Dax could ask more questions.

He stayed in place, leaning forward with his palms on his thighs. A still body was lifted from inside the truck and placed on a waiting gurney. Two medical workers hoisted the gurney and trudged through the debris toward the top of the incline.

The firemen gathered their supplies and followed suit.

"Wait!" he yelled, charging forward. "There was a woman in there. Where is she?"

Commotion stopped the EMTs, and Ben struggled to sit. "Dax," he said, the wind beating back his voice so it was barely above a whisper.

Dax ran to Ben's side, reaching him in time to keep him from hopping off the gurney as the medics fought to keep him still.

"She's gone, man. I woke up just in time to see her following a guy up the mountain. I tried to get out and couldn't. I'm so sorry, dude."

"Did you see what he looked like? Hear her say his name? Anything?"

Ben shook his head then winced.

"We need to get him in the ambulance then to the hospital," one of the medics barked.

Dax took a step away and let them continue. There was nothing more for Ben to tell him. Vanessa was gone, and if Ben was right, she'd walked away. But she wouldn't leave Ben injured and alone, wouldn't disappear without telling someone where she was going.

Confusion swirled inside his brain as he jogged back up the mountain to find Madden speaking with Mrs. Steele. The older woman stood under a yellow umbrella, bundled in an olive-green raincoat. "Is Vanessa okay? I heard the rumbling and came out to see if anyone was hurt. She'd just left. I saw the truck off the side of the road, but also the one leaving. I don't know which one she was in."

"You saw the other truck?" Dax asked. "What about the driver?"

"It's hard to see with all this rain. All I could make out was the color."

"What color was it?" Dax asked, but he already knew the answer.

"Black."

The confirmation hit him with the force of a hurricane.

Vanessa may have survived the landslide, but now she was in more danger than ever before.

Vanessa clenched her hands into fists in her lap. She tried to keep track of the twists and turns along the country roads, but she had no idea where she was. Her brain worked in overdrive to figure a way out of this nightmare, but the gun resting on Ethan's thighs was a constant reminder that she was screwed.

"Where are you taking me?"

He didn't answer. Just kept his gaze fixed on the road and his mouth shut.

His silence was unnerving. If she was about to die, she at least deserved to understand why.

"You could have let me stay in the truck. Why save me just to kill me?"

Nothing but the windshield wipers answered her.

Panic clawed inside her throat. She had to think of a different approach if she wanted Ethan to tell her anything. "Did Chip put you up to this? I mean I know my uncle hates me and everything, but I really didn't think he'd stoop this low. If the guy wants that old house this bad, he can have it. I'll pack up and move back to Chicago. Just tell him he won, okay? Then we'll forget whatever this is." She waved a hand between the two of them.

Ethan snorted. "He doesn't care about that stupid house. He just doesn't want you there."

"Why not?"

"Because we knew this would happen. Damn it, everything was fine." He smacked a hand against the steering wheel. "We cleaned up our mess and no one suspected a thing. Your mom threw a wrench in things, but as soon as she was out of town, we had nothing left to worry about. Until you showed up. You ruined everything."

Now that she'd loosened his lips, she struggled to keep up with the torrent of words pouring from his mouth. "I didn't ruin anything. I inherited property from my grandfather and moved in. That's it. What could I have possibly done that was so bad you've had to torture me?"

"You came back. That was enough."

Frustration ate away at her. She'd been stuck in the same loop of fear and confusion since she'd arrived in town, and she was sick of it. Ethan might put a bullet in her head. If she couldn't escape her death, she at least deserved to know why.

Wait. He could have shot her in Ben's truck. Hell, could have left her in the teetering vehicle, hoping nature would sweep in and finish the job without him having to further dirty his hands. He wouldn't answer her when she'd asked why he'd saved her in the first place, she might as well try a different approach. "You won't shoot me."

He finally glanced her way and pure rage shone from his eyes. "Wanna test that theory?"

"You need to be sure I'm dead, so leaving me in the truck was out because there was a chance I survived. You could have just shot me back there, but then once someone found me, they'd know it was murder. If you're going to get away with killing me, you need to make it look like an accident."

The word tasted bitter on her tongue as another accident floated back to the forefront of her mind. Pieces clicked together. She might be grasping at straws, but there was only one way to find out.

"Just like with Garrison."

Ethan clenched his jaw so hard she feared his teeth would burst through the skin.

She'd hit a nerve.

"I read about him in the newspaper. The article claimed it was a tragic accident, and he drowned in the river behind my house. Weird how he had an injury to the back of his head when they found him."

"That's not weird at all," Ethan said, his voice clipped and tight. "Maybe when he fell into the river, he cracked his skull, who knows."

"I wonder if the injury would be consistent with the size and shape of a hammer."

The color drained from Ethan's face. "You had to keep asking questions. Keep digging and digging. If you had stopped, things wouldn't have gone so far."

"If someone hadn't broken into my home and scared the hell out of me at every turn, I wouldn't have had to keep asking questions," she shot back.

He snorted. "It was too risky. There was no telling what was left in that house. Your mom…she left so much behind. I had to make sure there wasn't something inside to tie me to anything."

The scenery outside the window became more familiar, but she still wasn't sure where they were headed. But if she could keep him talking, maybe he'd slip up. Give her something she could use against him.

"Like the hammer and shirt?"

He squeezed his eyes shut for a beat before training his gaze back on the road. But this time, she saw sadness and regret. "You don't understand."

The defeated tone threw her off, but she kept pushing. "Then make me understand."

He returned to silence.

"Damn it," she yelled, slapping the dashboard. "What does it matter? You're going to kill me anyway. Shouldn't I at least know why?"

He blinked, as though surprised she had any fight left in her. "I don't want to kill you."

She couldn't help the cackle of laughter that shot out of her mouth. "Really? The gun on your lap says otherwise."

"I don't have a choice," he said on a long sigh. "Everything got out of a hand. From the beginning of this whole mess. Garrison…he was like a brother. I didn't mean to hit him so hard. I just reacted. And when things had gone too far, we had to finish it. There was too much at stake if we didn't."

The confession didn't surprise her, but one part stuck out. "'We'? You weren't the only one who hurt Garrison. Did my uncle help you?"

Ethan worked his jaw back and forth. "We did what we had to do."

"But why did you have to kill your friend? If you were all so close, why would you and my uncle hurt him? Dump his body in the river?"

He didn't speak for so long, she thought he'd refuse to answer. Refuse to finally give her the final piece of the puzzle.

"Because we had to save your mom."

The whispered words erupted in the cab of the truck like a bomb, destroying everything she thought she knew.

Chapter 25

Anger and fear fueled Dax as he stalked over Chip Kemp's front yard, not caring about the rain dripping down his back or his brother urging him to calm down.

"You can't storm up there and go off on this guy," Madden said, jogging to stay in step with him.

"I can do whatever the hell I want. My gut knows Chip's hands are dirty. Besides, what else should I do? Sit around and wait?" He hopped onto the porch and pounded his fist against the door. "Open up, Chip."

"You think he saved Vanessa from a car accident to bring her to his house and what? Sit at the kitchen table? Break bread?"

"I don't know," Dax yelled into the wind. "But I have no other idea where she could be or who she's with. So, either shut up or help me figure this out."

Before Madden could respond, the door swung open. Chip stood on the other side, his face red and twisted in fury. "What the hell do you think you're doing?"

"Where's Vanessa?"

"How should I know?"

Dax shoved past him and rushed inside. "Vanessa? Are you here?" He hurried past an empty living room to the kitchen.

"Get out of my house before I call the police," Chip shouted. "Vanessa isn't here, and why you'd think she was is beyond me."

Dax spun to face the older man, jabbing his index finger into his chest. "Because she's gone. Went off with a man after climbing out of a rolled-over truck on the side of a damn mountain."

"And you think it's me? That I lured your little girlfriend away and brought her home to hang out with my wife and daughter?"

Dax threw his hands in the air. Desperation pushed him closer into Chip's face. "You've been a pain since she's been to town. Making her feel horrible. Heaping guilt and your unwarranted anger on her shoulders. You're nothing but a bully, and I won't stand around and let you hurt her. Now, where is she?"

Madden clapped a hand on his shoulder and eased him back. "Chip, it's been a rough day, and now Vanessa is missing. We believe she is in extreme danger. Sorry to barge in like this, but you've been the only person whose name keeps coming up."

"I can't make myself any clearer. I haven't done a damn thing to that girl. I didn't break into the house. I didn't run her off a road. I didn't poison the damn goats." He ticked each offense off on a finger as he spoke. "What do I have to do to get you people to listen to me?"

Dax shoved a hand through his wet hair and fought the urge to tear through the house.

Diane appeared at the top of the stairs. "What's all the commotion about?"

Dax turned pleading eyes her way. Chip had treated Vanessa like dirt under his feet, but her aunt had showed kindness. A genuine excitement at getting to know her niece. "Vanessa's gone." His voice caught on the last word.

"What do you mean by 'gone'?" she asked as she glided down the stairs.

"She was in a car accident. When we got there, she'd vanished. Mrs. Steele spotted a black truck leaving the scene, and we believe she was in that truck," Madden said.

"Probably the same truck that ran me off the road yesterday," Dax stormed.

Diane stopped, her mouth wide in horror. "Oh my God. This is horrible. Chip, who would want to hurt that poor girl?"

Chip ground his teeth together. "Like I've been trying to explain, I don't know. I'm not involved in this mess."

"But you were involved in one before, weren't you?" Dax asked, studying Chip's pinched expression. "You mentioned earlier that you didn't want to clean up another one."

Frowning, Diane bounced her gaze between the men. "What is he talking about, Chip?"

Dax ignored her and kept pushing. "Would someone follow Vanessa up that mountain? Would they be concerned she went to speak with Mrs. Steele?"

The vein at Chip's temple jumped.

"Who'd want to run her out of town?" Dax stepped forward, pressing into Chip's personal space. "Who owns a black full-sized truck?"

"I'm sure a lot of people in this town own a black truck," Chip said. "All I know is that I don't."

"Doesn't Ethan borrow his stepson's black RAM from time to time?" Diane asked. "It's been parked behind the butcher shop the last week or so."

Chip shot her a warning look that had Dax fisting the neck of the older man's shirt.

"What is she talking about?" Dax asked.

Chip kept this mouth shut and raw hatred shone from his green eyes.

"Diane, what's the stepson's name?" Madden asked. "I'll tell Sanders to run down the information and see if we can find a location."

While Madden got the information from Diane and fired off a text message to Deputy Sanders, Dax never let his gaze stray from Chip's face. He ran through the conversation he and Vanessa had had with Ethan. "Vanessa and I talked to Ethan yesterday. He was pretty chatty. Mentioned something about honoring the bro code. Any idea what he was talking about?"

"No."

"Are you sure? Between you cleaning up a mess and him honoring some code, it has me wondering about what you two could be hiding."

"Enough." Diane marched down the rest of the steps and wedged herself between Dax and Chip. "I don't know what the heck's going on, but it's time you start talking. You've been acting strange ever since that sweet girl moved to Cloud Valley. I thought it was because of the way her mama left town, but now I'm not so sure. If my niece is in danger, I won't sit back and do nothing. And I won't let you stand there like a goddamn statue, refusing to answer questions. So, spill it. Now."

Chip squeezed his eyes shut for a beat, and when he opened them again, resignation sagged his shoulders. "Diane… I…" He lifted his hands and let them fall to his sides. "I don't know what to say."

"Try the truth." She rested a palm along his jawline.

He laid his hand on top of hers and sighed before circling his fingers around hers then dropping their joined hands to rest between them. "It's not an easy story to tell."

Impatience swelled in Dax's veins. "Just tell us how to find Vanessa."

Chip squeezed the back of his neck. "My sister left town because she was pregnant. Most people in town think she refused to tell anyone who the father was, but Ethan and I knew."

"It was Garrison," Dax said.

Chip nodded.

"Why didn't she want anyone to know?" Dax asked.

"Because the day he got her pregnant is the same day he died. Look, we were at our house. Mindy and Garrison disappeared. When Ethan and I went to find them, Mindy was struggling. Trying to tell him to stop…to stop…" He hung his head as his voice trailed off.

Bile sloshed in Dax's gut. "He raped her?"

Diane gasped and covered her mouth with a shaky hand. "That poor thing."

Chip cleared his throat. "Yes. I tackled him, got him off her. We started fighting and Ethan came running at him with a hammer. It just happened. He hit him too hard. We panicked and didn't know what to do so we rolled him into the river. Made it look like an accident. We buried the hammer and the shirt I'd been wearing in the garden, thinking no one would ever find it. Dad never planted anything there, and I never thought he'd leave the house to Vanessa. Ethan and I were both panicked."

"Panicked enough to kill an innocent woman?" Dax asked.

"Maybe," Chip said.

"Where would he take her?" Madden asked.

"I swear I have no idea. I never imagined he'd take

things this far. I haven't been Vanessa's biggest fan, but it was only because I didn't want her uncovering the truth. I never wanted her to get hurt."

Dax bit back a response about all the harm Chip had done. None of that mattered right now. "Does he own any property that's off the beaten path? Frequent anywhere outside of town where he'd take her?"

Chip shook his head. "He owns his home and the business, but both places always have people around. He wouldn't want his family to know. That's what started this whole thing. Him wanting to keep our secret from his wife and kids."

"I can't believe he'd actually hurt her," Diane said. "He's a good man. Always so kind. So thoughtful."

"He killed once," Dax said. "He'll do it again."

"But it was an accident. He didn't mean to kill Garrison," Chip said.

A thought struck Dax. "He has to make it look like an accident again. He'd take her somewhere she might find herself in trouble. Madden, can you pull up the video feed from Vanessa's outside cameras?"

"I can't, but Reid's at the office." Madden punched in the information then pressed his phone to his ear. "Reid, I need you to get on the computer and look at the security feed from Vanessa Kemp's outdoor cameras."

Time stretched on for eternity. Dax held his breath, silently urging Reid to hurry the hell up. He didn't know how long Vanessa had been with Ethan, but every minute was a minute too long.

"Call the sheriff's department. Now," Madden said then disconnected. "You were right. A black Dodge RAM drove up to Vanessa's house a few minutes ago."

Dax didn't wait to hear another word before he ran out the door and prayed he wasn't too late.

Little could shock Vanessa at this point, but pulling into her own driveway was the last thing she'd expected. "Why are we here?"

He shut off the engine and aimed the gun at her chest. "You ask too many questions. Just get outside and don't do anything stupid."

Saliva pooled in her mouth. She forced her jelly-like legs to climb out of the truck. She paid attention to every detail around her. Gravel crunched beneath her shoes. Frankie's frantic barks from inside the house competed with the sound of wind rustling the leaves. The rain had stopped for now. She searched for anything that could help her, give her the upper hand.

She came up completely empty.

Ethan gripped her arm and yanked her forward.

She dragged her heel against the loose stone. The least she could do was leave a trail to find her if anyone showed up.

Ethan towed her behind the barn and around to the patch of woods where she and Dax had found her little flock her first morning there. Memories burst forward, bringing tears to her eyes. That was the first time she'd witnessed his compassion, his kindness. He'd taken charge and hadn't just fixed a problem but had showed her patience and a willingness to help her help herself. How had she fallen so fast for someone she'd known for such a short amount of time?

And now she might not get a chance to ever tell him exactly how strong those feelings were. Regret washed in, weighing down each step. She'd searched her entire life for a man like Dax only to lose him before she really had him.

At least she'd gotten a chance to stare love in the face, to feel its impact and to experience what all those damn songs were written about. That's what she'd hold on to until the very end. But if she had anything to say about it, the end wouldn't be today.

"Hurry up," Ethan snapped, yanking her under the thick cover of trees.

She kept her mouth shut and followed behind him, mindful of her surroundings. The sound of the river gurgling downstream echoed ahead. Fear gripped her stomach, but she refused to show it. Refused to walk calmly to her execution.

"Are you going to do the same thing to me as you did to Garrison? Throw me in a river and hope everyone thinks I just slipped, fell in and hit my head? This time you can't make some stupid claim you're doing it to save someone. You're a murderer. Nothing more."

Ethan stopped and squeezed her arm so hard she yelped. "I'm not a murderer! I protected your mother. I loved her!"

Surprise number two was enough to make her stumble forward. "I don't understand."

He growled, yanking him toward her. "Chip didn't want us going after his sister. Told us all the time she wasn't up for grabs. Then she got all starry-eyed over Garrison. He thought it was hilarious. Laughing behind her back whenever Chip wasn't around. Acting like a clown. I told him to cool it. To leave her alone. She was so sweet, so innocent. He took all of that from her, and when I found him on top of her in the woods, I lost it."

He took a second to compose himself, inhaling deep breaths of air.

Her stomach dropped. "How did he take her innocence?"

Working his jaw back and forth, he snorted. "What do you think? He was on her, his pants around his damn ankles. She was crying. Yelling at him to stop. Telling him she wasn't ready. But he wouldn't listen. So, I hit him—hard enough to knock him out. There was so much blood. It got all over Mindy and Chip. We didn't know what to do so we threw him in the river. He deserved worse."

Vanessa pressed a hand to her mouth. Bile shot up her throat as the image of the blood-splattered shirt she'd found in her mother's room rushed back. She'd dreamed a thousand dreams over the years about her father. The type of man he was. What kind of job he'd had or hobbies he'd loved. She'd made excuses for why he hadn't tried to find her. Never had she imagined he'd been a monster.

Never thought her conception was a result of something so horrific.

"Not so chatty now, are you?" Ethan said, hauling her forward again. "Chip and I were terrified you'd look like him. That you'd be a constant reminder of what we did, and that eventually that would bring out the truth. We never thought you'd come back to town and wreak havoc on our lives. Asking a million questions like a damn dog with a bone."

Some of those questions came back with the force of a raging rapid. She tripped over her feet to keep up with him. "Mrs. Steele said my mom and Garrison spent time together. That they were at the beginning of a relationship when he died. Are you sure you saw what you think you saw?"

Maybe it was wishful thinking, but she'd believed the story she'd heard from Mrs. Steele. Could picture the two teenagers figuring out how to make things work despite her uncle's protests. Something that at the time probably seemed unsurmountable to two kids.

Red splotches invaded his cheeks. "You're lying. They weren't together and never had plans to be. He took advantage of her, and Chip and I stopped him."

"No," she said, inching closer to the drop-off to the river. Ethan wouldn't shoot her—couldn't if he wanted to make her death look like a drowning. If she ran, he'd easily overtake her. She had no weapon. Only one way of escape remained. "You and Chip killed him."

"Enough!" he yelled, causing birds to fly from the trees. "Let's get this over with."

She took another step back and her foot slipped on the slick grass. "What? No hammer to smash in my skull?"

Shaking his head, he released her arm, lifting his hand as if to slam it across her face.

Not waiting for the strike, she shoved his chest and threw him off balance. She held her breath and leapt into the frigid water.

Ethan's shouts sounded from above her seconds before a gunshot erupted, a bullet ripping into water beside her.

She dove deeper into the murky river. Rapids gushed over her head and sucked her under. Her lungs screamed, her throat burning for air, but she stayed submerged and prayed for a miracle.

Chapter 26

Eternity passed by the time Dax and Madden reached Vanessa's property. He'd placed a call to the sheriff's department about what they'd learned, but only Ethan's empty truck waited to greet them when they arrived.

Dax followed the sound of Frankie's frantic barks to the house. He checked the knob, but the door was locked. Not having a second to waste, he aimed his gun where the dead bolt attached to the wall and squeezed off a shot.

"What the hell, dude?" Madden yelled and jogged to his side.

Dax burst through the door, and Frankie jumped on his legs. "Vanessa! Are you here?"

Frankie barked and bolted outside.

"You look in the house in case she's here," Dax said. "I'll follow Frankie."

He didn't give Madden time to argue as he chased down the little dog. He ran past the barn and toward the woods, retracing the steps he'd taken only days ago when Frankie had led him toward the missing animals. If Frankie could produce a miracle and lead him to Vanessa, he'd cook the mutt steaks every night for dinner.

A low growl sounded from Frankie's throat, and he ran at full speed into the trees.

A gunshot exploded from inside the woods, and Dax's heart jumped into this throat. The tinny taste of fear coated his mouth, but he kept running. Kept pushing forward. He picked his way through overgrown brush and weaved through a maze of trees. Water dripped from the canopy of leaves and slid down his face.

Another shot went off. He ran faster, making his lungs burn and muscles scream. He spotted a flash of movement seconds before Frankie leapt into the air.

Then he saw him.

Frankie bared his teeth and attacked Ethan's leg.

Ethan shook off the dog then aimed a gun at Frankie. "You little bastard."

Dax closed the distance between them with his weapon trained straight ahead. "Shoot the dog and it's the last thing you'll do."

Shock registered on Ethan's face. "Dax! Thank God. I came out here to talk to Vanessa. I heard her screaming for help. She fell in the river."

Terror clamped onto his gut. If Vanessa was in the river, he had to get to her quickly. But first he had to get past Ethan. "So that was your plan all along, huh? Toss her in the same river as your friend and hope to God everyone in this town bought the same story. Make yourself look like some wannabe hero who tried to rescue her while all your secrets remain buried?"

Shock morphed into rage, and Ethan swung his gun at Dax.

Dax didn't waste another second. He pulled the trigger, hitting Ethan in the leg.

Ethan fell to the ground, the weapon bouncing away from his hand. A howl of pain hissed from his mouth. "You asshole!"

Madden appeared just as Dax secured Ethan's gun.

"He said Vanessa's in the river," Dax said. "You deal with him. I have to find her."

As much as he wanted to stay and inflict more pain on Ethan, he sprinted toward the hill overlooking the wide river. He squinted, searching for signs of Vanessa in the water. "Come on," he urged, adrenaline pulsing through his veins. He hadn't come this far to lose her.

Dark hair broke through the surface of the water seconds before disappearing again. She was several yards away, the strong current carrying her closer to the rapids every second. He ran toward the river's edge and jumped.

Icy water hit his body, engulfing him. He fought against the murky water, finding the surface and inhaling deep gulps of air before swimming downstream. He kept his eyes open as he kicked his legs with as much force as possible.

"Vanessa!" he yelled as he searched. The water carried him forward. He fought against fallen limbs and jagged rocks.

He spotted her again. Her eyes were wide and skin ashen. She held out her arms in time to catch a thick trunk of an upturned tree that hovered over the water. The river moved around her, trying to toss her around. Waves splashed over her face.

Aiming her way, he summoned every ounce of strength he had left and swam straight for her. His muscles ached and his heart hammered against his chest. The overturned tree grew closer. He reached for a limb with one arm, hooking it over the rough, wet bark, and wrapped the other around Vanessa's waist moments after she dipped under water once more.

He yanked her against his body, maneuvering her so her face tilted upward.

A hacking cough shook her shoulders.

"I've got you," he said. He held on for dear life. Waves beat against him and threatened to tear him away from his anchor.

"Hold on, Dax. I'm coming," Madden yelled.

Relief rooted in his soul at the sound of his brother's voice. He tightened his grip on the sturdy wood, but the slippery moss clinging to the side made it hard to hold on. "Help's here. You're going to be okay."

"I knew you'd come," she said, her teeth chattering. "I'm so cold."

"A couple more minutes and you'll be safe and sound."

Madden lay on his stomach and reached out over the water. "Can you move any closer?"

His muscles strained as he struggled against the rushing current. "Vanessa, I'm going to pass you to Madden. I need you to stay against the branch. He'll grab you and pull you to shore."

"What about you?"

"I'll be right behind you, honey."

She nodded then shifted to pull herself closer to the limb.

Dax unhooked his arm and braced his free palm against her back. He urged her forward, willing her to close the gap and get to Madden before another wave took her under.

Madden stretched forward and took hold of her arm. "I've got her." He pulled her up to the shore then returned to the edge of the riverbank, reaching out a palm.

Gritting his teeth, Dax placed one hand over the other and heaved himself toward his brother. The tips of his fingers brushed against Madden's.

The thick branch snapped and smacked him on the side of the temple before barreling over him. The heavy log pinned him under the water. Pain exploded inside his head. Water filled his mouth. He thrashed around the murky depths, but the wood refused to budge as it pushed him closer to the deadly depths of the riverbed.

"Dax!" Vanessa crawled onto her knees and lunged forward. The edge of the river slapped against her. Mud seeped between her fingers. Fear weighed her down as she watched Dax disappear under the water.

"Stay there," Madden said. He dove headfirst into the river.

Horror locked her in place as she tried to catch a glimpse of Dax. Her teeth chattered and shivers shook her shoulders, but none of it mattered. All that mattered was Madden pulling Dax from the raging river to safety.

Frankie's bark reached her seconds before he tore from the tree line and leapt onto her lap.

"Hello?" a man called out, hidden among the trees.

The sudden voice sent ripples of fear through her body. She searched for a weapon, anything to keep Ethan away. She'd jumped into the river, thinking he wouldn't shoot, but he'd proven her wrong. Bullets had splashed around her as she'd struggled not to drown. He might have missed her while she'd flailed in the water, but his aim would be better as she sat on the riverbed.

"Vanessa, it's Deputy Sanders. Where's Dax and Madden?" The deputy jogged down the grassy incline toward her.

The terror wrapped around her heart loosened a fraction. She jumped to her feet and pointed at the water.

"They're in there. Dax was struck by a tree. Madden jumped in to save him."

As if summoned by her words, Madden broke through the surface and pulled in a large breath before going under again.

Fear beat against the side of her neck with every thump of her heart. Dax had been submerged for so long. He needed air.

Madden popped up again, this time with an arm hooked across Dax's chest.

Deputy Sanders ran toward them, reaching out a hand. "Almost there, Madden."

Madden kicked his feet and moved his body to the shore.

The sight of Dax's ashen face and closed eyes sent a dagger of worry to her gut. She scurried to Deputy Sanders's side, silently urging Madden closer.

Deputy Sanders clasped Madden's forearm and hauled him up on the muddy shore.

Madden struggled for air and laid Dax on his back. "He's not breathing," Madden said between gasps.

"He needs CPR. Now!" Needing to act, Vanessa dropped to her knees beside Dax and sealed her mouth on his before breathing life into his body. She pulled back, anchoring her hands on his chest and pressing against his heart.

He lay still.

She repeated the process. Mouth to mouth. Hands to chest. "Come on, baby. You can't leave me now. I have so much to tell you. So much to share. Please. Open your eyes."

She prepared to lean forward once more when a hacking cough tore through his body. He surged up, expelling water from his mouth.

"Dax!" Relief brought tears to her eyes, and she threw her arms around his neck.

He clung to her, burying his face in the crook of her neck and greedily sucked in air. His body trembled, his skin ice-cold.

Deputy Sanders called out instructions to the communicator strapped to his shoulder then kneeled beside them. "Medics are coming."

Vanessa frowned as she struggled to wrap her mind around how things had changed so quickly. "How are any of you here?"

Dax pulled back and framed her face with his hands. Wet strands of her hair molded to her cheek. "We went to find you, but you were gone."

She gasped, momentarily forgetting about the terrifying landslide that had swept over the mountain. "Oh gosh, Ben. Is he okay?"

Dax nodded. "He will be."

Madden walked over, water dripping from his saturated clothes. "Once we found out Ethan had you, Dax figured he'd bring you here."

Wonder filled her. "You found me. You saved me."

The corner of his mouth lifted. "You got away from him, I just made sure he couldn't get to you before I dragged you out of the river."

She glanced behind her at the raging stream. "Garrison was my father. He threw him in that same river after he hit him on the head."

"I know, honey."

Tears filled her eyes, and she faced Dax again. "I have

so much to sort through, but none of that matters now. All that matters is you're okay. That you're here with me."

"There's nowhere else I'd rather be. I was stupid earlier. I was scared and guilt-ridden. I never should have—"

She pressed her lips to his. "You don't have to say any more."

"Yes, I do," he said, leaning his forehead to hers. "I'm sorry. Sorry for how I acted, for what I said. I'll never let my anger—my pain or my pride—dictate how I treat you. I thought I'd lost you. That I let you walk away and would never get a chance to tell you I've fallen in love with you."

Excitement and happiness burst in the pit of her stomach, and she wrapped herself around him. She held him tight, never wanting to let go. "I love you, too. I know it's so fast, but it's true."

"All right, you two," Madden said. "The medics are at the top of the hill. If you can manage, let's meet them up there so you can both get checked out. No need to sit here, soaking wet. Besides, I need to use someone's phone to call Lily and check on Pops."

Dax climbed to his feet then helped her up, keeping one arm secure around her back. Exhaustion and wet clothes weighed her down. Adrenaline fled from her system and left her shaky and tired. "How is your dad?"

"He'll be fine." Dax pressed a kiss to the top of her head. "He was worried about you. Worried I'd made a mess of things that I couldn't fix. It's a good thing you accepted my apology, or he might have kicked me out and adopted you as his own."

She grinned, relieved to learn Walter would be okay. "Well, after you jumped into a river for me, I didn't have much of an option."

He grunted. “Next time we swim together, I think we should find a pool.”

She hooked his arm around his waist and kept him close as they trekked up the riverbank and to the front of the house. Frankie stayed glued to her side. The taillights of an ambulance disappeared into the mist, and she sank deeper against Dax.

“Ethan’s been taken to the hospital then will be transported to the county jail,” Deputy Sanders said. “He won’t hurt you anymore.”

Dax steered her toward the second ambulance sitting in the driveaway. The back door was wide open, and a middle-aged woman stood at the ready.

“You two need anything else from me?” Madden asked.

“Nah,” Dax said. “Go tell Dad everyone’s okay.”

Vanessa untangled herself from Dax long enough to wrap Madden in a hug. “Thank you for saving him—for coming to save me.”

Madden gave her a quick squeeze. “That’s what brothers are for.”

Dax snagged her back against his side then stretched a hand toward his brother. “Thanks, man.”

She tried to step away to give the two men space, but Dax refused to let her go. Not like she’d complain. After her ordeal today, there was nowhere else in this world she’d rather be.

Madden slapped his palm in Dax’s and pulled him in for a quick half hug. “You’d have done the same for me. Take it easy for a while, okay?”

“I’ll make sure he does,” Vanessa said, snuggling into the heat of his body.

Madden dipped his chin then strolled to his truck.

Deputy Sanders appeared before they reached the impatient medic. "I hate to do this, but I'll need a statement from both of you."

She squeezed her eyes shut for a beat. For as long as she lived, she'd never forget the terror she'd endured, but the idea of speaking the experience out loud, of reliving every single detail, had her fisting Dax's wet shirt in her hand.

"Can you give us a little time?" Dax asked. "It'll be easier to go through everything in warm clothes."

"Sure," Sanders said. "I'll wait for you on the porch."

Vanessa sighed, wishing she could head inside right now. She wanted nothing more than to put the ugliness of the day behind her, but that wasn't possible. At least not yet.

The medic finally approached. "Who's first?"

"Him," Vanessa said.

He opened his mouth to argue, but she cut him off with one hard look. "You came for me. You saved me. Now let me take care of you a little. Let her give you a clean bill of health so we can dry off and get comfortable. Then I need to make sure and follow through on my promise to your brother and make you rest."

He tucked his thumb under her chin. "As long as you're beside me when I do."

She pressed her lips to his. "Sounds perfect to me."

Chapter 27

Dax handed Vanessa a fresh cup of coffee then sat beside her on the sofa.

Frankie lay on her lap, half of his fat little body covered by the orange throw blanket she'd draped over her shoulders. The dog refused to leave her side since Dax had pulled her from the river.

"We'll have to add rescue K-9 to his résumé now. He led me straight to you like you were one of the goats," Dax said, and took a sip from his own mug. The hot coffee was strong and bitter, the warmth coating his raw throat.

After changing into dry clothes and speaking with Deputy Sanders, the chill had yet to leave Dax's bones. He wasn't sure if it was due to his plunge in the icy river or listening to the details of everything Vanessa went through.

He'd held her close as she'd spoken, wishing he could absorb the pain that had made her voice shake. Wishing he could go back and change the way he'd handled his father's fall so he could have been with her.

But he couldn't do either. All he could do was support her as she waded through the aftermath of her trauma.

Vanessa scratched Frankie behind the ears. "Who knew he had so many skills? I just hope he can stick with finding animals and not me from now on."

"I don't plan on letting you out of my sight." Dax kissed her then set his coffee aside. "How are you feeling?"

She rested her head on his shoulder. "Physically, okay. Tired. A few aches and pains, but nothing too serious. Emotionally…well, that's a different story."

"Do you want to talk about it? I understand if you don't. It's been a long day. But I'm here if you do."

She let out a long sigh. "I can't believe after all these years, I know who my father is. And even though I have so many answers, there are still some unknowns. I don't think there's a way to get more clarity on exactly what happened between my mother and Garrison."

"Does it matter? Knowing the details won't change who you are. Won't change the way you feel about your mother or the relationship you had."

She shrugged. "I guess not, but I hate to think of her being hurt. I hate to think she experienced something so horrible just to be run out of town and forced to live away from her family for the rest of her life. She gave up so much to have me. All because she needed to keep this secret. I mean…did she look at me and remember all the bad things from her past?"

The question twisted his insides. He wished he had the words to wash away all the turmoil chugging inside her, but this was something she'd have to work through. No matter how painful. "I never got a chance to meet your mom, but I have no doubt she loved you so much. Enough to walk away from everything to give you the life you deserved. No matter what happened between her and Garrison, she raised you in joy. In happiness and love. Nothing you learn will ever change that."

Shifting to stare up at him, she smiled. "Thank you for that."

He kissed her, and Frankie barked in protest before jumping onto the floor.

Chuckling, she took a sip of her coffee then set it down beside his. "Sorry, boy." Leaning back against him, she rested her hand on Dax's knee. "I just wish my brain would shut off. I can't stop thinking about my aunt and uncle. What will happen to him now?"

"I don't know," Dax said. "That's for the law to figure out. Regardless of whether what happened was an accident or not, a life was taken. Lies were told to cover up the truth. Justice needs to be served."

"I really wanted to build a relationship with him—with my aunt and Autumn. Now that will never happen. Not if I'm the reason Chip ends up in jail."

He hated that even after everything she'd survived, she was still stuck in a place of uncertainty. She deserved more. Deserved to finally unpack all these damn boxes and make her new house her home. To figure out her future without the past dragging her down—heaping guilt on her shoulders for events she'd played no hand in creating.

"If your uncle goes to jail, it's not your fault. I hope that Diane and Autumn would see that, too, but if not, screw 'em."

"Screw them, huh? Just accept that the only family I have left in this world might never want anything to do with me?" A sadness that broke his heart coated her voice.

"Family isn't always blood. It's the people you surround yourself with. The people you choose to let into your life. I'm not saying you shouldn't feel loss, and even grieve that loss, but this town is full of people who'll have your back. *I'll* have your back."

"You've proven that," she said. "And I know you're

right. I guess I'll just have to see how everything shakes out."

"True, except for one person."

She frowned. "Who?"

"Mrs. Steele. You didn't get a chance to tell me about your visit."

The side of her mouth ticked up. "I've been a little preoccupied."

"Tell me now."

"I liked her. A lot. She was warm and sweet. She had nice things to say about my mother. The stories she told were very different than the picture Ethan and Chip painted, and those are the stories I want to be true. But even if they aren't, Mrs. Steele is my grandmother. I really want to get to know her."

"Do you think she'd want that, too?"

A beam lit up her entire face. "She said she did. We had this connection that I really hope doesn't go away once she learns the truth of what really happened. I really believed she could be my grandma. And now that I know she is, I'm so excited to see what kind of a relationship we can build."

"I'm sure it will be amazing, but for the rest of the night, I want to build on our relationship."

"Oh really?" Vanessa shifted to throw one leg over his lap and straddle him. Her damp hair fell around her shoulders, and she rested her palms on either side of his neck. "And how exactly should we do that?"

He stared up at her beautiful face and his breath all but left his body. He wasn't sure what he'd done right for her to walk into his world, but he'd be grateful every single day. "By telling you how damn lucky I am. When I didn't know where you were or who had you, my whole world crashed at my feet. If I'd lost you—" Emotion clogged his throat, stripping away the rest of his thought.

"You don't have to worry about losing me. I'm here with you, beside you, for as long as you want me."

"Then you better get comfortable, honey, because I never want you to leave." He captured her mouth with his and let his hands roam up the curve of her back. With Vanessa in his arms, his world was right how it was supposed to be, and he'd do everything in his power to keep it that way.

Three days later, Vanessa ran her fingers through her hair and combed through the tangles. She sat on the porch beside Walter and kept her gaze on the driveway. "Thank you for letting me meet Mrs. Steele here. She was uncertain about going back to the place where her son died."

"Not a problem," Walter said, petting Frankie, who slept on his lap. "I've known Mildred for years. She's a nice woman. I hope to get a chance to catch up with her a little bit before the two of you have your time."

"I'm sure she'd love that."

The front door swung open and a middle-aged woman dressed in purple scrubs stepped outside with a platter topped with refreshments.

Vanessa jumped to her feet. "Tia, you didn't have to do that."

Tia clicked her tongue. "Nonsense. I don't mind at all. The weather's finally turned and that sunshine is good for all of us. Especially Walter. He's been cooped up in that hospital and needs some good old-fashioned vitamin D."

"What I don't need is a babysitter," Walter said, crossing his arms over his chest like a petulant toddler.

Vanessa struggled not to laugh. Instead, she poured

him a glass of lemonade before reclaiming her wooden rocking chair.

Tia chuckled and shook her head, causing the dangling hoops in her ears to shiver in the sunlight. "Not a babysitter, a new buddy who gets to make sure you're doing okay. But since you're out here with this pretty little thing, I'll pop inside and get some stuff done." She shot Vanessa a wink then disappeared back in the house.

Walter grumbled under his breath and took a sip of his drink. "At least she makes some damn good lemonade."

Vanessa kept her thoughts to herself. While Walter had healed in the hospital, Dax and Madden had spoken with him about their living situations. She hadn't been in the room while they'd talked, but she'd heard all about Walter's reaction to hiring a home health aide to stop by the house every day.

Luckily, Tia seemed more than capable of handling Walter's surly disposition while he adjusted to his new normal.

Dax emerged from the barn and wiped his hands on the thighs of his jeans. His black cowboy hat shielded his face from the sun, and his blue T-shirt molded against every muscle in his chest. He grinned at her, the look in his eye telling her exactly where his thoughts were as he made his way up the porch steps. "Who made lemonade?"

"Tia," Vanessa said. "She seems really nice."

Walter snorted. "Sure. She's a real pleasure when chatting my ear off and making me do those stupid physical therapy exercises."

"God forbid she makes sure you're healthy and happy," Dax said. He placed a kiss on Vanessa's cheek then took the seat beside her.

"Yeah, yeah, yeah."

An SUV pulled into the driveway and straightened Vanessa's spine. She gripped the arms of the wooden chair. "She's here."

Walter set his glass down and rose. "That's my cue to step inside."

"You don't have to do that," Vanessa said. "You wanted to catch up with Mrs. Steele. Stay and chat a while."

He passed behind her and rested a hand on her shoulder. "I'll find some time to say hello before she leaves. This time is for you. You'll be fine. I promise."

His reassurance lifted her lips and helped calm her jangled nerves. "Thank you."

Dax jumped to his feet. "I'll help you inside, Pops."

Walter swatted away the offer. "I'm fine. I'll just head inside and find my new friend. You stay here with Vanessa." He disappeared into the house, Frankie following on his heels.

"Only if that's what she wants," Dax said, raising his brows in her direction.

"Always."

Mrs. Steele parked her SUV and climbed out. Her hair hung loose like the day they'd met, and she wore an oversized dress splashed with colorful flowers. She waved and walked toward the porch.

Vanessa stood and met her with a hug. "Thank you so much for coming. Did you have a nice visit with your sister?"

"I did," Mrs. Steele said, drawing in a deep breath. "But I must admit, my mind was a bit preoccupied."

"Do you want to sit?" Dax asked.

"Of course."

Dax ushered her into one of the vacant rocking chairs then waited for Vanessa to settle in the seat beside her before taking the chair on her other side.

Nerves danced in Vanessa's stomach, but she decided to dive right in. "I'm not sure what all you've heard about what happened a few days ago. We don't have to go into all of that, but I did get confirmation that Garrison is my father."

Mrs. Steele squeezed her eyes shut for a beat, and when she opened them again, tears slid down her wrinkled cheeks. She held out a hand, waiting for Vanessa to take hold of it. "What an unexpected gift, and I want to get into all of it. No matter how hard it is to hear. Maybe just not right now. Right now I just want to be happy that you found me."

The words released a torrent of emotions and washed away any lingering nerves. "Really?"

"Child, I have lived a lot of years on this earth wrapped in my grief. Longing for the life I wish I could have had with my dear boy. I'd give anything to have him back. To watch him grow. Nothing will change what happened, but now I have a piece of him. If you'll let me, I can watch you continue to grow into an amazing woman. Watch what you make of your life."

"I don't want you to just watch," Vanessa said. "I want you to be a part of it."

"Really?"

"Yes, really," Vanessa said, her chest tightening. "I've spent years writing letters with my grandpa, but I never had the kind of relationship with him I wanted. I missed out on so much. I'm learning why my mother made the decisions she did, and I can't be angry at her for it. But I want more than letters and stories. I want to know my grandmother."

Mrs. Steele lifted a hand to heart. "I never thought I'd be so lucky to be a grandmother. I tell you, fate has a sneaky way of bringing people together. Of righting the wrongs and putting us where we should be. I'll always mourn the time we've missed, but that will make me more grateful for what time we have left."

The sentiment lifted Vanessa's lips. A sense of peace settled in her soul. She might never have every answer she wanted in regard to what her mother had gone through, but that was all right. She had a new relationship with her grandma to build, the man she loved beside her, and a future full of possibilities in front of her.

Epilogue

Vanessa loved the view from her front porch. She breathed in a deep lungful of crisp, fall air. The leaves clinging to the trees created an explosion of colors. The cluster of purple and orange mums placed around the yard added to the festive atmosphere.

Dax stood beside her with his arm draped over her shoulder. "You ready?"

She tried to smile but feared all the nerves tying up her stomach made it come out as more of a grimace. "What if nobody shows?"

He grinned down at her then lifted his gaze to just above her head. "I don't think you need to worry about that."

She followed his line of vision and the truck trudging her way both relieved and increased her anxiety. "Okay, so people are here, but will they like what I've done?"

He placed a kiss on her forehead then took her hand, tugging her forward. "There's only one way to find out. Besides, this is a soft opening. Friends and family only. Do you really think anyone you invited today will be anything other than completely excited for you?"

He had a point, but that didn't mean she didn't want everything to go off without a hitch.

After things had settled down months before, she'd

dived headfirst into creating a space where she could welcome the community and offer everything from goat yoga to garden staples. While her contractor had gone to work on the barn, she'd toiled over the garden as well as putting together her new place.

She'd thought unpacking her boxes would do the trick, but she hadn't been prepared for the amount of time that went into making her grandfather's house her home. She'd poured through each room, taking care of the things her grandpa had thought important enough to keep. She'd cried, laughed and grieved different parts of the family she'd never know—the family she'd lost.

But in the end, she'd felt closer to them all.

And now with her heart at peace with her past, she couldn't wait to focus on her future.

As vehicles parked, she took Dax's hand and crossed the lawn to the barn. The siding boasted a fresh coat of red paint and new French doors trimmed in white led to the recent addition. She'd spent the morning with the animals, giving baths and placing fun bandanas around their furry necks, so she opted to head for the pristine yoga studio.

Stepping inside, giddiness swam in the pit of her stomach. Black mats marked the spots of future patrons on the gleaming wood floor. The ceiling pitched high in the center. Thick beams crisscrossed along the ceiling to add to the rustic charm. A mirror took up one full wall, while the others boasted framed black-and-white photos of the property and animals who lived on it. A cubby for shoes and purses sat beside the door, as well as a small seating area with a long bench and two armchairs.

Autumn sat behind the welcome desk at the front of the space with Frankie curled on her lap. Her dark hair was pulled into a high ponytail.

She waved. "Hey, guys. This is so exciting. We've put so much work into this place already. I can't wait to see how it goes. Mom said she can't wait for these yoga classes and will even try a class with the goats. She made me promise not to take any pictures." She lifted her hand to her mouth as if telling a secret. "Although I may have to sneak a few."

"Just don't get me into trouble," Vanessa said with a chuckle.

After the truth about her uncle had surfaced, she'd hated the idea of her aunt and cousin refusing to maintain a relationship. Luckily, her worrying had been for nothing. The three women had found strength in one another, forging a strong bond she'd be forever grateful for. A bond that was cemented with offering Autumn a job. She'd remembered her cousin's dream of earning a degree to help her transform her grandfather's property into a thriving business.

Now the two had combined their dreams for the future to build something beautiful they knew their grandfather would be proud of. And, hopefully, after Chip paid for the crime he'd committed as a teenager, he'd come around to seeing what a wonderful thing they'd brought into the community.

Dax fisted his hands on his hips. "You need help with anything, Autumn? Looks like you've got everything set up."

"I think I'm good," Autumn said. "Mats and bands are laid out, my playlist is ready, and I even turned on a diffuser. I figured the vanilla would combat the smell of goats in here. They're cute and all, but awfully stinky."

"You thought of everything," Vanessa said.

"Just followed the boss's orders." Autumn gave a mock salute.

Dax linked his fingers with Vanessa's and tugged her toward the sliding barn door that led to the animals. "There's one more thing we have to do before people come inside."

Frowning, she walked beside him and checked her mental to-do list. Not one task came to mind that she'd forgotten. Soft opening or not, she'd wanted today to go perfectly. Strived to give her friends and family a complete experience they'd fall in love with—then tell everyone they knew all about.

Goats and sheep greeted them when they entered the wide aisle. Bessie mooed in the far corner. Vanessa had never thought she'd love these animals as much as she did, but she didn't have time to fawn over them right now.

Glancing around, she searched for whatever issue needed to be attended. "What's going on? What did I forget?"

Dax spun her to face him and smiled. "I want you to take a moment before the craziness begins and appreciate how far you've come. I'm so proud of you. Of your determination and vision. Of how you made decisions with your head and your heart. You've built something amazing. Not only will it be a success, but I can see the potential for more. For this land to bring the community together the way you dreamed. I want you to soak all this up and enjoy it."

She took in a shuddering breath. "It's been a lot, but I think you're right. This is going to work. I feel it in my bones. Like this was my purpose all along. Cloud Valley has given me so much. A home, a place to live out my dream, and a man who's helped me every step of the way. I couldn't have done any of this without you."

"Yeah, you could have," he said with a wink. "I'm glad you didn't have to, but you could move mountains if you wanted. I'm just happy to be a part of it. And if you'll let me, I'd love to continue being part of your life. Every day. Forever."

Her breath stalled in her throat and her heart beat with the force of a hurricane. "What are you saying?"

He whistled, and Frankie charged into the aisle. Dax bent down and lifted a ribbon from around Frankie's neck. A solitaire diamond dangled from the ribbon. "I'm saying the day you walked into my life was the best day ever. You make me a better person. You've showed me what real love is, and I want to spend the rest of my life showing you how much I love you—making you feel as special as you make me feel. Vanessa Kemp, will you marry me?"

Tears misted in her eyes and she threw her arms around his neck. "Absolutely, yes!" She lifted onto her tiptoes and kissed him hard before pulling back and smoothing her palm along his jawline. "How did I get so lucky to find you?"

Smirking, he shrugged. "Your grandpa must have had one hell of a plan."

She threw her head back and laughed. "Must have."

Frankie barked as if in agreement.

Dropping her arms, she held out her hand to let Dax slide the engagement ring into place. She stared at the sparkly diamond and squealed. "It's beautiful."

"Not as beautiful as you." He hooked an arm around her waist. "Now, let's get this party started."

Grinning, she fell into step beside him back into the yoga studio, which was now full of her family and friends. Joy filled her until she thought she'd burst. She'd arrived in this town lost and searching for the right direction to take her life.

But she'd found more than a place to belong—she'd

found people to love, a home to cherish, and a man she adored.

A man who'd be her partner, her lover, her husband every day for the rest of her life.

* * * * *